Praise for Meg Little Reilly's *We Are Unprepared*

"Reilly shows the costs of ignoring major problems—whether in a marriage, government, infrastructure, or the environment."

—Booklist

"I couldn't stop thinking of Shirley Jackson's *The Lottery* as I read Meg Little Reilly's *We Are Unprepared*. Part environmental thriller, part exploration of marriage, it reveals the psychological storm that lies underneath the tranquil New England façade ready to sweep us into tribal life."

—Joseph Monninger, award-winning author of *The Map That Leads to You*

"Smart, prophetic, heartfelt; *We Are Unprepared* is just the book I've been waiting to read—both wake-up call and salve for these uncertain times."

—Robin MacArthur, author of *Half Wild*

"This intimate, well-crafted book is an important addition."

—Charlene D'Avanzo, author of *Cold Blood, Hot Sea*

"Frightening, fascinating, all too possible."

—Paula Treick DeBoard, author of *The Drowning Girls*

"Reilly gives us one heckuva ride... Cli-fi novels don't get much better than this."

—Dan Bloom, *The Cli-Fi Report*

Also by Meg Little Reilly

We Are Unprepared

EVERYTHING

THAT

FOLLOWS

MEG LITTLE REILLY

mira

mira

ISBN-13: 978-0-7783-6414-6

Everything That Follows

Recycling programs
for this product may
not exist in your area.

For questions and comments about the quality of this book, please contact us at
CustomerService@Harlequin.com.

BookClubbish.com

Printed in U.S.A.

For Josephine and Annabelle, who make me hopeful.

EVERYTHING

THAT

FOLLOWS

PROLOGUE

There is a moment in any event when momentum takes over and dictates the direction and force of everything that follows. It's the energetic tipping point, beyond which some things become irreversible. The outcome is not entirely prescribed by that momentum, but it can no longer be undone.

It's the backrush, the seaward return of a wave after it crests and topples on the shore. The strength of a wave determines the strength of its backrush, so even though we cannot know its precise path through the sand, there is no question about whether that wave will find its way back to the ocean. It is unstoppable by then, impossible to erase from history.

Like every wave that has ever landed ashore, there are moments in our lives when the energy crests and we lose control. We're in the backrush.

CHAPTER 1

It didn't seem dangerous until the rain started. Not really. Until then, the evening still felt largely unwritten and within their control. But as the fog changed to mist and then to hard wet rain that soaked their boozy skin, the night started to get away from them. Doors were closing, options vanishing. And by the time Kat was being pulled by Kyle unwillingly toward the edge of the boat, the approaching danger was inescapable.

Kat blinked the water out of her eyelashes. When her vision cleared, Kyle's face was just inches from her own. Someone watching from behind might have mistaken them as a couple in an intimate embrace, that suspension of breath before a first kiss. But that person would have been wrong. Their closeness was not voluntary.

Kat twisted her torso around and tried to get a clearer view of where behind her Hunter was seated, but Kyle's fingers dug harder into her waist. He was leaning back against the wall of the whaler's stern, pulling her weight toward him. All she could see beyond his body was the black, churning ocean.

Three of them were on the boat—Kat, Kyle and Hunter—

so maybe the encounter didn't really look romantic. Three people made it something else. But what, Kat couldn't pinpoint. She twisted around again, trying to catch Hunter's attention, but it was useless. Hunter had passed out somewhere around the last finger of whiskey and hadn't budged since. Now he was slumped along the white leather bench at the bow, his face pressed into the smooth cushions that formed a half-moon. He didn't flinch as the rain pelted his tanned skin.

Kat turned back to Kyle. His face was too close, distorted. The sharp angles of his jaw, his prominent nose and dark eyes. He looked surprisingly hideous at such proximity.

The night wasn't supposed to end this way. Nothing they planned pointed to this. It was supposed to be a celebration. And yet, there they were, alone on the Atlantic in the driving rain.

Kyle shouldn't have been there, either. That, it seemed now, was where they'd taken a wrong turn. If anyone were to be out on that fishing boat late at night, it should have been Kat and her boyfriend, Sean, and their friend Hunter. It was Hunter's boat. They were supposed to be celebrating her biggest sale ever: a large, blown-glass sculpture she called *The Selkie* was the size of a toddler and twice as heavy, and its sale would pay for a year's worth of rent. Glassblowers don't make a lot of sales like that—not even on Martha's Vineyard—and so a night of overindulgence might have been expected. But the party at the bar went on too long, and the after-party shouldn't have happened at all. With or without Kyle, the boat had been a bad idea.

Kyle's shoulders swayed with a gust of wet wind. He looked around nervously at the choppy waters and used one hand to steady himself on the edge of the boat before returning it to Kat's waist. Was that hesitation she saw? A second thought about where he was taking this? In his inebriation, Kyle seemed to be oscillating between asking permission and not asking. He was a beggar and a predator both at once. But his grip on her body didn't relent for long. Kat still felt trapped.

"Kyle, let's drive back in. It's starting to really come down."

"We will, we will," he said. "In a few minutes."

Even if she broke away from him, where would she go?

Kat was usually good at this—recognizing untrustworthy characters and threatening scenarios. It was a skill learned of necessity, unfortunately for her. But the whiskey had dulled her powers. And Kyle had seemed so desperate to impress, too passive to be a threat. She didn't see this move coming. She'd overlooked the signs, and at some point along the way, the evening simply got away from her.

It all started with the sculpture; she was sure of that. That was when her euphoria set in, which was roughly the same time that her good judgment left her.

"That's a heavy fucking mermaid," Hunter had said.

Six hours before, Kat, Sean and Hunter had delivered the eighty-pound glass artwork—her big sale—to the pristine summer home of a local art collector. It took all three of them to lift it from the dolly.

"It's not a mermaid," she corrected him. "It's a selkie."

Hunter rubbed his lower back. "I don't know what that is."

"It's basically a mermaid," Sean said from the doorway of the elegant home. He was ready to leave. Sean had seen the glass sculpture before. He'd seen it at every stage over the preceding months as Kat labored around it with pipes of molten glass and blowtorches. He'd told her he thought it was a risky idea, putting so much money and energy into an enormous work of abstract art on the hope that some crazy rich person would pay ten thousand dollars for it. People wanted fancy bowls and paperweights shaped like whales, he'd said. That's what sells. But he was wrong. He shouldn't have doubted Kat because she had created something extraordinary, and now a rich person *was* buying it, and for much more than that.

Kat called it *The Selkie* because, at the right angle, you could see the curve of female hips, shoulders and breasts. The bottom half looked more seal than human. From a different view, it was a smooth abstraction, with ribbons of gray-blue waves running through it. Haunting from every angle, it was technically interesting, but not the sort of thing most people would want to look at every day.

"C'mon, we have to get this dolly back to Kyle at the bar," Kat said. She had been eager to get out of the art collector's house too, and on to the celebration with their friends.

It wasn't always the case, but on some occasions, Kat found it strange to be alone with these two men, one of whom was her boyfriend. They'd been hanging out so much lately that it was beginning to feel like she was dating both of them... or like Hunter was their adopted thirtysomething child... or she was theirs. Most of the time she could ignore the odd feeling, but on that day, Kat wanted it to end.

They left the collector's house just as the sun was going down; Kat remembered the station of the sun vividly. As they stepped out into the overcast October evening, she felt a lightness that went beyond the lost weight of her artwork. She was high on the possibility that this sale could portend greater opportunities down the road: richer clients, bigger price tags, more ambitious works. She was also relieved by the sudden influx of cash into her checking account. It was a near guarantee that she could make it through another winter on the Vineyard without much trouble. The economics of her life were even more precarious than usual.

It wasn't just Kat. Sean and Hunter and all the locals were giddy to finally have their island back. It used to be that Labor Day meant the official end of the tourists and the start of the off-season, but these days, people just kept coming through September. The air stayed warmer and the beaches stayed busy. "Shoulder seasons," that's what they called fall and spring now, which just meant the restaurants stayed open for another six weeks. It's good for the year-rounders' incomes, but it also made Columbus Day feel like a miracle when it finally hit and most of the tourists left for good.

No one harbored hard feelings for the tourists; that's an important point on the Vineyard. No one here held a grudge for the summer dinks. It's a point of understanding among all the natives and loners, the fishermen, the environmentalists, the washashores and the weirdos who stayed all year that the economy relied on everyone's contribution. So thank God for the people who came, and spent, and left. Everyone's survival depended on it.

And on that night, just hours into the post–Columbus Day calm, the tourists were finally gone. The ferries were back to their limited schedules and many of the establishments had locked their doors for good.

"It's like the zombie apocalypse around here," Hunter had said as they walked. They were headed for a local bar called The Undertow.

An eeriness had descended on the suddenly empty streets, growing eerier as dusk fell, like an abandoned carnival in a horror movie. But most of the locals preferred it that way. They gladly kept the carnival running all summer, then relished the quiet of its abandonment. Anyhow, it wasn't entirely dead. A handful of restaurants and shops with loyal followings kept humming through the winter, including Kat's glass shop. What was left open was just enough for them. You could almost feel the electrical current of the island turn down as the last overbooked ferry cast off toward the mainland. The island, and its year-round residents, were shifting to their lower gear.

Sean had been walking in front with the dolly. Kat remembered the sound of it clanking along cobblestone. The narrow, winding side street opened up to the slightly wider Main Street, with its tiny ice cream shop and pricey boutiques. It was life in miniature, a movie set. Nothing in the village of Addison was convenient and nothing you needed was ever available—unless what you needed was fudge, a Black Dog sweatshirt or seashell art. Places like these—Addison, Edgartown, Tisbury and the like—weren't designed for real people anymore. They were performances of island life for outsiders, approximations of the real thing. Addison was on the southeast shore, just a short drive from the Edgartown ferry stop, and it was as picturesque as it was inconvenient.

"Gang's all here," Sean said when they got to The Undertow. They could see heads laughing through the windows on the second floor.

Kat didn't particularly like this bar, but there weren't many options in off-season. The first floor was a working fish market, so the whole place smelled of old oyster water. But it had great ocean views in three directions. And, because of the stink, it never got overwhelmingly touristy. All the servers and cooks from the other restaurants liked to come here after their shifts ended, so things didn't usually pick up there until late. Wednesday nights, it was an unofficial gay bar. Thursdays were open mic. It was one of the few places in Addison that felt like it belonged to the locals. All of which is why it was Sean's favorite bar.

Sean had grown up on Martha's Vineyard and detested anything designed to attract moneyed outsiders. He stayed unflinchingly loyal to all that was local and old. It was like a religion to Sean. His bars, his friends, his clothes, his old-man-on-the-sea beard, even his longtime girlfriend, Kat. He stuck with things that he valued as a matter of principle. Sean was a reliable rock and everyone fucking loved him.

It is entirely possible that on that night, Kat, without fully realizing it, was feeling a little suffocated by Sean's unofficial role as the mayor of the Addison year-rounders. Maybe she didn't realize it at the time, but she was pushing up against something. Maybe a part of her yearned to behave badly.

When they got inside The Undertow, Hunter and Sean joined the crowd at the center of the room. Kat went straight to her best friend, Erika, who was working on a whiskey sour at the bar.

"Where you been?" Erika said, leaning in for a cheek kiss. Too many windows were open in the bar, and Erika's skinny tattooed arms prickled with goose bumps.

"*The Selkie*! We just dropped it off."

"Good for you and good riddance. It can haunt someone else now." Erika maintained the possibility that every supernatural theory was a little bit true. She was particularly literate in Celtic traditions and felt sure from the start that invoking a sea spirit was terrible juju. Just asking for bad luck, she'd said, and there's no point in doing that.

"I think I'm going to miss her, actually." Kat put an arm around Erika and ordered a pilsner.

Erika, who worked at a restaurant, told a spirited story about the fight she'd had earlier that day with her boss, neither the first nor the last story of its kind. Kat listened and laughed while the sun finally went down outside and the boathouse lights cast a twinkly effect across the barroom.

"What's going on over there?" Kat nodded toward Hunter and a woman she'd never seen. The woman looked miffed as she spoke to him. Hunter had his hands in his pockets and his head hanging sheepishly.

"Exactly what you think," Erika said. "So I see Hunter's drinking again?"

"A little, I guess. I don't know." Kat watched him shift from one foot to another in discomfort. "He seems okay."

Hunter wasn't supposed to be drinking. He was just four months out of rehab and on strict instruction to lay low and stay sober, at least until his father got reelected. He was the only son of US Senator Briggs, of *the* Briggs family of Massachusetts. While not a committed drunk, Hunter was a consistent fuckup as only a rich, ignored and bored scion of America's ruling class could be. His latest infraction was a drunken joyride along some protected habitat farther up-island, which got him arrested and led to a very public apology and half-true confession of alcoholism, at the advice of his father's campaign manager. (Kat thought sex addiction would have been a more fitting label.) So no, Hunter shouldn't have been drinking that night. But he was fun and bad and generous with his affection. No one ever stood in his way.

Maybe if Hunter hadn't been drinking, they wouldn't have taken his boat out. That seemed to Kat, in hindsight, like another inflection point of the evening.

"A toast," Sean yelled from the other end of the bar as beer sloshed over his raised hand. "In congratulations to the talented Kat for sending her giant mermaid out into the world."

"It's a selkie!" Erika yelled.

The group quieted, their drinks raised.

Sean smiled wide. "And cheers to the good visitors of our fair island, for finally getting the fuck out."

"Hear, hear!"

Sean looked drunk already, though it was always hard to tell. He got rosy and cheerful on the first sip. Sean could toast the sun setting and rising again each day. And it was always he who made the toasts because there was an unspoken understanding among everyone that this was Sean's bar, Sean's world. He assumed a heartfelt responsibility for the people in his corner of the island that no one could ever match or dared try.

"Summer's over, go home," finished Kyle, the bartender. He was new to The Undertow, just a month or so into this job. Kat had only seen him a few times before that night.

"Summer's over, go home!" repeated the group. It was a rallying cry for the locals, but there was no malice behind it. On that night, it felt jubilant.

Sean took a seat at a sticky table in the center of the room and a dozen other revelers joined him.

Kat ordered three plates of fries and another round of pints from Kyle before sitting down.

They were ticking through everyone's plans for the coming months; that was the last thing Kat remembered really clearly.

Erika, who was normally a chef at a high-end farm-to-table restaurant, was moving to a fried fish joint in Oak Bluffs for the winter. Erika's friend Colleen was going to work at a gift shop on Chappy, which she was bereft about because Chappaquiddick may as well have been a different continent in the dead of winter.

Sean would be at the boatyard, of course, and also doing one-off refurbishing projects on some of the yachts in storage.

Sean's buddies Jeff and Rakim were going back to stay with their families in Quincy while they looked for work.

Hunter was reportedly perfectly happy with the landscaping job he'd picked up since rehab, which meant mowing grass in the summer and shoveling snow in the winter. It seemed a waste of all that expensive schooling to Kat, but Hunter said the physical work helped to keep him "on track."

Kat would be at the glass studio, cranking out the stuff that sells well in winter—holiday ornaments, cocktail glasses, champagne flutes—and minding the shop for whatever light traffic might wander in.

This was the rhythm of everyone's life on the island, driven by two tides, both beyond their control: the ocean tide and the tide of tourists. The latter rose like a tsunami in late May, multiplying the population sixfold and changing everything for four crowded, messy and occasionally dehumanizing months of the year. It assigned everyone to the category of buyer or seller, taker or giver. You were either there to play and spend, or you were there to serve—waitress, line cook, cashier, dockhand, ferry attendee, bar back, weed dealer or landscaper. And if you were any of those things, you were probably two or three of them because everyone had at least one side hustle. That's how you survived the year. And when that tide of consumers finally receded, what was left was the heartier life. It's a gnarlier creature that stayed on all year, with more grooves to show for the shifting salt and sand. The grooves were where the stories lived.

"Fries are here!" someone yelled.

Timofti, the Romanian line cook, brought three steaming plates to the bar and went back to the kitchen. He didn't stop to talk that night, as he usually did. Kat realized that most of the other seasonal workers were long gone, which meant that Timofti was probably in a legally gray area with his J-1 visa. The Undertow wasn't one to turn down cheap labor.

Kat stood up to get the fries. She remembered balancing the three plates on her arms, the way she used to do when she waitressed.

Kyle the bartender had called it "impressive."

Hunter came up behind her. "Only professional foosball players and chronic masturbators could do it better!" That was his joke about her forearms. They were, by comparison to the rest of Kat's reedy body, rather brawny. Hunter took the plates back to the table.

"I'm a glassblower," she said to Kyle by way of explanation. Kyle raised his eyebrows. "Cool."

This was the first conversation Kat had with him since he started working there. The sound of his voice was a surprise, deeper than his youthful face suggested.

Kyle had questions about glass working, which Kat remembered going on a bit too long about. He wanted to know what sort of tools she used, and how she got into it. He'd done some carpentry, apparently, said he built a doghouse for his mom a while back. Kat asked about the dog, but Kyle couldn't recall its name or breed. Just a mutt, he'd said. Kat remembered a few people coming up to the bar with drink orders, which Kyle filled, but he never took his attention away from her. Something felt familiar about him— the way he held himself away from the crowd, comforted by the barrier of the bar. Kat identified with that distance—as if he wanted to be there, but didn't believe he belonged there. She knew that feeling. It seemed weird that she'd never really talked to Kyle before. This intense, eager outsider was a curiosity to her.

Sean came over at some point and put his arm around Kat. She remembered feeling embarrassed by how intently she'd been listening to Kyle. Surely he'd noticed.

"What are we talking about?" Sean asked.

"Glass working," she said.

"And carpentry," Kyle added.

No one made eye contact.

Sean squeezed Kat's shoulders. He seemed satisfied with this answer, and had a few questions for Kyle about his carpentry. It was the sort of work Sean respected. He liked people who did things that *mattered*. Because to Sean, glassblowing and woodworking were the same; they both added real and tangible value to the world. Painting, building, fishing, cooking, child rearing—he considered all these to be critical skills, none lesser than the other. Most other things, though, were utter bullshit.

Sean had no patience for frivolity or vanity. He expected a lot from everyone and his righteousness would have been intimidating had Kat not passed all the high bars. She felt safe in his moral world. It was as if she wanted to soak in all of Sean's rules and boundaries to salve her younger self. His boundaries were something firm to lean against.

Kat went back to the table with Sean and rejoined the group. More pints came. It seemed like people were drinking fast. She remembered Sean running his hand down her long, sandy-brown hair as they both spoke loudly to other friends.

People continued to arrive and the room became hot. Someone bought another round. Three people with early morning jobs had to go, and others took their seats. Eventually, the only people left in the bar were their friends. All the faces were familiar, if not the names. They all shared the common ground of winters on the island and a friendship with Sean. Tequila shots were passed around. Kyle turned up the classic rock that played in the background, driving the volume of conversation up with it, until the roar of the room could surely be heard from the street below.

Kat remembered glancing at Kyle as he worked behind the bar. She was hoping to pick up their conversation later.

At some point, Timofti emerged from the kitchen, his coat in hand and face still dripping with sweat from the oven heat. He sucked two bottles of cold beer down at the bar. It must have been about midnight.

The lights came on soon after that.

People stumbled around looking for their coats.

There were back slaps and hugs as the crowd filed down the steep staircase to the cobblestone street below.

And then it was just Sean, Hunter, Kat and Kyle left in the bar.

Sean blinked into the screen on his phone. "Shit, I gotta run back to the boatyard. There's rain coming in soon and I didn't cover everything. I'll walk you home first."

Was that part right? Kat wondered. Had he offered to walk her home? He must have, but she couldn't remember for sure.

But she'd said no, that was okay. She'd be fine. It was just a short walk.

They kissed goodbye, probably, and then he was gone.

Her memory of this part of the evening wasn't great, but Kat could guess how that interaction had gone, and how Sean probably felt about it. He hated that they were still living in separate places. There were good reasons to live apart, like Sean's eleven-year-old daughter who lived with his ex-wife in Boston, and the convenience of Kat's current apartment right above the glass studio. But Kat knew those were thin arguments. They'd been together for six years. Sean was a thirty-nine-year-old man who knew exactly what he wanted. He had made it clear he thought they should be living together by now, if not married.

"Who's up for a nightcap?" Kyle had said. The lights in the bar were glaring on them.

"I am." Hunter was drunk. "Let's take a bottle to my boat."

Kat found her coat wedged between a stool and a filthy bar wall. "You should go home, Hunter. We probably all should."

"C'mon," Kyle said, pulling a half-full bottle of Maker's

Mark from behind the bar. "This might be our last night to get on the water this fall."

This wasn't hyperbole. Any day of the year, it could be ten to thirty degrees colder on the Vineyard water than the mainland. October at midnight flirted with the end of outside drinking season.

Kat remembered thinking as Kyle came out from behind the bar, that she'd never seen the bottom half of his body before. He was leaner and taller than she thought. And with the addition of a charcoal peacoat and long silk scarf, he looked significantly more polished too. He wrapped the speckled blue scarf loosely around his neck three times with great flair. It seemed a bit absurd to Kat, stepping into such dandy clothing after a shift at The Undertow. Who *is* this guy? she wondered.

"It's a plan, then!" Hunter led the way down the stairs to the street.

Kat followed while Kyle locked up.

She and Hunter stood alone for a few minutes and waited under the soft glow of the streetlights. A fog was just starting to roll in. Being with Hunter was like being with herself. It required no work at all.

"Hunter, you should go home," she said. Hopefully that's what she'd said. It's what her sober self would have said.

He put a firm hand on her shoulder. "I promise you I will, soon. Let's have one more round on the water to celebrate your big sale, and then I'll go home. You don't have to babysit me."

"I know that. But I don't want to contribute to your demise, either."

He cocked his head. "My demise will not happen with bottom-shelf whiskey. I promise it will be much more impressive. Anyhow, it's virtually on your way."

Kat should have listened to her instincts at this point. She should have recognized what an odd plan it was: the three of them, tipsy at best, on a boat after midnight on a cold and foggy October night. And hadn't Sean mentioned rain? She said nothing.

Kyle caught up with them and slapped Hunter hard on the back. "Let's go."

They walked down the center of the little street, past the last quaint shop, a bed-and-breakfast and a row of old Cape Cods in cedar shake.

After that, the sidewalk pitched up at a thirty-degree slope and there were no more houses; just tall grasses separating them from the Atlantic Ocean on their right. At the top of the hill sat the glassblowing shop, an aging Cape Cod that had long ago been converted to a glass studio and retail space. It was right at the edge of the sharp bluff, the only structure on that side of the road, alone and exposed at every angle.

The hanging wooden sign out front said Island Glass, though you couldn't make it out in the dark. The sign squeaked as the wind moved it back and forth on its hinges. The entire place was dark.

Technically, Island Glass belonged to Sean's mother, Orla Murphy, but Kat spent more time there than anyone. Her whole life was there. The garage was her studio, where she made all the inventory for the shop and had spent thousands of sweaty hours among the enormous and treacherous tools of her craft. A furnace, oven, refractory and dozens of smaller instruments were obsessively organized behind the faded garage door that opened to the street.

The main part of the house, the retail shop, was set farther back from the road, hovering at the edge of the receding ocean bluff. To get to it, you had to walk through the garage or around to the side entrance.

When Sean's father bought the house forty years ago, it had fifteen feet of grass on the ocean side, or so the story goes. They tore down the interior walls of the house and made it into one big open retail space, planted flowers all the way around the outside, and replaced the windows with Orla's exquisite stained glass creations. It still looked just like the pictures from those days, even as the frontage shrunk.

Island Glass was also Kat's home; she rented the small apartment on the second floor. It was never meant to be a permanent arrangement. When Orla had suggested that Kat rent the space seven years before, as she was starting her glass-blowing apprenticeship, it seemed like a smart option for the short term. But Kat grew attached to her life at Island Glass. She liked being close enough to the studio to blow glass until midnight if inspiration struck. And if Orla needed an extra hand in the shop at an odd hour, she could just holler up the stairs to Kat's door. Everything she loved was right there.

Kat felt a tug of sadness as they walked past the shop. It had been a hard week; they'd lost more of their oceanfront cliffs. Island Glass was a few feet closer to the edge than it had been a week before. She didn't want to think about those things now, though. She just wanted to keep celebrating.

Kat, Hunter and Kyle walked another five minutes in silence, looking out over the steep bluff of wet earth and beach grass. Kyle lit a cigarette and held his long arm out away from them between puffs. The wind picked up and they moved faster. Kyle's cigarette went out and he flicked it into the grass.

To their left, the houses had changed from cottages to estates, sprawling and set back, with landscaped yards and latched gates. That's how it is on the Vineyard: nothing is very far from anything else. And in the length of a scrub oak, you can pass from the rich to the überrich.

Kyle looked up at the estates. "One of these is yours, right?"

Hunter nodded ahead. "The next one." His was the grandest house in a long line of grand houses. "Technically, it's my dad's vacation home. I'm just camping out here indefinitely."

Kyle stopped and looked up at it. "Fuuuck."

Hunter kept walking. He regarded his wealth with a mixture of embarrassed humility and self-loathing. He took full advantage of the privilege, from extravagant spending on his friends to the unbridled indulgence for every chemical his body craved. He knew this wasn't the way most people lived, and he was grateful for what he had. But he wasn't proud of his wealth. Hunter knew he had done exactly nothing to deserve any of this, and he'd spent most of his adult life demonstrating an unworthiness to inherit it. He was as detached from the origins of his wealth as he was from his father, his father's second wife and the land baron ancestors who'd earned it all for his family. In fact, his *only* connection to those roots was his ability to spend their money. So that's what he did.

"Whaler's down here." Hunter led them away from the house and toward the bluff on the right, where a steep line of stairs pointed down to a private dock and motorboat.

Kat and Kyle followed. They walked in a line down the long dock, which bent and bowed ever so slightly, warped by years of changing seasons. The wind picked up, drowning out every sound around them but the banging of the boat against the dock. They braced themselves against a light, cold spray from the water's chop. And then it was calm again. Water lapped gently at the dock posts. The muted glow of a lighthouse pushed through the smeary fog. Martha's Vineyard was asleep.

Hunter stepped unsteadily into the boat, holding with both

hands to the steel rail that ran around the lip of the vessel. Kat remembered thinking he looked too wobbly to drive a vehicle on land or water, but she followed him anyhow.

He went to the cockpit, which had a low canopy overhead, and turned a key to activate a line of dim interior lights. White cushion seats and white walls glowed against the delicate chrome hardware. The cockpit, which was constructed of glossy grained wood, was at the center of the boat. Otherwise, the Whaler was entirely open. You could walk in a full circle around the perimeter if, Kat imagined, you were reeling in a particularly wild catch. It was a fishing boat, but not the utilitarian sort that the real sportsmen kept at Sean's boatyard. This was a vintage model, with countless upgrades and refurbishments that made it distinctly tonier.

The boat could comfortably hold four in the semicircle of the bow, where neat little cup holders had been carved into the wood paneling behind the seats. At the stern, you could lean right up against the wall of the boat and feel the rumble of the hulking outboard motor on the other side. Kat liked that feeling.

Every detail of the craft had been considered. It was so tasteful, Kat thought it a shame to leave it exposed to the elements, just sloshing around in the salt water, bumping up against slimy dock posts. She'd been out on it before and the luxury of it never escaped her.

Kyle was stunned as he stepped aboard. "This is incredible. Is it an antique or a reproduction? This is, what, twenty-nine feet?"

"Thirty-three. It's refurbished from the sixties, I think." Hunter didn't really care about boats, but even he was charmed by this one.

Kyle ran his fingers along a small brass plate fastened to the port side. It was engraved with the final lines of a Yeats poem. Kat noticed the stanza every time she was on the boat. It spoke of the "invulnerable tide"—an idea she'd never heard of before seeing it there, but wouldn't likely forget. Kat never really understood those lines, but she knew enough to know that they weren't about the ocean. The invulnerable tide Yeats was referring to was something darker, more ominous than that. It sent a chill through her each time she read it. Hunter said his father had a dark sense of humor.

Kat took a seat across from Kyle at the bow as the engine whirred, and Hunter steered them slowly away from the shore.

"I think we've got a little time before the rain comes, but don't go out far," Kat yelled toward Hunter in the cockpit.

Kyle took a slug of the whiskey and handed the bottle to her. "So where are you actually from?" he asked her. He had to shout to be heard over the wind and the motor. "Not here, I assume."

Coming from someone else, this would have offended Kat. But Kyle was also—obviously—not from here. She knew what he meant. "I'm from upstate New York. But I've been here for seven years. You?"

The wind picked up.

Kyle scooted closer to Kat. "I'm not from here, either," he said, and that was all he said.

She took a long gulp of the harsh liquor.

Hunter slowed down, then set the boat to idle and joined the other two at the bow, taking the whiskey from Kat.

She wanted to go back to what Kyle had said and press him on his origins, but she didn't. This avoidance of talking about the past was a familiar tactic to her. Kyle didn't seem to want to talk about where he was from and neither did she, which felt something like a secret agreement. Everyone was allowed to do that on the island. You could be whoever you said you were. Kat liked that about living among a mostly transient population. She liked the surrealism that thrives in vacationland. When you live in a place that serves as an escape from reality for so many, you can live forever in a world of make-believe. On vacation, you can take only what you want of yourself with you and leave the rest of it behind. And if you happen to live on the Vineyard all year, you can be forever suspended in a mythology of your making.

"Great fog," Hunter said, leaning back into the cushion. He took a gulp from the bottle, and then two more.

The interior lights by their feet illuminated the thick, wet air around them.

Kat stood up and reclaimed the bottle, taking a sip for herself. As she sat back down, she could feel Kyle's arm draped behind her, apparently ready to receive her.

She sat forward.

Kyle inched closer.

This was her fault. That was Kat's first thought: *this is my fault.* She had been too interested in engaging him in conversation back at the bar, too solicitous. Of course his arm would be there.

"Hunter, we should head back before the rain comes," she said.

Hunter closed his eyes and drifted toward sleep.

"Tired already?" Kyle said to her. His voice sounded different.

"Yeah, I really am. Do you mind if we go back?"

"We will." Kyle reached out and tried to pull Kat's shoulders back toward him.

She stood up and kicked Hunter's shoe. "Hey."

Nothing.

"Passed out." Kyle shrugged, a small grin on his face. "We may as well enjoy this."

Kat pulled the whirling hair away from her face and tried to sound casual. "Kyle, I'm unavailable. You know that."

He leaned back and spread his long arms out like a raptor. "Then why are you out here with me?"

"I'm not out here *with you*..." she started.

But why *was* she out there? It suddenly seemed wildly inappropriate. Kat and Sean had an adult relationship and were free to be friends with whomever they chose. But in the black of night, with a man she hardly knew, it suddenly seemed like a gross miscalculation on her part. She should not be there. Sean wouldn't have done it. She wished he was there with her now.

"We're going back in," Kat said sternly, and she walked around to the cockpit.

She could hear Kyle stand up and move toward her. She ignored him. It was time to drive back to shore.

At the controls, Kat leaned in close, trying to make quick sense of what she was working with. She'd driven a few boats before, but never this one. She couldn't tell if the components were unfamiliar, or if they were just arranged differently. Kyle said something from behind her, which she couldn't hear over the intensifying wind.

"Can you check on Hunter?" Kat yelled in an attempt to keep him at a distance.

They both looked over at Hunter, slumped in the seat by the bow, his mouth hanging open slightly.

Kyle laughed. "He looks comfortable enough."

Kat squeezed the release lock and went to move the lever up to a start position, but it seemed to already be in place. Right, they were idling. She pushed hard on the lever, jiggled it a little, and then harder still. It wouldn't shift into run mode. Then she remembered something about the choke. Maybe that was the problem. Kat fiddled with the key, hoping to activate an automated choke at the ignition, but there was no give. Could there be a switch? She had the vague idea that chokes on old boats were switches. Kat didn't want to ask Kyle for help, though she knew he was right there behind her, watching her struggle. There was no choke switch. Or maybe there was, but she couldn't find it in the shadow of a stranger, under a starless sky, with the wind screaming into her ears and the fog building.

Kat spun around. "Do you know how to do this?"

Kyle furrowed his brow. "Not this kind of boat, I don't."

He could have been lying, enjoying the trap he'd ensnared her in, but it didn't seem like he was lying. Kat detected a hint of embarrassment in Kyle. It was the deepening of his voice and the suggestion that he knew all about *other* boats, just not this one. Unfortunately, she believed that he couldn't get them back to shore, either.

Kat walked to the bow and began shaking Hunter, saying his name over and over with increasing volume while he swayed obliviously in her hands.

This is when her heartbeat picked up. If she'd been sober, alarm bells would have been sounding in her head too.

Then Kat remembered the motor. Maybe there was some switch on the motor that would make it go. She could just drive them home directly with the outboard, as she'd seen people do with smaller boats. That could maybe be an option.

Kat walked to the stern and leaned over the back, trying to discern the edges of the black motor against the black choppy water. She reached out, running her hands along the smooth of its plastic. What she was looking for, Kat had no idea. All she could see were dark propeller blades turning slowly, passively in the waves.

"What are you doing?" Kyle asked from directly behind her.

He seemed nervous too. The whiskey bottle in his hand was almost empty.

Kat stood up straight and turned around, searching reflexively in her pockets for her cell phone as she did. It wasn't there. She remembered accidentally leaving it at her apartment when she'd started out that evening. Everyone she knew was either with her or going to be at The Undertow that night. Who would she have needed to call? She wished she'd remembered her cell phone.

"I'm figuring out how to run this."

"C'mon," Kyle said, putting his hand on her shoulder. "Let's sit for a few and get to know each other better. Then we can prop Hunter up and make him drive us in. We're not far out. There's no rush."

But there *was* a rush. Kat could feel it inside of her. She needed to get off this boat, away from this man. She tried to step around him to get to Hunter. She would slap him awake if need be. But Kyle moved in front of her and blocked her path.

"Don't go." The expression on his face was serious now. His voice sounded angry.

"Kyle."

"Don't go." He dropped the empty bottle with a thud on the floor of the boat.

She was cold suddenly. Was it beginning to rain?

Kat tried again to move Kyle aside with her hand, but his sturdy body didn't budge.

"Kyle, c'mon." She shoved him harder and got free for a moment, taking one step forward until she felt the length of his long arm wrap around her waist and yank her back to him.

With one quick motion, he spun her around, so they were

looking directly at each other, just inches apart, as he leaned his back against the wall of the stern.

It was definitely raining now.

And that was how they ended up there, with wet faces so near, Kyle's hands gripping the sides of her waist, holding her in place against him at the back of the boat.

She strained her head to look back at Hunter as she considered her strategy. Screaming probably wouldn't help. So Kat decided to pretend to be accommodating, for now. If she could get Kyle to relax a bit, maybe she'd have a chance to get to Hunter and wake him up.

"I think you know why you're out here with me," Kyle said.

She shook her head. "No. This isn't what you think it is."

She could feel the rain coming down on the shoulders of her jacket.

Kyle pulled her closer, so their hips were touching, their bodies supported by the low wall of the boat behind him.

Kat could smell his whiskey breath, tinged with tobacco. The buckle on his belt pressed into her stomach.

Kyle looked around, blinked a few times. For a moment it seemed that he was as surprised as she that he was holding her hostage. Kat could see now that he was very drunk and not entirely aware of his surroundings. But then he smiled oddly, and his hesitation was gone, his control regained.

Kat considered crying, but she couldn't will the tears through her fear.

Kyle leaned back against the boat farther, holding her tighter. His long, stupid scarf had nearly unraveled from his neck and it billowed out behind him over the dark surface of the water, whipping against the edge of the motor.

Kat tried to pull away again, but his left hand clamped

harder around her hip as his right hand moved too firmly behind her head, his fingers lacing through her hair.

It was that feeling, the uncompromising slither of his fingers on her scalp that finally triggered something inside her. This was not going to happen. Whatever Kyle had in mind for that moment, a feral instinct in Kat was not going to let it happen.

Kat shoved him with a sudden, hard push. He tried to hold on and yank her closer, but she drew her hands up in defense.

"Nooo!" Kat yelled.

From behind her she could hear Hunter's feet on the deck, but Kat's instincts were already set in motion by then.

And just as a gust of hard rain blasted them from the south, rocking the boat, Kat reached up again and thrust one forceful hand out in front of her—in a stop signal or a push, she didn't know which. She could feel her palm press against Kyle's sternum for the briefest moment as she made contact. Then all at once, his eyes grew wide, his grip on her released and his torso tipped back, back over the edge. There was no pause. He didn't hover. In a flash, Kyle's entire body disappeared through a wall of hammering rain, over the stern of the boat and into the ocean.

Kat fell forward, and it seemed for a moment that she might go over as well, but Hunter caught her with one arm and steadied himself with the steel rail. He'd been a half beat behind her.

Kat stood there at the back of the boat while all the blood in her head drained to her feet. She stared down into the black water trying to see through the dimpling, rain-battered surface to the spot where Kyle had disappeared so quickly. He'd gone down inexplicably fast. She scanned the chop, expecting to see him surface. But nothing. Not a trace.

Hunter leaned over the edge too and scanned the water.

Then he vomited. They both stared at the water for another full minute, searching.

Finally, Hunter stood upright, wiped his mouth and said, "Let's go."

"What?" Kat whispered.

"It's pouring," he said. "We're not that far out. He can make it back on his own. He's probably already started."

Kat shook her head without a word. *No, no, no, no, no.* She knew that wasn't right.

She looked down again through the steady rain at the turbulent water and screamed, "Kyle!"

Silence.

She screamed his name again. Then she looked back at Hunter, who was rubbing his face violently with both hands.

They couldn't just drive away. That isn't what you're supposed to do. A man was overboard, in the water. He was out there alone somewhere. You aren't supposed to leave people out there. But what exactly *could* they do?

Hunter was insistent. He pushed Kat gently aside and went straight to the wheel. With a few quick motions, the boat was humming again and he started to steer them back in the direction of the dock, or where he believed the dock to be. It was so much harder to see now through the driving rain.

Kat felt a confusion mixed with a terrible dread, but she also thought perhaps Hunter was right. They needed to get to shore. Get help. If Kyle was swimming back at that moment, he'd have a better chance of surviving with a search team and medical help. Yes, they just needed to get back and get help.

What other options were there? Kat knew that even if one of them dove in, they probably wouldn't find Kyle, not in this weather. And they would have a solid chance of drowning in those conditions. No one else needed to drown today.

No, she reminded herself, no one *had* drowned today. It was still possible that Kyle had surfaced and was swimming back to shore. But if they could drown, couldn't he? Their fear of jumping in after him seemed in itself confirmation that she didn't believe it was survivable. And what about how quickly he'd plunged overboard, as if some creature from the deep had reached up and yanked him in. Where had Kyle gone?

Kat imagined Kyle's body rocketing headfirst toward the seafloor. How was what she'd seen even possible? The only thing they had any certainty about in that moment was that Kyle had entered the water. They didn't know that he was dead. But how could he not be?

The rain was coming down in sheets now and the ocean moving in enormous, terrifying swells. The boat rose up with each wave, and then smacked back down to the surface, another sheet of seawater washing over their already soaked bodies. Water sloshed around their feet and the cold wetness crept farther up their legs. It felt surreal, as if the boat was going slower than it should have been, like the shore wasn't getting any closer. Something was holding them out there it seemed…with him. But that made no sense, Kat reminded herself. They were headed for shore. They would be back in a matter of minutes.

Kat didn't feel the pelting rain or the heaving of the boat. She didn't feel anything but the palm of her right hand, the palm that had touched Kyle in those last seconds. It was *her* hand that felt the wet wool of his peacoat, and her hand that blocked—or pushed—him into the ocean. But the strange force that had surged up through her body and exploded into Kyle's chest had come from someplace else. It came from her past, from the person she used to be. That person wasn't violent, but had grown up in a violent world that demanded an unflinching self-preservation. That person could sense malice in its most subtle form; had sensed Kyle's malice toward her on the boat. Kyle was an imminent threat. Although Kat had worked hard to distance herself from her past, apparently that instinct still lived deep inside her, ready to react to threats. It may have killed Kyle.

"Watch your foot," Hunter said as he looped the fat rope around the dock post, just as he had unlooped it less than an hour before. He stepped carefully onto the wet dock and offered Kat a hand. She was stunned by how sober and present he suddenly seemed.

"We can cut through the preserve," she said. "It's the fastest route to the station. Or, no, maybe we should just run to your house and call from there. Yeah, let's do that."

A car drove along the road above them, the headlights futile blurs in the dense rain. Hunter pulled Kat toward the stairs, under the shadow of the bluff.

"Wait," he said into her ear.

"What? No. We have to go now!" Shivers were reverberating through Kat's entire body, fear and frigidity weakening her more with each moment they stood there.

"Please, Kat," Hunter pleaded. He was holding on to her shoulders, more desperate than forceful. "Let's wait until morning. He's probably swimming in now. He's almost certainly swimming in. And…if he's not…well, there's nothing anyone can do for him."

"No, we can't wait!" She looked up toward the empty road. "C'mon, we're wasting time. We have to—"

"Kat, I'm fucked up right now! If we go to the police, it will be in the papers. Another scandal for Senator Briggs's drunk son. And my father will lose this election. I'll be cut off for good. I'll go to prison for sure this time."

Kat was confused. She looked up at him, but could barely

find his eyes in the blackness. "But this was an accident. No one's going to jail."

He shook his head. "Not with the amount of alcohol in my system. Kat, I've used up all my accidents. It will be the end of my life. *Please*. I'll face this, but I'm begging you for just a few hours to sober up. It won't make any difference to Kyle. He's either going to swim to safety, or he isn't."

Kat could hear the terror in Hunter's voice, but she couldn't make sense of it. This didn't have to be the end for anyone—even Hunter, who was an idiot, but not a criminal. It was an *accident*.

"I promise I'll face this," he said again. "I'll do the right thing. I just need a few hours to get it together."

And then she thought she understood: Hunter must think it's his fault, that *he* pushed Kyle overboard. Hunter had lunged at them in a stupor and watched Kyle's body go over the back of the boat. Maybe he thinks Kat witnessed him push Kyle into the ocean. Maybe that *is* what happened.

Kat looked out toward the water as her brain held the thought. She'd been assuming it was her fault, but she was drunk too and couldn't be sure of anything... Maybe it had been Hunter's fault.

"C'mon." Hunter began walking up the steps. He interpreted her hesitation as assent.

Kat followed him up, unsure of what would come next. The more she played the time on the boat in her mind, the hazier it became. Her hand...Hunter's clumsy body falling toward them...and the bullet-quick speed with which Kyle plunged into the water and disappeared... Just a series of flashing images. Only the panicked expression on Kyle's face was still clear in her mind. If they went to the police now, she had no confidence in her ability to describe what she'd seen…or what she'd done to Kyle. And had she been the one to do it or was it Hunter?

Kyle might be alive, she reminded herself. She should assume that he's alive. And if he is, he'd know what happened out there. He'd tell the police that he'd been pushed. No, she thought again, maybe he wouldn't tell. Because Kyle would also be ashamed of his drunken aggression. Probably. Maybe. Kat didn't know anymore what was a greater threat—Kyle's death or his survival. She felt nauseous.

At the street level, all was quiet except for the sound of the steady rain. Every nearby house was dark. Hunter looked down at Kat as she took the last step up. Water was dripping from his eyelashes, his hair and chin.

"I'll call you in a few hours," he said. He paused for a moment and then walked away without looking back.

"Hunter," Kat tried to say, but no sound came out.

This wasn't right, doing nothing. It left her feeling at odds with herself. You're supposed to act, to do something at a moment like this. She knew she should go after him. They needed to go to the cops together and explain…what exactly? Someone went missing overboard? If Hunter felt that he was the reason Kyle was in the water, then he probably was, right? She wasn't sure that he was, but she wasn't sure of anything. Could she go to the cops alone and turn her friend in for fleeing the scene of an accident? Is that what they'd call it? Or would it become manslaughter if Kyle didn't turn up? No, she mustn't think about the consequences right now. The only thing that mattered now was Kyle's survival. She definitely needed to go to the cops. But her feet wouldn't walk in that direction.

Kat stood dripping, convulsing with shivers, as she watched Hunter disappear into the enormous Briggs family vacation house. She saw one small interior light blink on, then blink off again thirty seconds later. He was going to bed. Kat could hardly see through the rain dripping down her face. She wasn't doing the thing she knew she was supposed to do, and in *not* doing it, she was choosing to do something else entirely.

Kat turned to her left and began walking slowly home, one foot in front of the other, along the wet sidewalk. She just kept walking, thinking of nothing but the motion of her legs and feet. Never stopping.

When she got to the glass studio, Kat unlocked the door and went inside.

She had done nothing, which was a choice in itself.

CHAPTER 2

Kat closed the door behind her and walked into the dark glass studio. She always went in that way at night—through the garage and up the back stairs—so she could double-check that the furnace and the white-hot glass reheater (the "glory hole") were set low. Living above machines set to thousand-degree temperatures had made her a little paranoid. But on that night, it was also the best way to minimize the possibility of anyone seeing her slip inside and sneak up to the apartment.

She walked dripping through the dark garage with her trembling hands outstretched to catch a stray chair or wooden paddle that may have been in her way. Too much had happened in the preceding hours for her to remember where she'd left everything.

Kat banged her right knee into something rock solid. It was the edge of the annealing oven. There were three bowls in there, maybe a few paperweights too. She'd made them the day before. It was a fleeting comfort to remember these small details of her normal life, the person she was before she left a man in the ocean.

Kat ascended the stairs slowly with waterlogged sneakers. At the top, she went straight through the dark apartment to the bathroom, where she closed the door and turned on the light.

She hung her head over the toilet with her hands on either side, retching but producing nothing. The room was spinning.

Kat dropped to her knees, closed the lid of the toilet and rested her head upon it.

Why was she there and not at the police station? Why had she let Hunter talk her into this? Kat could feel a viscous string of saliva slide from the side of her mouth onto the cool porcelain, but she didn't move. Kat didn't know if she'd watched someone die, but she'd surely watched someone disappear. And although she'd done nothing intentional to harm Kyle, there was a distinct possibility that he had been harmed—fatally, perhaps—and she was paralyzed by her own guilt.

It wasn't all new guilt. It was new mixed with old. The old guilt was shame, actually. It was the practiced shame of someone who'd grown up covering for, and protecting herself from, a delinquent parent. Her mother's crimes had been minor, but capacious. They demanded constant caution on Kat's part to avoid prying questions from teachers, social workers and classmates. It wasn't only the petty thievery and insurance fraud in lieu of real jobs; it was also her mother's regular disappearances with shady new boyfriends, and worse, her cruelty toward Kat when those boyfriends eventually left her. Kat had endured it all until the day she turned sixteen and left her mother. Kat woke up each morning with an unspecific feeling that she was guilty by association, complicit in the chaos around her. She thought she left that feeling behind, until now.

Kat was guilty of nothing in her childhood, but the stench of her past was hard to wash off. It was that shame that made going to the police station difficult for her right now, even as she knew it must be done. Kat had left her past behind, but apparently she hadn't shaken the feeling that people like her—people on the margins, victimizers and victims alike—were all guilty of something. Those people didn't usually fare well with police encounters. So all it took was Hunter's gut-wrenching appeal for her to acquiesce to his wish.

But now, as the room spun around her, it was reality that made her panic. Kat and Hunter—one or both of them—might have directly contributed to Kyle's demise. Their actions were most certainly provoked, but how much that mattered now, Kat didn't know. If Kyle was dead, Kat realized that every version of this story from here on out would implicate her. The decision to go home and not report his fall overboard was irreversible, and becoming more treacherous with each minute she spent on the bathroom floor.

And goddamn Hunter was at home, probably passed out. She hated him at that moment. She almost blamed him for whatever may or may not have happened to Kyle, but it wasn't her nature. Kat had tacitly agreed to Hunter's plea to run, and now she was wrong right along with him.

The worst thing—the thing that Kat could hardly bring herself to consider—was the possibility that Kyle could be dead, but his death had been preventable if only they'd gone for help. If he did drown, Kat prayed that his death was sudden and decisive. And if it hadn't been fast, she hoped to never know the truth.

Kat couldn't shake the vision of Kyle's wide, panicked eyes in the final moment before he went over the edge. One second her palm was still touching the wet wool of his coat. Then he was gone. Dead, maybe.

The pale blue and green tiles of her shower stall blurred before her. She heaved, expelled what bile was left in her stomach and passed out on the cold bathroom floor.

Six hours later, a fist pounded on the front door of the shop, sending a bolt to Kat's fogged consciousness. The first thing she saw as she opened her eyes were those blue and green shower tiles…and then she remembered the puking… and the wet trek home…until she'd walked backward in her mind all the way to the panic in Kyle's eyes. The memory of his eyes sent another tsunami of guilt over her aching body.

Another friendly knock came from outside.

Kat pushed herself up and reached for the knob of the bathroom door. She needed to go see who was there. She had to act normal. She was an innocent person who'd made a mistake. She had no reason to avoid a knock at her door in the early morning. But then she saw her reflection in the mirror—her stringy hair matted around her forehead and lidded hangover eyes. On one cheek was a fresh bruise from when she'd passed out on the tile, and on the other, the dried stomach bile she'd been sleeping in. It wasn't an innocent look. She waited for the knocking to stop. Then she counted to one hundred and left the bathroom.

The apartment was flooded with morning light. The storm had moved on.

Through a kitchen window, Kat looked down at two men and a woman standing at the side entrance to the shop. The people who'd been knocking, she presumed. They all wore the same windbreakers, which said Woods Hole Erosion Team across the back. She'd seen them around town for the past three days, ever since the landslide on their beach. At the reminder of the landslide, Kat felt another wave of panic, this one mixed with despair. There were suddenly too many unsolvable problems before her. And those problems were intersecting in troubling ways. Ever since the landslide, area beaches had been crawling with police, scientists and cleanup crews. People were watching those beaches with greater attention now. They were seeing things that might normally go unseen. Things, she worried, like late-night boating excursions.

No, she reminded herself. There was no one else on the beach last night. She definitely hadn't seen anyone else.

Kat watched the three windbreakers below. They were discussing something; it looked lighthearted. The older man told a joke and the other two laughed. The woman pulled out a flyer and stuck it in the doorjamb. They walked away, laughing again.

Relieved, Kat went to the kitchen sink and drank a tall glass of water. Then she walked back to the bathroom, turned on the shower and let it run while she peeled the damp clothes from her body. She needed to see Hunter, but she couldn't leave the house looking filthy and wild. She just needed a few minutes to pull herself together, then get out there into the world and do what needed to be done.

The sun was shining brighter when she emerged from the bathroom and she worried that she'd taken too much time. Kat wanted to look like she was in a rush when she arrived at the police station. She *was* in a rush.

A walk to Hunter's house at a brisk speed. Nothing strange about that.

By Kat's calculation, it was 7:50 when she knocked on Hunter's door. She knocked loud and without any pauses because the minutes were moving faster than she'd anticipated, and 8:30 was her new arbitrary deadline for getting to the police station. After that, it would look too casual, like it hadn't been a priority.

The door swung open and a tall man in a pressed oxford shirt greeted her.

"Please. Come in," he said.

"Is Hunter here?" Kat had never seen this guy. She stepped inside and let the man close and lock the door behind her.

"Hunter's resting," he said calmly.

A family doctor, she considered…but he didn't *seem* like a doctor. His clothes were too sharp, his wristwatch too ostentatious.

"I'm an associate of the senator's," the man explained.

Kat looked past him, around the grand entrance of the house, up the stairs. "May I talk to Hunter, please?" She didn't want to act alarmed before this stranger.

"Let's have a quick chat, first."

She glanced over her shoulder at the door, then back at the man. "Okay."

"I know about the accident," the man said, rolling up the cuffs of his powder blue shirt. His forearms were covered in dense white-blond hair that crept up his knuckles. The hair curled around the enormous face of a gold Rolex.

Kat considered running. "I'm not sure what you mean."

"Yes, you do. But you're safe here, Kat."

"Who are you?"

"Like I said, I'm a friend of Senator Briggs. I help out where I can. And, Kat, you and Hunter need help right now. So listen to what I'm about to tell you."

She stared at the broad and solid creature, a Scandinavian brick with fluffy white eyebrows.

"Let's just assume Kyle Billings is dead," he started. "He was a very disturbed young man who was attempting to assault you. Hunter thwarted his attack, and there was an accident in the process. Nothing could be done. In all likelihood, a life has been tragically lost, but we have a chance now to save the lives of the people who remain. Let's stop the bleeding, shall we, Kat?"

She looked into the man's eyes and tried to understand what was happening. He was telling her the story of last night, giving her the script. But that isn't exactly how things had gone down. Or was it? Kat didn't move.

"Can we agree that the death of Kyle Billings—if it happened—is a tragedy, Kat? And that we don't need to compound that tragedy? That won't help anyone, will it?"

She heard nothing beyond the name: Kyle Billings. She'd never known his full name. Kyle Billings, Kyle Billings, Kyle Billings. Kat rolled it around in her head. With a last name, he became a son, maybe a brother, an old friend. He was a person connected to other people, a person with a past.

"Kat, are you listening?"

She nodded.

"I know this is difficult," the man said, though he didn't seem particularly troubled by any of it. "So we'd like to offer you a gift of thanks for your discretion."

He reached into his back pocket and handed her a small, folded piece of paper with only the following written on it: $1.3M.

Kat stared at the paper for three seconds, confused. And then alarmed. "A million dollars?"

"One point three, yes."

"This is a bribe? What is this for?"

The man folded his arms, annoyed by her indelicacy. "It's a gift of thanks…for keeping this between us. And I'm sure you understand why this is the best tactic for everyone. The Briggs family has a lot to lose, as you know."

"No, no, no!" Kat pushed past the man and ran through the foyer. She looked around the living room and kitchen, then ran upstairs.

Every bedroom was empty and orderly, with piles of nautical-themed throw pillows arranged atop beds. Why did they need so many rooms if no one was ever there? And which one was Hunter's? At the end of the hall, Kat nearly crashed into a stunned young woman wearing a T-shirt bearing the logo of a Portuguese soccer team. She'd been cleaning the last room, Hunter's bedroom, it seemed. He wasn't in there.

Kat flew down the stairs, past the man and out the door. The fresh air felt good in her lungs.

Kat looked up and down the street with squinty eyes. It was unusually sunny and warm for mid-October, a completely different place than the street they'd shivered along the night before.

Kat crossed the road and looked down at the water. There was Hunter, sitting in a lawn chair on his dock, looking straight into the sun.

"Let's go, Hunter," she yelled as she ran down the stairs. She looked around and whisper-yelled the rest. "We need to tell the police what happened. He might be alive."

Hunter didn't move.

"Hunter!"

Still nothing.

Kat walked the length of the dock and stood in front of him, blocking the glare of the sun. With her shadow cast across him, she could see the hollows of his eyes. He looked awful.

"This was your solution?" Kat held up the paper from the white-haired man. "You want to pay me to keep quiet?"

Hunter met her stare, but he didn't move. "I don't like it, either, Kat. I had to tell my dad, though. This could cost him the election and end his career. It's bigger than us."

The boat thudded gently against a dock post beside them.

It made her sick to see it there. It was covered now. Kat wondered if the man with the arm hair had covered it for them. That seemed like something that would fall to him now.

"Hunter, we have to take responsibility for this! If they find the body and track us down, this is going to be a million times worse."

He stood up slowly. "How would they track us down? No one knows that the three of us went out last night. And it was raining too hard for anyone to hear us. The universe is handing us a fucking lifeline here, Kat. Let's take it."

"No. I'm going to the cops. I'm going right now."

She turned to leave and he grabbed her forearm. "Please don't. This will be it for me. I'll go to prison, and I will have officially ruined my father's life which, despite the fact that he's an asshole, I don't want to do."

Kat considered telling Hunter that there was a chance that it was she and not he who pushed Kyle into the water. Last night, she'd been sure of it. But her muddled thinking made her question her memory. Maybe it didn't matter who pushed him. And maybe a small part of her wanted to leave some room for the possibility of her own innocence.

Hunter had every resource in the world to weather a criminal conviction. What did she have? No money or family or connections of any kind. She sure as hell wasn't going to take the fall for a crime she had only *maybe* committed. No, she was just going to tell the police a sanitized version of the story: that Kyle had been drinking, the weather turned bad, he lost his balance and he went overboard. Then he disappeared into the water. They looked for him, then returned on the assumption that he was swimming in. She would emphasize that it was all an accident.

"You can come or not come, but I'm going to the cops

right now, Hunter. I don't want your money." Kat walked back along the dock and started up the stairs.

"You think you're going to get off free here?" he yelled.

She turned around. "What?"

"You're in this now, Kat. Forget the money. The money doesn't change any of it. You're a highly suspicious person now."

"No, Hunter, I'm not."

"Then why did you go home after we got back to the dock? Why didn't you call for a rescue? Why'd you go to sleep, and take a shower this morning, and change all your clothes?"

"I didn't..."

"Seems like strange behavior for an innocent person, is all I'm saying."

Hunter wasn't enjoying himself. He was doing what he needed to do to keep Kat from reporting what happened. She could see the self-loathing on his face. But he was still doing it, and it was working. She was nervous now.

"But it was an accident," Kat whispered.

Hunter shrugged. "Maybe it was and maybe it wasn't. Who knows..."

"We do! We *know* that it was an accident!"

"Our version of the story isn't worth as much as it used to be."

Kat shook her head. She couldn't believe he was doing this. She wanted to hate him for it, but it looked more desperate than diabolical. He was a grown man too scared and sorry to get caught for screwing up again. She hated Hunter for provoking empathy in her, even as he put their lives at risk.

"No." She shook her head.

He stared pleadingly.

Kat climbed the stairs slowly, waiting for Hunter to change his mind about it all, which he did not. He let her go.

And Kat didn't walk toward the police station. She went home instead. She was still sure that telling the police was the right thing to do, but she was too frightened to do it.

As she walked through the garage studio, Kat could hear her phone ringing upstairs on the kitchen table. Shit, Sean. They were supposed to meet for breakfast, as they always did on Wednesdays. Shit, shit, shit. She knew it was him even before she got to the phone.

"Hello?"

"Kat, finally. Is everything okay? I've been calling for an hour."

"Yeah, fine. Sean, I'm so, so sorry for missing breakfast. I feel really sick today and slept right through everything. I guess my phone was off. I'm so sorry."

"God, how much did you drink last night? Did you stay out late? I thought you were heading straight home."

Kat did a fast scroll through all the faces she'd seen in the last twelve hours, assessing how far she could take this lie. "I was. I went home soon after you. I think I have, like, a cold or something. The tequila shots probably didn't help. I'm really sorry to miss breakfast."

"It's fine." Sean seemed annoyed, but satisfied with this response. "Are you working today?"

In all the confusion, she'd forgotten to open the shop. She and Orla took turns in the off-season. Traffic would be light, but they couldn't afford to miss even the occasional shoppers who might pass through.

"Yep, I'm going to open it in just a minute. I'll take it easy today, try to rest up."

"Okay, just stay out of the garage. You don't need to be sweating in front of an oven if you've got a fever."

She hadn't said that she had a fever but that worked nicely. "I'll come by later with a grilled cheese from Stoney's," he added.

"No, don't bother." Did she say that too forcefully? She really didn't want to see him in person. Lying to Sean's face would be too hard. Best to just avoid him for a while. "I have no appetite right now and I'm no fun. I'll call you later."

Kat and Sean hadn't spent a full day apart—a day without the briefest check-in or stop by—in longer than she could remember, and this felt like a bad time to start.

"Okay. I've got a couple of big boats to put to bed for the winter, so this will be a long day at the boatyard anyhow. Love you."

"Love you too."

Kat walked to the kitchen sink and drank another sixteen ounces of tap water. She could hear it gurgling through her hollowed insides. She was starving, but couldn't imagine eating actual food.

Kat went back down the stairs and out the door. She walked around the house to the oceanfront side, which was now a mere four feet from the edge of the cliff. She stepped over the orange police tape that had been put up after the landslide, and sank into an Adirondack chair. The sun was strong, but through the chair's old wood she could feel moisture from the previous night's rain. It must be one of the last things to dry, after the sidewalks and roofs, the towels left hanging on porch railings, and boats left uncovered. All the untreated Adirondack chairs on the island still held the story of the night before.

She figured it would only take three steps to go over the edge from there. They should get a railing or something. Kat made a mental note to talk to Orla about that. At the very least, they could build a wire fence to warn people of the drop-off. Kids couldn't be out there anymore. Kat always assumed that one day she and Sean would have kids, and they would hang around the shop after school the way Sean had done with Orla. Was that off the table now? If Kat had maybe killed a person and certainly evaded the authorities, did that disqualify her from being a parent? The implications of the night before kept coming at her, like unexpected punches to the gut.

Last night had been horrible, but each successive realization at the consequences of last night was worse. Suddenly the entire path of her life was unfolding in Kat's mind and the sweeping breadth of her one terrible, drunk decision was becoming clear. Why hadn't she just run to the police station? Why wasn't she headed there now?

A willet soared above the shoreline, searching for something to dive at with its needle-sharp bill. It went south for a while, then came back and made a ninety-degree turn toward the shallow water. An unsuspecting fish, murdered. Sean's daughter knew about all the birds on the island, which meant that Kat and Sean did too. What had she told them about the willet? It often searches the shores for food at night, she'd said. And it sees everything.

Someone must have seen them out there.

CHAPTER 3

Lying on her back fully dressed in her unmade bed, Kat tossed a tennis ball back and forth between her hands. Left, right, left, right. It made a gentle thud against her palms with each catch, quiet enough not to drown out the sounds of the voices below.

Through her bedroom window, Kat could hear men talking down on the beach, right in front of the glass shop. She couldn't discern the words, but the cadence of their conversation was growing familiar to her after two sleepless hours staring at the cracked ceiling above her bed. People had been on that beach, on and off, for the past three days, ever since the landslide. It was an assortment of local cops and municipal employees tasked with "risk assessment," as they called it. They were taking pictures and measuring cliff moisture. They were trying to figure out where things got away from them, when the threat of catastrophe turned from possible to imminent.

Kat was doing the same.

She'd made it through the day. She'd opened the shop, gone through the motions with the four customers who actually bought things and watched the hands of the clock go around. No one had mentioned the disappearance of Kyle Billings. No one had come to arrest her. Nothing was different, and the silence of all that nothing was unbearable.

Alone in her apartment, Kat was playing the muddled reel of the accident over and over in her head, pausing from time to time, with the tennis ball in hand, to examine and replay the images. She was looking for an explanation for what had become of Kyle, other than the obvious one.

The whir of car wheels spinning in sand rose up from the beach. There was too much pressure; Kat could tell from her bed. They needed to let more air out of the tires.

Had that SUV been on the beach last night? She'd seen it come and go, and now she couldn't remember if it had been left parked on the beach. No, she would have remembered seeing it. Then again, it was pretty far down, and the fog had been thick…maybe it had been there. She wanted them all to leave her beach and the fragile, exposed wall of their cliffs. She wanted everything to be as it was.

The landslide happened three days before, on the last full day of bustling summer crowds. It felt like a thousand years ago to Kat. She could hardly remember anything before last night. But she remembered the landslide.

They were just finishing an early breakfast. Kat, Sean, Sean's mother, Orla, and Sean's daughter, Weeta, were on their last bites at the diner when the parade of sirens went by. They paid their bill and, along with several other patrons at the restaurant, walked out the door to follow the noise. They didn't know at the time that the sirens were headed for the doorstep of Island Glass, Orla's shop.

By the time they got down to the beach, two dozen people were already there. It was mostly cops, coast guard specialists, scientist-looking types with clipboards milling around and shocked residents still in their pajamas. The officials all wore tall boots for trudging through the loose, wet sand while they cordoned off the area with orange ribbon. The damage stretched from Island Glass down several hundred feet. Every inch of land along the way was now five feet closer to the water's edge, including Orla Murphy's glass shop and studio. Where there had been overgrown beach grasses, there was now freshly exposed bluff that seemed still to be in motion, with small pockets of sand tumbling here and there.

Kat remembered clearly the sound that Orla made as they stepped onto the beach and she sucked in the air around her.

"Oh Lord," Orla said.

Soft waves lapped up around their feet in rhythmic regularity, searching for places to pool on the uneven sand. The delineating line between ocean and turf had disappeared into a mess of crumbled beach wall. It was disorienting.

Sean placed a firm hand on his mother's back as they approached a police officer in a raincoat. "Excuse me...was this a landslide?"

"More of a buckling," the cop told them, his eyes on the orange-tape operation ten feet away.

"Is it over?" Kat asked.

The cop shrugged. "No way to know, really."

Unsatisfied, Sean walked past the man. Weeta followed quickly, almost forgetting how the wet sand was ruining her new Converse high-tops. Kat and Orla walked three steps behind.

A young woman in tall rain boots and a windbreaker jogged toward them from the water. "Excuse me, you can't be here!"

They stopped and considered the woman who, despite her authoritative tone, looked barely old enough to drink. She had a long blond ponytail that brushed over a backpack she wore high and tight.

"The public can't be out here."

Orla pointed up to the street level. "That's my place."

"Oh."

All five of them looked up at the raw edge of the bluff twenty-five feet above their heads, where a grassy lawn had broken clean off and fallen to the beach earlier that morning.

"You live here?" The woman's clear, smooth forehead wrinkled in concern.

"No, it's my business. It's a glass shop. We make everything in the garage. Can you explain what happened? How bad is this?"

No one mentioned that Kat *did* live there, on the second floor. And as of that morning, she could probably see straight down into the water from her bedroom window.

"I'm so sorry," the young woman said. "This is pretty bad. The rising tides have been undercutting your cliff for years, basically eroding this coast from the bottom up. This morning the top layer finally gave way. It just slumped and fell."

"I know all that," Orla clipped. "But they said this wouldn't be a concern for twenty more years. Why is it happening now?"

The young woman took a long breath. "That's what we all thought until recently. But then some monster storms have come through in the last few years, and sea levels rose a bit faster than expected... It's a confluence of things. Usually, there's a triggering event."

"Well what triggered this?"

"I don't know." The woman looked around, apparently hoping to be rescued from this excruciating conversation.

"And what's your job here?" Kat asked.

"I'm a grad student."

"Oh, for fuck's sake!" Sean stormed away, toward a gaggle of uniformed men. Weeta followed.

The young woman frowned at Orla and Kat. "I'm finishing my PhD in coastal erosion. I've been studying its effects here for two years. I probably know more about it than anyone on this beach."

"Sorry, we're just in shock," Kat said. "Can you tell us if it's safe to go back in the house?"

The woman stared at the wall of the cliff, and they followed her gaze. Kat noticed for the first time the clear lines of fine sand and clay, a layer cake of Vineyard history holding up her life, or *not* holding it up. That house contained Kat's whole existence.

"I don't know. That's not my call. You're probably safe for now because the weak part of the bluff has fallen off. But the erosion will continue. You need to plan for that. The part we don't know is how waterlogged the clay might be. See those layers? They absorb a lot of moisture and sometimes when the clay can't hold any more, it just…mobilizes."

"What does that mean?"

"It means a landslide, or an eruption of some sort. One way or another, this house isn't going to be here in twenty years. It might not be here in five."

Orla looked out at the water. She was approaching catatonic. That house was the embodiment of her. It was the business she'd built with her late husband; the place she'd spent thirty years mastering the skills her father taught her and his father taught him. She'd helped her son, Sean, with his homework on the porch after school and mourned the death of her husband by working endless hours in the scalding garage studio. And after his death, she found hope again by teaching her young apprentice—Kat—the craft. Glass working was the thread that connected the Murphys of eighteenth-century Waterford, Ireland, to Orla, Sean and Weeta. It was their story, and that was everything to Orla.

Kat looked at her watch. It was almost ten. Time to open the shop.

"Let's go back," Orla said.

The others nodded.

Orla, Kat, Sean and Weeta walked back along the beach the way they'd come, past the strange new topography of their waterfront, to the warped staircase that led up to the road. No one spoke as they walked along the sidewalk toward the shop.

All three adults knew that this, or something like this, was always a possibility. Life on the Vineyard was not fixed. Even Weeta knew that things were shifting and eroding imperceptibly all the time. But the Murphys didn't dwell on the idea because what on earth could be done about it, anyway?

Movement was the norm, disconcerting as it was. It connected the locals, was something to observe and discuss at the diner. The sands were always shifting in small ways, rearranging the face of their beaches. But the Vineyard also had a fantastical history of large shifts, like when it disconnected from its sister island Chappaquiddick. The two islands spent eight years apart after a major storm destroyed the connective land between them a while back. And then they came together again just a few years after that, and all the islanders just shrugged and went on with their lives. One would think such perpetual motion would prepare its inhabitants for a dramatic change, but man is still more inclined to expect the inertia of sameness despite all evidence to the contrary.

At the front door of the shop, Kat hesitated.

"We have to see," Sean said. He went ahead of her and turned the key in the lock.

Inside, the sun was blasting through the stained glass windows on the waterfront side, casting a blanket of multicolored shadows over every surface in the room. The open space was sparsely decorated with only smooth cubic furniture that displayed the bowls, vases and glassware. A row of colorful sand dollar ornaments hung along the wall, blending with the rainbow dapples from the windows. It was an extraordinary effect, famous now among locals and tourists. The shop opened every morning at ten and, during the high season, it wasn't unusual to find a line at the door when they opened. No one was outside on that day.

"It looks the same," Weeta said. They had all been expecting something different.

Orla went to the window and looked out at the breaking waves.

Sean put his arm around his mother's shoulders. She wasn't a small woman, but she looked it then.

"What are we going to do?" Kat asked their backs.

"We'll figure something out," Sean said.

Orla shook her head. "No, we won't."

"Of course we will, Mom."

"I don't think so. I have no savings and neither do you, Sean. There's nothing we can do...nothing but wait."

"You have insurance," Kat said.

Orla turned. "Not for this. No one on the water has that kind of insurance anymore."

"We'll figure something out..." Kat's voice trailed off as she noticed Weeta standing beside her with wide, frightened eyes.

Weeta was so tall and thin, with straight black hair that almost hit her waist. It was easy to forget that she was only eleven. She had been with Sean every other weekend ever since he split up with her mother, Beth, when Weeta was just a baby. It was becoming clear to them that any day now she might protest the arrangement, demand to stay back in Boston more often with her mom and all her friends. Sean dreaded that day.

Weeta was short for Weetamoo, named after her great-grandmother on Beth's side, the Wampanoag side. This was their island first. Weeta didn't look a thing like Sean, but they couldn't have been more alike. Kat used to think it strange, that some unlikely negotiation of dominant and recessive genes produced offspring so physically different. But she'd been wrong; Weeta was Sean's daughter in every way. Ethical and opinionated, stubbornly righteous, but a friend to everyone. She was, like Sean, a connector of people. He was fully devoted to her. It was one of the things Kat loved most about him.

"Don't worry," Kat assured Weeta. "We'll figure this out."

"Maybe I can help," she said. "I can get a job or something. I can ask my mom."

Sean looked at her. "Don't do that, honey. We'll make it right."

No one really believed that.

Just then, three loud knocks startled them as a rotund police officer opened the front door. "Orla," he boomed.

"Hi, Tom," she sighed.

Everyone knew Orla and her glass studio.

Tom the police officer looked sorry for his presence. "Orla, you can't be here anymore."

She put her arms out in defeat. "Well, where can I be, then? Really. What am I supposed to do?"

He yanked his beige pants up with a hard tug of the belt. "Okay, we'll keep an eye on your cliff, let you know if it looks like things are changing. I can't get a straight answer from anyone about what we're dealing with here. The erosion committee is hiring a full-time person and we've got some experts from the city camped out here for a few more weeks. So you can stay for now. But if they say it's not safe anymore, you gotta go. I'll drag you out myself if I have to."

"Understood."

"Stay off the beach, though."

"I will."

Sean shook the man's hands and walked him out. No one said a word. When he returned and it was just the four of them again, Orla was fighting back tears. Kat put her arm around Weeta, who was looking down at her dirty high-tops. They would never be white again.

Orla smiled a sad smile at Sean and adjusted the collar of his jacket. It was a small, involuntary gesture, bursting with pride and ownership. Kat wondered at the time what it was like to experience the feeling of having created another human from your own flesh, how excruciating it must be at times to see them out there in the world, vulnerable to everything. And for a child, how it must feel to be connected to the body that created you, forever tethered by an invisible line of closeness, of dependency.

Kat had never experienced that magnetism. Biology doesn't promise a connection, only life—and even that, it hasn't perfected. For Kat and her mother, the connection stopped at birth.

Kat lived with her mother for sixteen years in Buffalo, New York. Boyfriends came and went, but it was mostly just the two of them. Her mother wasn't a bad woman; Kat always considered her more underdeveloped than evil. She had a short attention span and poor impulse control, bouncing around between illegitimate moneymaking schemes and loser guys, dragging her resilient daughter around with her. Kat's mother always regarded Kat as a means to an end. She made Kat pretend they were sisters in public. She had her shoplift makeup when money was tight. At thirteen, Kat was tasked with driving her mother and her low-life friends home from the bars in the early morning hours. No one in their orbit had real jobs and most had done time. It was a workable, if cold, arrangement in the early years. Then her mom got increasingly depressed and verbally abusive. More than a few of her boyfriends tried to force themselves on Kat. As a result, Kat developed an ability to spot lechers and sadists in an instant. She could see trouble from a mile away. If anything good came from Kat's childhood, it was a ferocious will to survive. Kat was a survivor.

Still, she occasionally felt overwhelmed by a desire for more closeness when she was around the Murphys. Kat loved them all so much. They'd taught her how to love. She was so grateful for Orla's guidance and faith in her; she could hardly believe her luck in finding them all. And she was grateful for Sean, whose love for her seemed proof that Kat hadn't been permanently damaged by the damaged woman who'd raised her.

The Murphys knew how much Kat loved them, but they didn't know how desperately she needed them. She'd only ever shared the rough contours of her past.

"We'll figure something out," Kat said. She'd do anything for these people.

A muffled trill of a cell phone broke the silence, and everyone's hand moved to their pockets.

It was Kat's. "Hello?"

"Kat Weber? This is Betsy Klein... I met you at the shop recently."

"Of course! Betsy, how are you?" Her heartbeat quickened as she walked through the side entrance door, to the relative privacy of the yard. Betsy Klein liked to buy things, big things.

"I'm great. Listen, I've decided that I'm going to do it. I want *The Selkie*. I couldn't get it out of my head since I last saw it at the shop, and Kenneth says he's given up on trying to regulate my art habit, which is great news for both of us. So anyhow, can you have it here before next Saturday? I'm having a little cocktail thing at the beach house, and I would love to have it here for that. What do you think?"

Kat's head was spinning. *The Selkie*! It had been sitting in the corner of Island Glass for six weeks, inspiring awed comments but not a single offer. Kat wanted to bring it down from its price of fifteen thousand dollars and just get it out of there before she began to really regret having put so much time and effort into it. But Orla wouldn't let her do it. Orla thought it was extraordinary—it was—and she wouldn't let her sell it for less than fifteen thousand. The right person will understand it, she'd said. Just wait. Kat didn't know if she was happier about the vindication of her hard work or the fifteen thousand dollars. She really needed the money. And the *meaning* of the money…it felt something like being a professional.

"Yes, yes of course! I can deliver it in the next few days. Let me make a few arrangements and call you back with a time."

"Fantastic," Betsy said. For her, this was as easy as booking a manicure. "I might be in Newport for a few days, but I'll send you the house code and I'll leave your check on the kitchen table. You're the best. Talk soon!"

The line went dead before Kat could thank the busy lady. She put her phone in her pocket and watched two cars go by. The drivers in each slowed down and strained to see what was going on down by the beach with all the cops. Kat wondered if she was allowed to be overjoyed by the sale of her selkie, in the wake of an avalanche. No, it was just a "buckling." Maybe she was allowed to be happy in the wake of a buckling.

"Everything okay?" Sean asked from the doorway.

She spun around. "I sold *The Selkie*."

He put his arms out and stepped toward her, enveloping her in a bear hug and lifting her feet briefly off the ground. "That's amazing! For the full fifteen K?"

"Yup."

He lifted her again. "Yay, yay, yay! We should celebrate!"

"I don't think today's the day for that." Kat pulled away from him and looked back at the house.

"Yeah, you're right. But when?"

"After we deliver it. I'll feel like celebrating once it's safely at its new home and the check is cashed."

"Good. Okay, then let's deliver it Tuesday and we'll celebrate then. I'll tell everyone to meet us at The Undertow. I don't know who's working that night…maybe that new guy, Kyle." Sean was still grinning. "Man, we needed this today. We really fucking needed this."

The memory of that call, and the look on Sean's face, made Kat smile. She tossed the tennis ball from her left to her right hand, and back again, smiling up at the crack on the ceiling. She could still hear the men down on the beach, though it was getting dark.

Sean was right. They really needed that win—the sale of *The Selkie*, the fifteen thousand dollars and the celebration that followed. All of those things were good and right. But the celebration had gotten away from them and there was no going back in time. So many things were beyond their control now.

Kat felt sure she'd never sleep again.

CHAPTER 4

Kat slid her hands as high up the hot iron rod as she could tolerate. She rolled it around and around in the molten glass pool, then pulled the glowing blob from the furnace and twirled slowly. The trick, Orla taught her, is to keep turning if you want something remotely spherical later. If the phone rings and you look away for five seconds, gravity will have its way with your hot glass, and you'll never get it back to that perfect orb again. She had learned to be faster and smarter than the temperature around her because every second spent away from the heat is a second closer to hard, immovable glass.

She moved her hands back a few inches and inserted the rod into the blazing glory hole. She used to cringe at the name—*glory hole*—but had mostly forgotten its prurient origins by now. She rather enjoyed the unsubtle reminder that hers was a masculine art. The weight of its tools, the danger it posed and the commanding power of bending glass. It wasn't for wimps. Orla liked to tell the story of begging her father to teach her the trade. He thought it unseemly for a woman to work glass, but eventually acquiesced and took great pride in her skill. Kat imagined herself as the next installment of this fabled past, in spirit if not genealogy.

Until she moved to Martha's Vineyard at twenty-one with the vague idea of being a cocktail waitress, Kat had never considered how something like a water glass came into existence. Glassblowing was never her plan. And art wasn't even a consideration. She'd known a few artists from her one semester at community college, but they'd faded from her life after she dropped out, and she'd always had a low tolerance for the cultural trappings of art. It seemed to demand more angst than she was capable of producing. The idea that she'd find a way to make a living in a creative pursuit was once unthinkable to her. But Orla needed help and Kat needed direction. She fell in love with the craft first. Then she found herself deeply attached to her mentor. And finally, she fell in love with her mentor's son, Sean. With the Murphys, and their island, Kat had created a full new life for herself.

She eased the rod and round ball out of the glory, dipped it in a bin of blue glass shards, and stuck it back in the hole again. The blue shards melted around the clear glass and eventually blended into a uniform periwinkle. She pulled it out, inched her hands to the cool end of the rod and, with one hard puff, sent a blast of breath through the hollow pole to the blue glass ball at the other end. A tiny bubble of her own breath grew slowly inside the ball, expanding it. Kat never stopped turning.

Orla always said that if you can do all the things at once—the turning and the blowing and the eyebrow-singeing fire time—and still maintain a clear artistic vision, then you can be a glassworker. It was an art, but it was also a muscular trade, and not many people could do both. When Kat accepted the apprenticeship seven years earlier, she suddenly felt an uncanny sureness of her ability to summon immense physical and creative strengths. Glass working was an art that made sense to her—it produced something real—and she was good at it. After one year, Orla entrusted Kat with most of the basic inventory for the shop. After three, she happily admitted that Kat was a better glassblower than she was herself. And after seven, Orla was sure she'd never met anyone so talented. The difference between Kat and the rest of the world, she liked to say, was that Kat *needed* to wake up each day and mold it to her will. Everyone else just wanted to.

That was all true, but Kat also liked the way her busy mind quieted before the lethal heat. It demanded every aspect of her physical and intellectual attention. Total immersion.

It was so consuming that Kat could nearly forget on that night what had happened out on the water with Hunter and Kyle. Not entirely, but nearly. And if she stared long enough into the blazing vat of liquid glass, she could almost scorch the image of those final moments with Kyle from her mind's eye. She hadn't heard from him or about him since that night, but she also hadn't dared go back to The Undertow. She hadn't really gone anywhere in the two days since the accident.

When the ball was cool enough to cut from the rod, Kat looked around for the right tool. Where had she left it? Why wasn't it in its proper place? She'd been out there too long, running on coffee and insomnia. She wasn't thinking straight anymore.

Just then, something slammed against the garage door. Kat jumped and drew her arm back, smashing the glass ball into the wall of the oven. It fell and broke; not shattering, but cracking neatly like a hot egg.

"Kat, are you in there?" It was Sean. He'd been calling her all day. "Kat, open the door!"

She stepped gingerly over her broken ball and went to the

door. When she opened it, Sean was standing in the black night with a six-pack in his hand.

"Hey."

"Hey, why aren't you answering your phone?"

"Sorry, I lost track of time. Kind of, um, in the flow with this project."

"Huh." Sean frowned. "All day? What are you working on?"

Kat didn't want to talk about what she was working on. She wasn't working on anything. She'd been hiding in the studio for six straight hours, trying to forget what had happened and trying not to think too hard about why she never went to the police station. She was working to drown out the guilty voices in her head. The problem was that every time she left the garage—to pee or eat or attempt a fitful sleep—she was flooded with worries about what would come next. Did Kyle make it back? Or was his body still out there? Either way, there was still a shoe to drop, another chapter in this story. No one had come to arrest her, but that didn't mean she and Hunter had gotten away with it. For now, she thought, it was best to stay the course and wait quietly for a sign.

Kat needed to talk to Hunter. They hadn't communicated since their argument on the dock. She wanted desperately to be in touch with him, to consider their options and make a plan. But she also worried that contacting him might create a guilty trail if they were ever under suspicion for something. Then again, maybe *not* talking to him was more suspicious. And maybe he was halfway to Costa Fucking Rica by now, being relocated by his father's handlers. She was a little worried about him, but mostly she was angry with him. A different person would have blamed Hunter for all of it, but Kat wasn't one to shirk responsibility. She would own what was hers.

Sean was still hers and he was standing before her, waiting for an explanation.

"Sean, I'm sorry. I haven't been feeling well, but I should have called you."

"Yeah, you should have. So I can come in?"

Kat led him through the garage, over the cooling glass shards, toward the door to the house. "Be careful here."

"What happened?"

"It's nothing."

They went up the stairs to her apartment, where forty-eight hours of clothes and dishes had been left unattended. She was surprised to see that it was almost eleven.

"Jesus, you must have been sick," Sean scoffed.

Kat forced a smile. "Delirious, really. Sorry it's so gross in here. Can I have one of those?"

He pulled a beer from its plastic ring and handed it to her. "So you're better?"

The feeling she'd been avoiding was pushing up from her stomach now, constricting her windpipe and sending a flood of blood to her face. Kat wanted to fall into Sean. She wanted to just explain it all and unload some of that feeling onto him. She wasn't better and she needed to tell him so. But that was the weaker option. As soon as he knew, he would have an opinion about how to move forward. He'd be a liability to this secret and a party to it. She pushed the feeling back down with a dry swallow.

Kat sat on the couch and took two sips of the beer, though she wanted to drink it all at once. It seemed like Sean was observing her as she drank. He was in search of a better answer for what was going on with her. Or maybe he wasn't at all and she was just paranoid.

He sat beside her and opened his own beer.

Kat leaned in toward him. The cold outside air was still on

his clothes and face, in his beard, which she liked as much as she could like anything at that moment. She kissed his cheek and he turned for her mouth.

It didn't feel right to fake this, but Kat decided that she should probably take off her clothes. That's what she normally would have done in such a situation, and she needed to behave as normally as possible.

"You smell like a campfire," Sean said into her neck. The studio always gave her a whiff of char.

She smiled and pulled off her shirt. "You smell like you."

They both undressed and then moved to the carpeted floor with slow and synchronized motions, followed by more frenzied ones, as always. Her head wasn't in it, but nothing about Kat's physical response to Sean would have indicated that. Everyone hit their marks and had their uncomplicated pleasures. Thank God. Their sex life had always been robust and satisfying; never too adventurous, but a steady and nourishing diet. It was a comfort to know she could get right into it without much trouble. This was all very normal behavior, normal enough to quiet any of Sean's suspicions. The whole act made her feel like a liar, but she was glad to pull it off.

When they finished and dressed again, Sean kissed her head and went to the bedroom. Kat could hear him crawl under the down comforter. She would have preferred to be alone on that night, but saying so was not an option, so she joined him.

Sean murmured an "I love you," grunted comfortably and fell quickly to sleep beside her.

Kat liked the warmth of his fuzzy back against hers. That feeling was real. Maybe this could work, she thought. Maybe Kyle's body had disappeared forever, and she and Hunter could keep this secret, and they could go on with their lives as normal. Sure, there would be news about the disappearance of a local man, probably a search party and some media attention. But what did that have to do with any of them? Nothing at all. They didn't even know Kyle Billings.

Kyle Billings. Kyle Billings. Kyle Billings. That was his name. He was a person who had existed and then stopped existing. Everyone on the island would know his name soon. Tragic story, what happened to that kid, they'd say. And Kat would just be one of those people who knew his name because she'd seen it on the news. She would shake her head and think of the family, just like everyone else. Nothing strange about that.

Kat slid out of bed and walked into the living room. She turned the TV on so low it was almost inaudible, then sat on the edge of the couch with a blanket wrapped around her shoulders. When would they find his body? Didn't Kyle have any friends to report his disappearance? He'd been gone for two days now. Something would have to break soon.

Kat flipped through the channels, looking for local Boston news, but it was all *Law & Order* reruns and infomercials at that hour. Martha's Vineyard public access was showing the Coastal Erosion Committee meeting from last week. Al Sweeney was lecturing a group of people in a semicircle of folding chairs about ocean acidification, and Kat wondered if maybe Orla should start attending.

She stretched out on the couch and watched the meeting at low volume, which was a bit like watching footage of astronauts in space. They were just figures moving in slow motion, far away from her life. Al Sweeney made a labored point involving lots of hand gestures, then someone else cut in and a civilized argument ensued. It didn't matter that she couldn't hear them because the footage of Kyle's plunge was playing on a loop behind her eyes. God, she was tired. Someone else took the floor at the committee meeting and read from a sheet of paper for a while. Kyle's eyes were big and white. Al Sweeney had a few follow-up questions. A gentleman excused himself from the meeting and everyone nodded. And then Kyle fell into the water. And then Kyle fell into the water. And then Kyle fell into the water.

And then, finally, sleep. Somewhere between last week's minutes and official adjournment, Kat's body relented.

"Kat, wake up. Kat. Kat, wake up."

She opened her eyes and squinted into the bright apartment. Sean's face was over her. He was unhappy.

"What is it?"

"Why are you sleeping on the couch?"

"Sorry, I couldn't sleep. Is that what you woke me up to ask me?"

"No. Hunter just came by looking for you."

Kat tried not to look alarmed as she sat up. "Really, what did he want?"

Sean walked around looking for something. "He didn't say. Have you seen my wallet? He seemed surprised to see me here though, which I thought was weird. Jesus, it's messy in here, Kat!"

"Hmm, I don't know what he'd want."

Sean found the wallet in a couch cushion and stuffed it into his back pocket. He looked directly at her. He was definitely pissed off. "So you don't know why he was looking for you?"

"No, I don't."

"Okay, well I'm gonna go to work and you should get in the shower because the shop opens in fifteen minutes. Aren't you working today?"

"Yes…wait, no, I'm not." Kat couldn't remember what day it was. "Your mom is opening up. But I have some work to do in the studio. Jesus, I didn't mean to sleep that long."

"Yeah, alright, well…" Sean looked around like he was waiting to say something or hear something. "I'll call you later."

Kat waited two minutes on the couch after he left, just to be safe, and then jumped up and slid into her jeans. Sean was mad, but she couldn't think about that right now. She needed to find Hunter.

Ten minutes later, she was back at the large red door of the Briggs family summer home. She only landed one knock before Hunter cracked the door and pulled her in.

"You should have called first," Kat admonished.

Hunter didn't respond. He walked her through the foyer and into the bright kitchen. A morning talk show flashed silently on a wall-mounted TV. They both took a seat at the table.

"Sorry, I just needed to talk," he said.

"Did something happen?"

Hunter shrugged and ran a hand through his greasy blond hair, which stood wildly on end. "I don't think so. But doesn't that seem weird? That nothing has happened yet?"

Kat studied the worry lines on his forehead. She'd never noticed them before. "Yeah. It does. I've been watching the news obsessively."

"Me too." He looked exhausted, but there was a nervous energy coursing through him.

A large restaurant-grade espresso machine hissed on the granite countertop. Hunter loved kitchen gadgets. He spent most of his free time—and he had more of it than most—refining his cooking skills.

"Can you make me one of those?" Kat asked, nodding at the espresso machine.

Hunter jumped up, apparently relieved to have something

to do with his hands. He opened cupboards and drawers until he found the right measuring tool. He knocked a coffee cup over with his elbow and barely noticed. There was a stack of pans in the sink. It looked like he'd been cooking all morning. Kat watched his back as he packed espresso grounds into the filter, more forcefully than necessary, it seemed. Dry stains flashed in the armpits of his shirt.

"Are you high?"

Hunter pressed a button and they waited for fifteen loud seconds as hot water pushed through fresh grounds.

"Don't do that, Kat." He put a small ceramic cup of inky liquid before her. "We've got bigger problems."

"Yeah, we do." She put her head in her hands.

"And no, I'm not high."

Kat couldn't muster the will to care either way. "Hunter, I thought you said this was going to go away. You were so fucking sure of it!"

He paced in front of the sink. "It might still go away." Back and forth, back and forth.

"So what's wrong with you, then?"

Hunter stopped. "It's just booze and espresso. I swear. This is stress you're looking at."

Kat believed him. There was something about the unwashed mess of a person before her that seemed too vulnerable to lie.

"Do you want some?" he asked.

She nodded, and he put a half-full bottle of Patrón before her.

Kat poured two fingers into a nearby water glass and winced as it went down.

"I don't think I can live like this, Hunter. My heart stops every time the phone rings. And Sean... God, I feel bad about Sean."

"I know. Me too."

"Have you talked to him?"

Hunter shook his head.

"I just… I can't get it straight in my head," she went on. "I'm so confused now about why we did what we did…and, like, what part of it was the real crime. I don't think any of it was a crime, really. But when you add it all up…the accident, and then the fact that we didn't go to the cops…it feels like a crime in sum, you know?"

Hunter poured tequila into a coffee mug and leaned against the kitchen counter. "Going to the cops benefits no one. It just fucks things up more."

"It benefits Kyle's family because they deserve the truth."

He shook his head. "You're not that naive, Kat. The truth isn't a fixed thing. The truth will end up being whichever part of our story the cops decide to believe, or a prosecutor decides to prove. Right now, there are only two people with the power to define the truth—you and me. If we tell, the whole world gets to decide what's true. And their truth won't look a fucking thing like what we experienced that night on the boat."

A hot, heady anger shot through Kat's body and she stood up. "You think that, Hunter, because people like you are in control of the truth. You get in trouble and your dad's staff make it go away. The truth is only flexible for people like you! I don't have the same power."

Hunter stared in confusion. "Yeah, *exactly*. So why would you go to the cops if you don't have to? You'd be more fucked than me."

"Because when we get caught for hiding all this, we'll be in more trouble than if we just come forward now. It will be exponentially worse because of the cover-up. But you'll still have that power—the money and connections and clout—

and I won't. Only one of us is taking a real risk here. And if you think I care enough about you to—"

"Wait!" Hunter walked to the wall-mounted TV behind her.

"No, you should hear this!"

"Kat, wait," he yelled without looking away from the screen. Hunter was fumbling for the volume. "I think they found the body."

She spun around and they stared side by side at shifty local news footage.

The sound came up just as images of a white-capped shore changed to police cars. A body bag was being hoisted into the back of a police van. It was black, with a zipper that ran the full length of it.

Body Washes Up on Katama Bay Beach, the chyron said.

"Oh my God."

"Nooo."

A cheerful anchorwoman appeared before them. "The body of an unidentified man was found at a popular swimming hole in Katama Bay early this morning. According to police sources, a Martha's Vineyard resident was fishing when his dog first spotted the body. Authorities have not yet identified the man, who had no wallet or personal belongings on him, and are looking for leads."

A toll-free number appeared on the screen.

"Police are calling the cause of death drowning and have no reason to suspect foul play at this time. We'll update you as the story develops." The news reporter nodded in conclusion and a commercial for natural dog food replaced her.

Hunter turned the TV off and looked down at Kat. "Holy shit."

"I know." She felt like she was going to pass out again. "It won't take long to figure out it was Kyle now."

"Yeah, but do you know what else this means?"

She paused. "That they're not looking for us."

He nodded.

No reason to suspect foul play. That's what the news reporter said. No reason to suspect foul play…for now, anyhow. If no one had a tip about seeing three people out in Hunter's boat, or two hysterical people arguing on the street later that night, then they would surely have no reason to suspect foul play. It was possible now that no one knew anything. Not certain, but possible.

Hunter sat down.

Neither of them spoke for a full minute.

Kat looked into her glass. "Do you think he was dressed?"

"What?"

"When they found him. Do you think he still had those same clothes on? Or do they fall off eventually?"

"I assume they fall off."

"Really?"

"How the fuck would I know? I've never been involved with something like this before." Hunter's forehead was shiny with sweat.

"I don't know. I was just thinking how undignified it would be if they found him naked. It's so sad."

Hunter stared at her. She was making him nervous. "Pull it together, Kat. This can't fall apart just because you feel sad. We don't have the luxury of weakness."

She'd never had that luxury, not even before all this. "I'm fine. I was just thinking about him. I'm allowed to think about him."

"You probably shouldn't."

"Hunter, I'm fine. I promise."

He ran a hand through his hair. "So we're on the same

page now? You understand why we don't need to go to the cops?"

"What are you going to do, kill me if I disagree?"

"That's not funny."

And it wasn't; she knew it. This was torturing Hunter too. In a way, she was grateful to him for keeping her from the police. They might be on the brink of getting away with it, so thank God she hadn't upended their whole lives just because she wanted to unburden her soul. The logic repulsed her, but it was still true. "Yeah, I'm with you."

"Then will you take the money?"

She shook her head. "No. And why do you want me to? I'm not going to tell anyone about this. You don't have to pay me."

"My father is adamant. It's…insurance, so you can't change your mind. He says we're all more secure this way. Just take it, Kat. It could change your life. Buy a house. Buy a car, whatever. It will give my family some peace."

"That's messed up."

"I know."

Kat wouldn't allow herself to consider the ways in which a million dollars could change her life. When she was a kid, she had to ration out the peanut butter jar to be sure she had enough to get through a month of packed lunches. She rationed tampons in high school. The sneakers on her feet at that moment were almost three years old. And now there was *this money*.

She couldn't take it. She couldn't take it and she couldn't think about it because thinking about it might push her closer to taking it and that was not an option.

"No, I don't want it. But thank you, I guess."

"Think about it."

"No."

Hunter lifted the mug to his lips and finished his tequila. He didn't want to fight.

"What do you think we're supposed to do now?" she asked.

"We have to wait. Be normal and wait."

Kat wished she hadn't had the tequila so early in the day. She felt nauseous and hungry again.

Hunter watched her eyes scan the countertops. "Want me to make you an omelet?"

"Yes, would you?"

Hunter was a startlingly good cook, and he knew it. He'd had a few kitchen jobs during his time on the island, before he switched to landscaping, but always got himself fired for some dumb infraction. He liked to buy expensive culinary knives, which he kept obsessively sharp. The three of them—Kat, Hunter and Sean—had finished off countless late nights with his mushroom omelets. Those nights seemed very far away now.

Hunter adjusted the gas flames and dropped butter into the pan. "I don't have anything left in my fridge, so it's just eggs today."

CHAPTER 5

Erika wiped the bar space around Hunter's sweating sauvignon blanc. "Oysters are in. They're small, but good this year. You want a dozen?"

It was the third day in a row that Hunter had been at The Lobster Claw getting slowly and genially drunk at her lonely bar. Bartending at The Lobster Claw was Erika's winter gig. The pay wasn't great, but she appreciated the slower pace after four busy months of high-end cooking. It was just her and Hunter on that day. He was grateful for her presence, which was both intimate and unquestioning. He could see why Kat called Erika her best friend.

Hunter looked through the windows behind the bar at the late October dusk. "Is it early for oysters?"

"Yeah, by a couple weeks. You want a dozen or half dozen?"

"Half, thanks." Hunter wasn't hungry, but sitting at the quiet off-season bar was becoming a formal occupation as he waited helplessly for news of their fate. He hadn't been to work at the landscaping company since the day Kyle went overboard and no one even bothered to call and inquire about his whereabouts. That was the privilege and burden of being a Briggs: his father got him the job by calling in a favor, and no one dared reprimand him when he screwed it up. They were probably happy to have him gone. The job was a bad fit. At first he'd tried to make conversation with the young Brazilian and Eastern European guys when they gathered in the morning for their assignments, but they weren't interested in talking with him, so he eventually stopped entirely. He just did his work and tried to stay out of everyone's way. He'd actually liked that job, the freedom from supervision and ability to make his own hours. It was just him, alone outside, moving as fast or—more often—as slow as he wanted to. Despite his reputation, Hunter actually liked working and being useful. But after everything that had happened, he couldn't stand to be alone with his thoughts, so he never went back again.

Erika frowned at her phone. "You seen Kat lately?"

"Hmm." Hunter reached for his water glass. "Not in a few days, I guess. Why?"

"Something's going on with her. She's been hiding out all week. Said she was sick, but I don't know. You think she's mad at me for something?"

Hunter considered running with this idea but it seemed too mean. "I doubt it. She's probably just wrapped up in some new project. You know, like she was with the mermaid."

"The selkie, yeah. I still can't believe those people paid fifteen thousand dollars for that creepy thing. Fucking rich people…no offense."

"None taken. They're the worst."

Erika filled his empty glass with pale, cold wine. She smiled. "Probably not all of them."

Hunter liked the expert motions of her skinny, inked arms. She looked older than her thirty-seven years, but she seemed like someone who'd be fun in bed. He'd never tried; it was too complicated, given her status as Kat's best friend. Those situations were best avoided, in Hunter's experience.

As he drained his glass, the door opened and three red-cheeked people burst in from the cold air. Two men and a young blonde woman convened loudly at the other end of the bar as they shed winter layers.

Erika placed a tray of oysters on ice before Hunter and headed to greet her new customers.

A Scotch for the old guy, a stout for the young guy and a local ale for the woman. Hunter strained to hear their conversation but got only bursts of laughter. He couldn't size them up. They wore sporty outdoor clothes, but didn't seem like winter recreationists or fishermen. None of their faces were familiar.

Erika laughed with the threesome. They asked her a few questions in hushed voices as Hunter looked on.

Erika nodded back. "Yeah, I knew him," she said to the young woman. Erika was usually the loudest person in her bar. "But I didn't know him well."

The strangers asked a few more questions.

"It's awful, I know," Erika agreed.

Hunter held his breath as the woman said something else.

"No one knows," Erika answered. "It's *so* tragic. I heard that his parents could barely afford to have the body sent back down to Florida, not that the body looked any good by then."

Hunter hadn't heard that bit of gossip. He'd never discussed Kyle's death with Erika; it simply hadn't come up yet. But it probably would. News like that travels fast on the island. Hunter wondered how many people were talking about Kyle right now, in bars and coffee shops around the Vineyard. He could almost hear the low chatter of gossip and speculation if he listened hard enough.

Erika and the three drinkers shook their heads in what-a-shames and then moved on to something else.

She returned to Hunter at the center of the bar. Erika pointed to his empty glass. "I'm not refilling that until the sun is down. You'll thank me for pacing you."

Hunter ignored the comment and nodded toward the others. "What was that all about?"

"Oh, you know… Kyle Billings. It's so tragic."

"Yeah, it really is." Hunter reached for his empty glass in vain. He wanted Erika to stop talking but she had more to say.

"To think that he was just out swimming on a cold October night… There's no way he wasn't on oxy. Or fentanyl. It could be fentanyl. It's all over the island. I didn't think he was the type, but you never know with that shit. He was definitely on something if he was out there in the water in the middle of the night in fucking October."

Hunter tried to look disinterested. "Is that what they're saying?"

"They're just saying he drowned, but there's always more to the story."

Hunter agreed. A lot of people were dying that way on the island, he said. And yeah, it was so incredibly tragic, the way addiction could take a hold of someone that way. He knew firsthand.

Erika leaned in closer over the bar as Hunter talked. He never discussed his time in rehab—mainly because it was a cynical political ploy to smooth things over after his latest public embarrassment. And he was only there for alcohol, his second DUI in three years. Hunter didn't know a thing about opioids. But his confessional tone was working to keep Erika distracted, so he kept going. It was a genius improvisation, really—except that it somehow made him feel even more deplorable than he had five minutes before. To think that Kyle's story was now an overdose story...that his family might believe it...to perpetuate that rumor seemed particularly evil. But he kept going.

"What was rehab like?" Erika whispered.

Hunter looked past her to the view of the water through the window. "It was humiliating, being monitored and analyzed all day. Knowing you can't leave. It was infantilizing." That much was true. "But obviously, I'm one of the lucky ones. It ends badly for so many people."

Erika put a hand on Hunter's and gave a little squeeze.

He looked down at the spiderweb tattoo on her bony knuckles and thought to himself that no one deserved to die an undignified death more than he. Erika should poison his sauvignon blanc. She should push that little oyster fork into his aorta until he bleeds out at The Lobster Claw.

"I appreciate your support," he said.

Erika smiled and walked down to the end of the bar to settle the strangers' tab.

The old man and the young man had left, but the woman stayed with the last few sips of her beer. She watched the television screen mounted high on the bar while Hunter watched her.

She wasn't dressed for a bar. She wore bulky winter boots and the bottom three inches of her pants were wet. Hunter liked the way her silky wisps of blond hair had pulled free from her ponytail.

"You want another?" Erika asked her.

She thought for a moment.

"Everyone will have another," Hunter announced. "On me."

The woman looked at him and smiled. "Okay, but only because I'm a poor student. I'm going home after that."

"Fair enough. What are you a student of?" There were four empty bar stools between them and he had to speak loudly.

"Marine geology. I'm trying to finish my PhD. That was my mentor." She nodded at the door where the men had left. "I was working down in Aquinnah, but now we're going to start focusing on Addison."

Erika put another full glass in front of them each and gave Hunter a "be careful" expression, which he pretended not to see. It was no mystery to anyone where Hunter would try to steer things from there, because his schedule in recent days had taken on a certain predictability in the preceding week and a half. He usually got politely drunk at The Lobster Claw; then exceedingly drunk at whatever establishment where most of the locals were drinking; and finally, he tried to take someone home. The last stage had only worked twice, but he considered that a respectable response rate. Not that this was a game to Hunter. He could pretend to himself that it was a game and play the role of bored island playboy, but it was all driven by a desperate desire to never be alone with his racing thoughts. It was sanity.

"And what's your story?" the woman asked.

Erika walked away to greet some new arrivals.

"I'm between commitments at the time."

The woman squinted at him. "That sounds leisurely. Do you live here?"

"I do, yeah. For now." Hunter made the decision at that moment to pursue her. Smart and pretty was nice, but her outsider status was the biggest attraction. She didn't know anything about Hunter, which was a fresh start, even if only for a few hours. "I'm staying at my family summer home. I would tell you more about it except that we don't know each other's names and it's getting awkward."

The woman smiled and revealed charmingly sharp incisors at either end of her wide grin. "I'm Ashley. You?"

"Hunter Briggs." He didn't intend to say his last name, but it was one of those names that was usually said in its entirety.

Ashley raised her eyebrows. "Like *Senator* Briggs?"

"Sometimes, yes."

"Wow, that must be something. Political blood. Are you going to follow in the family footsteps and run for office one day? I think political dynasties are profoundly un-American, but I did vote for your father in the last midterm."

Hunter drank and considered ways to reroute the conversation. He didn't like talking about his dad. "We thank you for your support. And no, I didn't get the politician gene. I think it skips a generation."

"I'm not sure about that." Ashley smiled into her beer and drank.

Hunter could usually tell if people were enamored by the low-grade celebrity status of his family. There were easy flags to spot, like immediate requests for pictures and premature flirtatiousness. Ashley didn't seem particularly interested in his celebrity, which was a good thing. You can't take star fuckers home.

"I think I need some food," she said. "Would your oysters be offended if I ordered a plate of nachos?"

Hunter's oysters sat untouched before him, which he felt a bit ungrateful for, but he couldn't bring himself to eat them. He hadn't eaten much that week. The oysters were beginning to dry and shrink up in their half shells. He wished for Erika to make them disappear, but she was darting around the room as it filled for dinner.

"Nachos sound better. Can we sit together at a proper table or do we have to keep yelling across the bar like this?"

Ashley thought for a moment. "I don't know."

"We're just talking about nachos, a casual appetizer. Either one of us can bolt at any moment if it gets weird. I won't be offended."

"Fine," Ashley said, sliding off her bar stool. "But we're going dutch on the nachos."

"I would insist on it."

Hunter gathered his coat and hers and they retreated to a small table against the wall of windows where they finished their drinks and commented on the view. It was a nice night; one of those clear autumn dusks that reflect lights off the water from a quarter mile away.

"So what are you really doing here?" Ashley asked as their tower of gooey hot chips arrived. "Are you hiding from something?"

"More like they're hiding me. I've been...immoderate in the past."

Ashley frowned sarcastically. "How terrible for you, sequestered out here in an exclusive vacation spot. Tell me more."

"Hey, I'm not complaining. But that's the answer to your question. I tend to fuck things up." Just saying that aloud felt dangerously close to honesty or a confession of some sort. Hunter veered quickly from the topic. "Anyhow, the island doesn't feel so glamorous in January."

Ashley coaxed a cluster of cheesy chips from the side of the mountain. "That's true. I love it here in the winter. I had this vision when I started my degree a thousand years ago that it would be all sunny, beachside research...but I quickly learned that it's impossible to get anything done in season. Plus, I can't afford it."

"So what exactly are you studying?"

"Coastal erosion. I've been collecting incremental data for years and then, you know, that buckling happened."

The cliffs in front of Island Glass, Orla's business and Kat's apartment. That's what she was talking about. Hunter wanted to bring this connection up but he did not. He felt too buzzed to calculate the risks of mentioning an association with Kat. Probably there were none, but better to err on the side of caution. "So do you spend a lot of time on that beach?"

"I will once the authorities let us in. For now, me and a few others from my department are working farther south, looking for other points of weakness."

Hunter exhaled and drank.

"Anyhow," she went on, waving greasy fingers. "I'm probably going to be here for another two months or so. I'm supposed to defend my dissertation in January."

"Good, then we'll have time for a few more drinks."

Ashley smiled a big green-light sort of smile and Hunter was relieved to know that he could probably put off the unpleasantness of being alone for another night.

They ordered a chocolate molten cake to share and drank more wine. Ashley talked about her younger siblings, her childhood home in New Hampshire and the slog of her PhD. Hunter watched her eat and tried hard to stay lost in her fast, emphatic conversational style. They were both quite drunk.

To his surprise, Hunter didn't need to concoct a clever explanation for why they should have one more drink together at his house. She just followed along in step as he led them home.

It was cold out, almost freezing with the windchill, so they walked quickly and said little along the way. As they passed the glass shop, Hunter noticed that the upstairs lights were on, which meant that Kat was in her apartment. He didn't turn his head toward it, though, for fear of being seen. He wanted to keep Kat out of all this.

Inside the house, they took off their coats and ascended the stairs. Hunter didn't even bother with extra drinks because this drug of distraction was better than anything in a bottle. It didn't always work that way—the first sip of a cold old-fashioned could outshine awkward sex if the Bourbon was good enough. But this woman, and their energy together, was all the drug he needed at that moment.

He pulled off her sweater and laughed to find a layer of thermal underwear beneath, the waffled kind he'd worn on ski trips as a kid. They were ripe with the smell of her earlier adventures. She was unapologetic about it all and he liked that. Hunter thought the local girls wore too much makeup, which was probably a snobbish holdover from his prep school days, but you can't reprogram some things. Ashley reminded him of the girls he used to pursue, when he was younger and quick to fall in love.

Hunter kissed Ashley's naked legs, knees and thighs, working his way up her body and through his A-game stuff. But she intercepted his advances with her own moves and eventually he was out of his head and totally in the act. They were both drunk, but it didn't feel like drunk sex in the out-of-body way he usually settled for. She was energized and athletic, a real go-getter. It was almost comical. She insisted on reading the expiration date of the condom, which struck him as hilarious. Ashley was above him, and then below. It was exhausting, but also a relief to have someone really running the show. He was happy to follow.

Ten minutes later, the entire episode concluded in a conventional but thoroughly satisfying missionary position.

And it was exactly three seconds after ejaculation that Hunter remembered all the horrible things he'd been trying to forget. The investigation of Kyle's death was still open. The boat was still banging against the dock posts. This little adventure had changed nothing. Hunter's body was calm but his mind wasted no time getting back to its baseline of panic. He needed a drink. He needed Ashley to leave so he could pour himself something tall. He liked her and hoped for an encore one day, but wanted her to get the fuck out at that moment.

"That was fun. I suppose I should go," she said, moving not a muscle in her body. She was splayed out under the down comforter with her eyes closed.

Hunter got out of bed and walked toward the bathroom. "Yeah, it was fun. Can I call you again?"

If she answered, he didn't hear her before the bathroom door closed. He peed and splashed water on his face. When he returned to the room, Ashley was halfway dressed, watching local news on a small TV that sat on a dresser.

"Why do they think he was swimming in Katama Bay?" she said, one sock in hand at the edge of the bed.

"What?"

"This guy who died—Kyle Billings. Why do they think he was swimming in Katama Bay?"

Hunter turned his back to her and rifled through drawers. What was going on? Why was she asking these questions?

"Oh, I don't know," he said. "I haven't been paying much attention. Do you want me to call you a car?"

"No, I'm fine to walk." Ashley continued to watch from the edge of the bed. "I just know for a fact that a Katama Bay swimmer would have been carried farther south by the current, if that's actually where he started from. It doesn't make any sense." She pulled her sweater over her head.

Hunter walked to the doorway. "I heard he was on oxy or something, so who knows."

Ashley considered this information. "Still, the current…it wouldn't matter. He had to have been farther north if it took two days for the body to wash ashore in that place. That's what the coroner said, that it had been about two days."

Hunter crossed his arms over his chest. "Kind of a morbid thing to be hung up on, don't you think? You're like some kind of citizen investigator. You sure you don't want a car?"

"I guess it is. I don't know. But it's going to drive me crazy if I don't figure it out." Ashley shrugged. "Anyhow, thanks for tonight."

"It was fun."

Ashley stood on tiptoes and kissed Hunter on the lips. Then, mercifully, she saw herself out.

Hunter stood in the doorway of his bedroom in his underwear, waiting and thinking. He listened to her feet walk along the hallway, down the stairs and then out the front door. She was gone.

Hunter stayed completely still, trying to understand what had just happened. Either Ashley had observed a real crack in the local police assumptions about Kyle's death; or worse, she knew something herself and was testing him. He tried to remember precisely how he'd responded to her questions, the body language he'd used. Those things would matter if she was testing him.

Hunter showered and dressed, giving Ashley plenty of time to get to wherever she was going on that night. He paced around the kitchen with a Bourbon in hand for five more minutes, just to be safe. But as he closed the front door behind him, Hunter couldn't resist breaking into a sprint.

It took three minutes to get to Island Glass. Along the way, he passed a middle-aged couple and a man in a Bruins hat. All three acknowledged Hunter with a nod as he huffed past them in the dark cold. He noticed all of these things now— witnesses and their response to him. A second look from a stranger could send him into a paranoid tailspin for hours.

As Hunter knocked on the side entrance to Island Glass, it occurred to him that Sean could be up there. He had no plan for such a scenario. Why did he keep forgetting about Sean? He should have called first, but he hadn't used his phone in days. I should use my phone, he thought then. Not using it would look suspicious. Hunter knocked again.

The door cracked open and Kat's eyes peeked out.

"Yes?"

"Is Sean in there?"

"No. What do you need? It's late."

Hunter knew she wasn't really mad at him so much as scared of their association, but her coldness still stung.

"I need to come in."

Kat sighed and waved him in. They went up the back stairs and into her apartment. It was Hunter's second time in Kat's apartment and he was surprised to find it in such disarray.

"Okay, so what's going on?" She went to the sink to fill a kettle with water.

"Were you sleeping? I'm sorry if I woke you up." Hunter knew he hadn't woken her. It was clear that Kat wasn't sleeping much.

"You didn't wake me up. So, what is it?"

"Well. I met this girl tonight—a woman, I mean." Hunter didn't want to tell any part of the story he was about to tell. Even the benign aspects embarrassed him slightly with Kat. He wasn't sure why. "We were at The Lobster Claw, having wine and nachos… Oh, and by the way, Erika is worried about you."

"Yeah, I miss her." Kat sighed. "Is that what you came to tell me?"

"No. Right." Hunter tried to collect his thoughts. "So anyhow, this woman seemed nice and interested…a real person of substance, you know?"

"So you slept with her."

Was that jealousy Hunter detected? Not likely, but it was… something.

"I did, yeah. So anyhow, we were just talking afterward and the TV is on and there's a thing about Kyle and then she just starts talking about how there's no way he was swimming on the beach they think he was swimming on because of the currents or the tide or something. She said it's not possible—she seemed really sure of it."

Kat stared at Hunter as the kettle began to whistle behind her. "How would she know?"

"She's a scientist. She knows about this stuff."

The kettle screamed and Kat spun around to move it to a cool burner. "I don't understand what you're telling me."

"I don't really know," Hunter started. "But it seems like she's going to look into this. At the very least, she's obviously comfortable talking to any willing stranger about it. What if she's telling people this theory all over town?"

Kat crossed her arms and closed her eyes tight. When she opened them again, she looked very angry. "Hunter, what the fuck? Why are you out getting drunk and talking to people about this?"

"Kat, I swear to God I haven't said a word about anything to anyone. I never will. She just brought it up out of the blue!"

"But doesn't it seem weird that you guys just met and she had all these ideas about Kyle? Doesn't it seem fucking weird, Hunter?"

It did seem weird. "I don't know. I guess so. I don't think she was, like, following me, if that's what you're suggesting."

The look on Kat's face changed to disgust. "Oh, you don't think so? Because your judgment is so reliable? Did it ever occur to you, Hunter, that this would be a good time to give it a rest with the girls? Sorry, the *women*. I don't usually care if you fuck your way through the whole island, but now you're putting us in danger."

Hunter knew she was right. But her tone...it was too cruel. His whole body stiffened in defense. "Well, what should I do, Kat? Should I stay home and rot in my house forever like you? Just hide out until the last few friends I have give up on me? I mean, what's your plan here?"

There was a noise at the street level that they both ignored.

"Fuck you for trying to turn this on me, Hunter! This is all on you." She began collecting dirty dishes from the counter and putting them indelicately into the sink. "And now this woman knows something...or she suspects something... Fuck it, I'm going to the cops. I can't do this."

There was that sound again, a knock.

"You're not going to the cops," Hunter scoffed. "You know exactly what happens if you try to tell your nice little story to the cops now. So just stop threatening me with that. This is as much yours as it is mine. If you really wanted to come clean, you would have done it that night. But you didn't. And you won't."

The thumping stopped, a door creaked and then there were footsteps pounding up Kat's stairs. They were Sean's footsteps.

He got to the top of the stairs and looked from Kat to Hunter, then back to Kat. "What's this? What's going on?"

Kat let forth a burst of exasperated air and ran her hands through her hair.

Hunter said nothing. He was waiting for her.

"What's going on, Kat?" Sean demanded.

"It's Hunter's drinking," she blurted. "Have you noticed that he's kind of spiraling right now? I thought someone should say something. That's what we're arguing about."

Hunter shook his head and looked out the window toward the black ocean. It wasn't fair that he should be the foil, but he understood the importance of keeping Sean out of this. It was a good lie, but it felt awful.

Sean's cheeks were red. He looked like maybe he'd had a few drinks himself. "I don't think that's what you were arguing about."

"It is," Hunter said.

Kat nodded.

The three of them stood looking at each other in the middle of her tiny, cluttered apartment.

"I don't think so."

Kat should go to him, that was what Hunter thought. She should put her arms around Sean and burst into tears, maybe accuse Hunter of coming on to her. That would really sell this story. But she didn't do that and, although their secret was in peril, Hunter was glad.

"No." Sean clenched his fists at his sides. "No, I get it. I knew about you guys. I saw it, but didn't think you'd really... But clearly I'd underestimated... You know what, fuck you, Hunter! And you, Kat..." He swallowed and shook his head.

Kat looked panicked. "No, Sean, that's not it! Hunter and I would never."

"For real, man," Hunter said. "I wouldn't. I swear."

Sean's eyes darted back and forth between them. It seemed like he was almost there. He wanted to believe them. But Hunter recognized that sick, suspicious sense that the world might be keeping secrets from you. Sean wasn't wrong about that; they *were* keeping secrets from him.

"No," Sean whispered. "Fuck you both."

He thudded down the stairs. Kat went after him, though not as fast as she could have. Hunter could hear her calling after him into the dark from the doorway. She was barefoot.

Running after him would have been a dramatic gesture. It might have been a good idea, but she didn't do it.

Hunter couldn't decide if he wanted Sean to believe their story. He knew he should. Sean was his friend and it had been awful to watch him feel so betrayed. Plus, he *wasn't* sleeping with Kat. There was no betrayal. But it was also true that Sean was in the way. Kat and Hunter needed to get through this time on their own. They needed to get to the stage when Kyle's death was a closed case and distant memory. Then—maybe—things could get back to normal between the three of them. Until then, Sean was a threat.

"I'm sorry," Kat said when she returned. "I didn't handle that well."

"I'm sorry too. Do you think you guys..."

"I think he'll come back. I hope." She sat down at the table and rubbed her face. "The sad thing is, I'm more worried about everything else right now than Sean. I'm worried about this scientist."

"Ashley."

"Yes, *Ashley*." She stretched the name out slow and sarcastically. "So what are you going to do about her?"

"What can I do?"

Kat considered the question. "You can keep sleeping with her. Keep an eye on her, you know?"

Hunter sat down. God, he was tired. He looked around the kitchen.

"I don't have anything to drink," she said.

He shook his head. "It's fine. That's not... Anyhow, I don't think I can sleep with her again. She scares me a little."

"You can take her to dinner."

"Yeah, I could do that. I was thinking about doing that anyhow, before all this, so maybe it's not a completely dishonest thing to do."

"I think you have to."

He nodded, strangely grateful for the assignment. Hunter generally considered himself to be more of a burden than a help to the people around him. He was certainly a burden to his family. He was occasionally a burden to his friends—something he'd learned early in life could be alleviated through extreme generosity. But he did not take this burden lightly. It was a source of great shame, in fact. And so when opportunities for sacrifice presented themselves, Hunter tried to take advantage of them. It seemed stupid to consider sleeping with a beautiful woman a sacrifice, but he wanted badly to never see Ashley again, and so it actually was. It was his contribution to their safety.

The thing Hunter could never adequately explain to Kat was that even this mess with Kyle had been, in a way, an attempt at sacrifice. Not Kyle's death—that was a mistake. But Hunter's decision to keep it quiet was intended to be an offering to his father. He knew his father wouldn't want him to go to the police. He knew all the ways in which he'd be fucking things up for his father's reelection campaign, his awful stepmother's social standing and the esteemed Briggs family name if he went to the police. He actually *wanted* to go to the cops and just pay the price of a clear conscience. But he'd screwed up so many times in recent years, and he felt that the least he could do was give his father the choice for how to move forward. No one thanked him—and no one should—but he believed in his heart that keeping quiet was a small peace offering to his family.

Kat thought he did it because of the money. Hunter told her he'd be cut off from the family if he tanked the campaign, which is probably true, but it wasn't the reason he did it. It just seemed easier than trying to explain that his asshole father was still his father, and if there was a chance to do the right thing—or not really the *right* thing, but the diplomatic thing—he wanted to try.

Kat stood up, so Hunter stood up. It was midnight and they both looked like hell. He forced a thin smile of solidarity. It was just the two of them now. There were only two people in the world with this secret.

And then Kat leaned in and let her forehead smash into Hunter's shoulder. She pressed hard and exhaled. He could feel her breath through his shirt, a shuddering, pained breath, like she'd been holding it in for days. It would have been normatively acceptable to put his arms around her upper body at that moment as a gesture of comfort, but he couldn't do it, not moments after being accused of betrayal by Sean. Kat probably understood. So he just stood there, with the weight of her head on his shoulder.

When all the breath had been drained from Kat's body, she sank back into her chair.

Hunter turned off a few lights in the apartment, walked down the stairs and out the door.

Every night ended alone, no matter how long he put it off.

CHAPTER 6

The sun was just appearing above the high tide, which meant that Sean had been sitting on the dock of the boatyard for about six hours. He had two wool blankets wrapped around himself, and a hat on his head, but he was still freezing in the deck chair. The sun's return was a relief.

Sean couldn't stop thinking about the sound of their voices as they'd argued. Kat's resentment and sarcasm, Hunter's seething pauses. It wasn't the sound of platonic friends fighting. Sean was absolutely sure that what he walked in on the night before was something intimate, even if it was angry intimacy. He was less sure of what it meant.

There was only one logical response to what he'd seen, and that was to accuse them of an affair and storm out. But an affair seemed unlikely to Sean...more likely now, but still improbable. Hunter might be capable of such a thing; it wasn't a pleasant thought since Sean had really grown to trust the guy. Kat, on the other hand, didn't have such deceit in her. He was almost sure of that. And it wasn't just the deceit. Kat wasn't one to squander a good thing. She had a strong sense of gratitude and everyone who knew her knew that she was grateful for the life she had on the island. It seemed so unlikely that she would do something as self-destructive as cheat on him.

And yet, he'd seen what he'd seen. There was something exclusive between Kat and Hunter. Maybe they were considering an affair, or he was propositioning her and she was declining. Maybe something had happened already and they were considering how to break the news to dumb, oblivious Sean.

That was how Sean spent the night at the boatyard, going around and around with his thoughts. Every time he began to relax and consider that what he'd seen was a mirage, his imagination would kick in again and the terrible possibilities multiplied. He imagined their naked bodies together, her smooth skin against his. Worst of all, Sean imagined them laughing to themselves about what a fool he was for not knowing. He couldn't go home alone and he didn't know who to talk to about it all, so he'd just sat down in a deck chair and drifted in and out of nervous, frigid sleep on the dock of the boatyard all night long.

A blurry figure walked down the beach toward Sean. As it drew closer, he realized it was his mother on one of her early morning walks. She started taking those walks when his father died years before. She'd walk up and down the beaches, along the grassy pathways and boardwalks, sometimes for miles. Vineyard beaches weren't the sort you could jog mindlessly along. They demanded more attention than that—an intricate and changing series of sands, cliffs, marshes and craggy rock borders. Orla liked the distraction.

As soon as she recognized him, Orla climbed up the dock and went to her son. "Early day for you, love." Her forehead wrinkled in concern.

"Yeah. Late, early, I don't know."

She tilted her head and a salt-and-pepper lock of hair blew across her face. Orla had a weathered, unadorned beauty that Sean thought exquisite. "Sean, what is it?"

He looked away from her at the water. "I don't really know. I don't think I want to talk about it until I know what it is."

"Something about Kat?"

"Yeah."

Orla nodded because that was enough for her. She had always needed fewer words than Sean, less of a crowd, more time in her head with her art. It allowed for a very low-key parenting style, which had felt alternately liberating and aloof to his younger self.

"Maybe a walk?" she asked.

Sean agreed and hoisted himself out of the deep chair. He wasn't eager to feel the movement of his frozen bones and stiff muscles, but he needed to do something.

Orla led the way along the concrete path that snaked through overgrown bushes. Beneath their feet was a dusting of the coarse, ubiquitous Vineyard sand that Sean hardly noticed anymore. That sand lived in every pocket of every pair of pants he had ever owned. It collected in the heels of his shoes. Sometimes it was in the center of a fresh sandwich or a crevice of warm skin. Sean figured he was about one percent sand by now; no point in fighting it. If you live on the Vineyard long enough, the borders between you and the land start to blur. Nothing felt impermeable to Sean anymore; that was the lesson of the sand.

"Looks like that storm spared us," he said from behind his mother. "Just kept moving eastward."

"Thank God. We can't take any more of those storms." Orla's steps sounded more labored than usual.

"Because of the cliffs, you mean?"

She sighed. Orla was anxious about it. They all were.

Sean meant to revisit the question of their collapsing bluffs, but he'd been so wrapped up in Kat's baffling behavior that he'd briefly forgotten.

His mother was still in a state of denial. She wasn't ready to really think about the unsteady earth their glass shop sat upon. To broach the grief of her threatened shop would mean broaching other grief too—the memories of her late husband, the futility of her life's work. She wasn't ready for that.

"You and Kat can figure this out," Orla said, changing the subject. "Whatever it is, you guys can figure it out."

"Mom, I know you love Kat, but it's complicated." For the first time, Sean was beginning to resent Kat's closeness to his mother.

"It's more than that, Sean. She's also wonderful with Weeta. And she's a thoughtful person. She's focused and serious. I like that too."

Sean knew this. But he didn't know it all. He didn't know that Orla had planned the next chapter of her life around an assurance of Kat's presence. Orla was passionate about her art, but levelheaded about life, and she knew what happened to so many old people on the island. They disappeared. One day, apparently, you just decide that the air is too cold or the medical services too thin. Maybe an adult child drives you to a pleasant apartment complex in a Boston suburb, one with ramps at low levels and MedicAlert buttons in every unit. Regardless of how it happens, it seemed to Orla that the whole world had conspired around this idea that there's a day upon which island life is no longer appropriate.

Well, not for Orla. No way. That day would not come. She was going to live every last day on the island and die there like her husband had. It would have sounded morbid to explain, but the idea made her happy. Orla would stay until the earth or the ailing cells in her body took her. She wanted her final move to be from her Vineyard home to wherever it was her husband now resided. Heaven, probably, though who knew what really happened after death; she didn't bother much with religion anymore. But this plan would only work if Sean didn't stand in her way and there was someone to take over the glass shop…if it was still there when the time came.

And Kat, like an angel sent from heaven, could help her with both of those things. She could have Island Glass when it was time; she *should* have it. Kat was better than anyone she'd ever worked with. She was better than Orla. But she also understood something that Orla's own son did not. She understood the idea of making one's fate her own. There was a knowing in Kat—a knowing what she needed and wanted in this world—that Orla shared. And Orla was confident, irrationally perhaps, that Kat would respect that about her. She was sure that when it was her turn for the great elderly golf cart roundup, Kat—and thereby, Sean—wouldn't make her get on it. Kat would be an advocate for Orla when that day came.

Sean didn't know any of these things about his mother's plans. He only knew that he loved Kat, and Orla loved Kat, and they were all supposed to be a family. Until now. He wasn't so sure now.

"Who's that?" Orla put a hand up to block the sun in her view.

In the distance, they saw a small woman kneeling in the sand twenty feet from the water's edge. At first it looked like she was praying, or perhaps crying, until they saw the tiny containers lined up before her. She was working on something with great attention.

Orla stepped off the boardwalk into a patch of dense bushes and walked toward the woman. Sean followed. It wasn't the sort of thing they would have done in July, when the hordes of unfamiliar faces took over their island. But in late October, unfamiliar faces were more of a curiosity. One stranger on an empty beach demanded investigation.

"Hi there," Orla yelled.

The woman looked up, startled. Her blond hair was tucked into a red woolly hat. "Hi!"

"What are you doing out here?"

The woman stood up and dusted sand from her backside. "Sedimentology. I'm just collecting samples right now… Hey, I remember you guys!"

There was something familiar about her, but Sean couldn't place it.

"From the beach," the woman explained. "I was down there on the morning of the buckling. That was your waterfront, right? I'm sure you don't remember me. You were probably completely shocked that morning."

But Sean did remember her now. It was the way she spoke, fast and expressive. He had the vague sense that he'd been rude on that morning.

"I've been meaning to track you down, actually," the woman went on, packing her things into a knapsack as she talked. "I really need to get onto that beach to take some pictures and samples. The Vineyard cops still have it cordoned off."

"We can let you on," Sean said.

"Really? That would be great."

Orla looked skeptical.

"Of course we can," Sean added. "The cops won't bother you if you're with us. It's a ten-minute walk from here if you want to go now."

"Yeah, that would be great!" She put her arms through

the straps of her pack and smiled eagerly. "I'm Ashley, by the way."

"So who are you here with, Ashley?" Orla was tired of having experts on her beach, delivering grim information she was helpless against.

"I'm a marine geology student with Woods Hole. I've been studying erosion patterns."

Sean smiled and went in for the shake. "I'm Sean, and my mother's name is Orla. The house on the cliff is her glass shop. It's basically our whole life." He didn't mention his girlfriend who lived above it all.

"I understand." Ashley nodded sympathetically, but with no less urgency. "And I appreciate your help."

Orla nodded and set out on their walk, with the other two behind.

Ashley chatted throughout about how much she loved the Vineyard and how cool it was that they got to live there all year. She described the town in New Hampshire that she'd grown up in and the occupations of each of her brothers. The wind from the ocean made it difficult to hear every word of it, but if Ashley knew that, she didn't seem to care. It was just polite talk to pass the time.

They walked along the paved pathway for a while until it changed to sagging boardwalk, the wood still wet with morning. Grasses pushing up through the cracks had turned an anemic shade of yellow in the autumn cold. The boardwalk ended at the place where the bluffs took a steep turn upward toward Island Glass. Instead of following it up to the shop and studio, they turned right, toward the shore.

"Here we are," Orla said, ducking under a barrier of orange ribbon.

Ashley looked up at their cliff.

The upstairs lights were on in the house, which meant

that Kat was awake, but hadn't opened the shop yet. Sean wondered if Hunter was up there with her.

Ashley nodded, as if it all made sense to her. "It's like the Gay Head Lighthouse. Different topography, but similar layering here."

"How do you mean?" Sean had heard something about the Gay Head cliffs being in danger, but it never occurred to him that this was a similar situation.

Ashley ran her hand along the wall, and wet sand fell to her touch. "I think we've underestimated the groundwater effect. In both places, it seems like the water is exacerbating erosion faster than expected."

Sean watched her examining the wall. In a matter of seconds, Ashley had changed from a chatty girl to a formidable expert. She was alluring in this light.

"Can you tell us how bad this is?" Orla asked. "How long it will hold?"

Ashley shook her head. "No one can really do that. It might hold for two years if we do nothing. It could probably hold much longer with groundwater mitigation. But then, if we have a really rainy season… Well, I hate to prognosticate."

Orla nodded. She didn't want to hear these things but she was coming around to their truth. She seemed to be coming around to Ashley The Expert too.

"I'd like to come back this afternoon with all my stuff if that's okay."

"Of course it's okay," Sean said. "If anyone stops you, tell them we gave you permission."

Orla looked up at the shop. "I should help Kat open up. Ashley, it was nice meeting you. I don't mean to be rude. I'm glad to know all this. It's just a lot to take in right now. Sean's probably your best resource. I'm in a bit of a fog."

"Of course. Thank you again."

Sean leaned in and kissed his mother on the cheek. "I'll call you later."

She walked away from them, toward the long, warped staircase that led up to the street.

"I didn't mean to upset her," Ashley said when they were alone.

"Don't worry about it." Sean didn't have the energy to explain what all this meant to his mother.

Ashley looked around impatiently. "Anyhow, I should go. You guys have things to do."

The sun was well above the water, which meant that Sean would need to be at the boatyard for work soon. He had two boats scheduled for detailing before being put to bed for winter. Still, he hesitated. "I'm going to get a cup of coffee. You want one?"

Ashley smiled. "I would *love* coffee."

Sean couldn't tell if her enthusiasm was for him, for coffee or just her personality. He liked it.

They walked together up the stairs to the street and then in step toward the only coffee shop that was open in town at that time of year. Ashley clearly knew where she was going, which granted her a patina of localness and an upgrade in trustworthiness by Sean's accounting. Anyone who chooses the island's harsh winters and empty streets over the more photogenic seasons probably had their head on straight.

At the shop, they ordered two drip coffees and went back outside to sit on the cold iron chairs that were left over from summer.

Sean pulled the hood of his coat up over his head and looked into his cup. "So you're here a lot?"

"Back and forth all season," Ashley said. "It was getting tiresome, actually. I can go a whole week in Aquinnah and barely talk to another human. It makes you a little crazy. But then the buckling happened on your beach and my research got a whole lot more interesting."

"Glad we could help."

"Sorry, I didn't mean it like that. It's really awful."

"Yeah, it is."

Neither wanted to talk about the buckling.

Ashley looked around, searching perhaps for another topic. "Hey, what about that body they found on the beach? That's pretty crazy."

"Kyle. Yeah, really sad. I didn't know him well, but everybody kind of knows everybody here, eventually. Wicked sad. I hear it was drugs, maybe."

Ashley cocked her head. "Maybe."

Sean turned to her, eager to focus on something that had nothing to do with himself. "What? You think it was something else?"

"I don't know anything." She put her hands out to disavow any theories she might have on the matter. "And I probably shouldn't talk about it. It's just… I know these ocean currents really well, and I know that something as big as a human body wouldn't have washed up on Katama Beach unless it floated down from much farther up shore."

Sean raised a skeptical eyebrow. "Oh, you know better than the cops? They've been finding the stuff that washes ashore for decades here. They know these shores."

"Yeah, but they're still relying on old current patterns," Ashley said. "Those beaches have changed in the last thirty years and the water isn't moving the same as it used to. I don't expect the cops to know that. It's not their job. But I'm telling you they're wrong."

Sean took a sip.

"I don't know," Ashley said into her cup. "It's none of my

business. And it's kind of a creepy thing to keep bringing up with people, I guess. But it's driving me crazy."

"Hmm." Sean didn't know what to make of this information. He hadn't thought much about Kyle Billings's death and he didn't have an opinion about who knew the most about ocean currents. "Okay, well, I have no reason to doubt you, Ashley The Oceanographer. I haven't thought much about it."

"Of course. You've got a lot to think about right now." She took another sip. "It's not, like, an obsession of mine or anything."

"That would be a little morbid." Sean didn't have much to add to all this Kyle business.

Ashley turned to him suddenly. "You know Hunter Briggs?"

Sean stiffened. "Yeah, why?"

"I don't know. He's the other person I brought this up with and he said it was morbid too. We were out the other night and it just came up. I figured you guys knew each other because everyone seems to know everyone here." It seemed like a story she'd been waiting to tell someone.

"Yeah, I know him." Sean felt an irrepressible anger well up inside of him at the sound of Hunter's name. They were out together—that's what Ashley said. Had Hunter slept with her already? He didn't want to think about Hunter, but he couldn't stop now. "So what's up with you and Hunter?"

Ashley pulled her hands into the sleeves of her coat and held her coffee with fingerless mitts. "I don't know, probably nothing. He couldn't push me out the door fast enough, so I'm guessing it was the last I'm going to hear from him."

Sean wasn't sure how to feel about this information. If Hunter was sleeping with Ashley, then there was a possibility he *wasn't* sleeping with Kat. On the other hand, he could be sleeping with both of them. And did Hunter Briggs have to fuck every female Sean had ever felt anything for? Not that he had *feelings* for Ashley, but he had something. And now suddenly it felt like he'd been relegated to the friend zone, a sympathetic shoulder for her to cry on about Hunter.

Sean stood up. "I should probably get to work."

"Already?"

He didn't really want to go, but his mind was reeling again. He was back to Kat and Hunter and—

"You wanna come to Katama Bay with me?"

"What? No, I have to work."

"Skip it." Ashley shrugged, like someone who didn't understand the rules of real jobs.

Sean found her maddening and magnetic all at once.

"It will only take an hour or so. I want to take a few soil samples."

Sean frowned. "Does this have something to do with Kyle Billings? This is some Nancy Drew shit?"

She shrugged again. "Maybe. So what? Come with me anyway."

Sean didn't really need to open the boatyard yet. Nothing on the schedule was urgent. He exhaled in defeat. "Yeah, I guess so."

Ashley smiled. She stood up and tossed her coffee cup in the garbage bin.

Sean did the same. He followed her lead toward her car.

And like that, they were a strange sort of friends, bonded by curiosity and private turmoil.

Sean sat in the passenger seat as Ashley drove them to Katama Bay. She talked ceaselessly and exceeded every speed limit, accelerating into every curve. Clouds moved into the steel sky above them and strong winds bent the trees along the road. It was exhilarating and strange to be there in the car with Ashley. She was new, and sitting beside her made the island feel new. It made Sean feel new.

Being with Ashley on that day wouldn't solve any of the problems in Sean's suddenly heavy life; he knew that. No, she was a break from those things. She was something else entirely.

CHAPTER 7

Kat leaned her head against the cool glass of the ferry window. A nearby baby cried while the parents argued in hushed tones. A young man wearing a backpack and a ring through the center of his nose chatted with the leathery older guy who always seemed to be on the ferry. Kat had done this ride a million times, but she hadn't done it—or much of anything—recently. Leaving the apartment was work now. Even the nearly empty ferry of late October felt too loud and bright to her on that afternoon.

She tried to focus on the dark, choppy water outside. The gulls that normally balanced atop the buoys were all gone for the season. Kat had only left her house three times that week, for provisions at the co-op and some library research, and it seemed she'd missed the last gasp of autumn.

It was good to be out. They needed new wood paddles for the stemless wineglasses Orla wanted to make, so Kat had been sent into Boston for supplies. There was no way she would have done it without Orla's prompting, but it still felt good to be out. She was glad she had done it, but she was even gladder to be on her way home.

In a previous life—the one she had before she'd pushed a man to his death—Kat liked these excursions into the city. She usually recruited Erika to join her. They'd try a new restaurant and do some window-shopping. When the weather was nice, they'd buy sandwiches to eat in Boston Common. It was a periodic reminder of her native continent and its inhabitants. Today's trip wasn't so blithe. She didn't even bother inviting Erika.

Kat reached into her bag and pulled out the book she'd acquired on the mainland: *Bird Species of Osceola*. It wasn't exactly what she'd been looking for—Kyle was from somewhere west of that—but it was the closest she could find at the big chain bookstore next to the glassworks supply shop. And she learned years ago that when you were on the mainland for something necessary, get something unnecessary as well because you wouldn't have that opportunity again for a while.

Kat flipped through the pages of dense text. She studied the glossy photos of Florida bird life. Apparently, the Osceola National Forest and Okefenokee Swamp regions of northern Florida are known for their vast array of bird species. Their crane population doubles in the winter when northern cranes come down to join the native sandhills. Kat studied the various pictures of sandhills on wet, scenic beaches. Ugly birds, really. Sandhill cranes can live to be twenty years old and they're doing just fine, but the whooping crane—a close relative—is nearly extinct today. Kat wondered if Kyle had noticed any of this when he was growing up there. Most kids wouldn't have, but maybe he was more of an observant type, the sort of boy who might notice the disappearance of whooping cranes.

She circled a section about flash floods in low-lying areas. It seemed pertinent to understanding who Kyle was—the fact that he'd moved from one wet place to another. But maybe it wasn't. She didn't give a flying fuck about the waterways of upstate New York, so why would he care about the Oke-fenokee Swamp?

Kat knew it was crazy to obsess over a dead man she hardly knew, but she couldn't stop. All she saw when she closed her eyes was his petrified face in the moments before his fall. She imagined his mother wailing as she got the news of his death over the phone. In this vision, Kyle's mother is sometimes sitting at a kitchen table smoking a cigarette with her girl-friends. Other times, she's walking down the grocery store aisle and she just crumples to the floor with her cell phone at her ear. There are a million possible formulations for how a person can receive tragic news while going about their day. Kat was working her way through all of them.

The images of Kyle's mother, his childhood home and former life were coming into focus with Kat's obsessive re-search. You can learn a lot from online obituaries—that's where she started. After that, she went to social media, which was full of old photos people had scanned and posted. And she was alarmed to learn that there are aerial photos online of basically every house on earth, if you look hard enough. It's all there. It's not like she was doing anything creepy or illegal. Just searching the internet, and checking out a few books here and there. The microfiche options at the library had filled in some gaps with archived newspapers and such... But that was basically it. This book was the first actual pur-chase associated with her Kyle inquiry, and it was only twelve dollars. Kat considered her research more of a casual hobby than an obsession.

A sullen teenage girl from the adjacent ferry booth stared at Kat, who was circling factoids with a red Sharpie. Kat stared back and the girl finally looked away.

Kat dug into her bag, looking for the pages she'd printed

up. Sometimes if she examined the big, pixelated image of Kyle—the one she'd blown up from The Undertow staff photo that was posted on their website—she could sort of tap into who he was. She'd squint her eyes, blurring Kyle to just a blob of pink skin and dark hair, then refocus and hope to see something new in his face, something that helped her understand who he'd been. Did he look like the kind of guy who would have cared about the native wildlife of northern Florida? Did he seem like a man who would have forced himself upon a woman?

The teenager was looking at Kat again. She could feel it.

Kat stared at the printout. The other bartenders' faces had been scribbled out, but she could still see half of fat old Jerry's smile, which was distracting. Kat dug into her bag for the black Sharpie. She fished around and the ferry lurched as it pulled into Vineyard Haven. Her marked-up photo slid off the table and under the bench seat in front of her.

As Kat jumped up to retrieve her paper, the sullen teenager jumped faster, eager to see what this strange lonely woman had been obsessing over. They reached for it at precisely the same moment and as each pulled a corner, the page ripped down the middle.

The girl pulled her hand back and made a weak expression of apology before looking down at the torn page. She looked right at the picture of Kyle and then back up at Kat. And for a moment it seemed that she recognized the man in the photo. Was that possible? Could she have understood who and what she was seeing in that brief glance? But then the expression on the girl's face turned to pity, or maybe it was disgust, and she went back to her seat. Maybe she wasn't interested in any of it.

Kat's fear of looking like a crazy person was suddenly subsumed by her fear of looking like a suspicious person—someone who might know something about Kyle's death. He was fresh on everyone's mind. The case was still open; the cops were still looking for answers; and Kat was still waiting for a shoe to drop. Everyone on the island knew who Kyle Billings was now. His image had been on TV for a week. Local stations all used the same old picture from a previous job, before he'd gotten the shorter haircut and filled out in the arms. Kat felt a little sorry for Kyle about the picture they used because he was actually much more handsome than that.

The vibration of the ferry quieted to a hum and everyone headed for the doors. Kat stuffed her book and printout pages into her bag, checked on her new glass-working paddles, and felt for her phone. It was all there. She reminded herself that she hadn't committed any crimes on that day and didn't need to be so goddamn nervous about just riding the ferry like a normal person. *Carry on*, she told herself. *Carry on as usual.*

At the place where the hulking ferry met the edge of Martha's Vineyard, a team of strong men and women in waterproof onesies moved quickly at their respective tasks—ushering the passengers off, directing the cars, securing the watercraft. No matter how few unimpressed locals happened to be on that ferry on any given day, every one of those workers were in place and ready to do their elegant dance. All day, in season and off. Kat loved the intricate coordination of it all. She smiled at the man directing a mail truck off the boat and breathed a quiet sigh of relief, because although she had no concrete reason to be nervous, a part of her wondered if the gatekeepers to her island might not let her back in once she'd left.

"Ma'am, this way," a man said from behind.

She spun around. "What?"

"Please come this way." The ferry worker pointed to a pathway that had been laid by little orange cones and Kat realized that she was about to walk into a small construction zone.

"Sorry, thank you," she muttered.

She walked behind a handsome middle-aged couple carrying three overstuffed canvas bags with their initials embroidered in large letters. Going to West Chop, probably, with those clothes and that look. She had come to know all the slight variations in well-heeled islanders. They were headed to the taxi stand.

Kat went to the #1 bus, which was spewing loud breaths of steam into the cold air as it idled. She showed the driver her ticket and walked to the back. There were four other people on the bus, pretty standard for an off-season weekday. None of them were tourists. Kat sank into the soft cushions and exhaled. Twenty minutes along Vineyard Haven Road and she'd be back home, thank God. Leaving her house and her island now felt like an ordeal and she wondered if it was possible to never do it again.

Kat had never been on an island before she moved to Martha's Vineyard. She only picked the Vineyard because someone at her old waitressing job told her you could make a killing as a server in places like that. She was estranged from her mother by then and had no reason to stay in the Buffalo area, and so she went. The idea of living on an island had been vaguely intriguing, but there was no way for her younger self to know precisely what it meant to be a resident of such a place. Because it was so small, and the borders clearly delineated, it struck Kat upon arrival that inhabitants regarded Martha's Vineyard as a sort of kingdom all its own. It wasn't really Massachusetts or New England or America any more than the Tower of London was Europe. It even had its own moat and drawbridge. And unlike the theoretical legal borders that separated most US states from one another, nature marked the precise moment at which you arrived on an island. You stepped off a boat, bridge or ferry—all borders which required tickets and permission from the gatekeepers—and then you knew that you were *there*. It seemed to Kat that Vineyard residents regarded every place on earth as either *there* or *not there*, and after seven years of residency, she couldn't imagine why anyone would choose the latter.

There were other places like this, of course. Kat understood that people from New York City regarded it as the center of the universe. Erika said it was because of Wall Street and fashion. But Kat had come to believe that the real reason they thought this was because this was how islanders regarded their kingdoms: as separate and special places from the rest of society. She went to New York once, three Christmases ago with Sean. It was wonderful, but it wasn't the Vineyard. Even the Big Apple, apparently, was just *not there*.

Kat stepped off the bus onto the cold, wet sidewalk in Addison. She was already starting to feel better. She could be home in ten minutes, back at her computer. Orla wasn't expecting her in the shop for the rest of the day, which meant hours of uninterrupted time to read through her new bird book and research every little thread of curiosity that might get her closer to who Kyle Billings was. She knew so much about him now, but still couldn't quite hold him in her hands. There was no ribbon of consistency connecting all the phases of his life—not one that Kat could find anyhow. She hadn't identified the thing that defined him and followed him all the way from northern Florida to the Vineyard. She could have said the same thing about herself until she'd learned to blow glass. Once she'd discovered glass working, Kat's passions revealed themselves retroactively. She suddenly understood what she'd been searching for in her past. Maybe Kyle had still been searching too.

Kat considered what discovery might have been waiting for Kyle as she walked home. It was raining slightly, cold rain that would have been snow if it was just a few degrees colder. Kyle never got a chance to figure out what the aimlessness of his youth all meant. Maybe that was too dramatic, though. Maybe he hadn't been the sort to indulge such romantic ideas. Kat would never know. She only knew that the ugly moments before his death, and his aggression toward her, were fading quickly from her memory. All that was left were the hints of goodness she thought she'd seen in him. Kat couldn't hold on to the fear that had led her to push him. Her psyche wouldn't allow it. And why? He'd been threatening her. He might have raped her. She dismissed the thought as quickly as it came. It didn't seem fair anymore. Kat was justified in protecting herself in that moment—she was sure of that. But it was also true that Kyle hadn't actually done anything. Not yet. Maybe not ever. And so it seemed only fair to give the memory of Kyle the benefit of the doubt. It might be nuts, but it was fair.

"Kat!"

She looked up from her feet into the icy rain.

Sean stood before her. He had a smiling blonde woman at his side and a bag of takeout from Stoney's in one hand. They hadn't seen each other in a week but he didn't look as bereft as Kat imagined he would be. He looked almost cheerful.

The smell of hot french fries rose up from the bag.

"Hey!" Kat ran a hand along her wet ponytail and smiled at the woman. "Hi, I'm Kat."

The woman put a hand out. She said her name, which Kat forgot almost immediately.

"Have we met?" the woman asked.

"I don't think so." Kat's head was spinning. This woman did look familiar, but there was no way they had met before.

"She's studying our beach," Sean explained. "We're just out for some provisions."

Kat nodded, though it didn't make a smidge of sense.

"The buckling," he added.

"Right, I figured." Kat turned to the woman. "So you've talked with Orla, then? About the cliffs?" *Those are my cliffs*, Kat wanted to say, *mine and Sean's*.

"I'm trying."

"Yeah, she can be tough." Kat looked back at Sean. It was all too strange. This was their first encounter since their fight and it didn't feel like the right sort of encounter. "We're all pretty nervous about the cliff..."

The woman's eyes widened as something became clearer to her. She was realizing that this was Kat—the girlfriend. Or ex-girlfriend. Kat wondered how Sean had characterized their status. She almost enjoyed watching the woman squirm before her.

The rain had picked up and they were all wilting under its weight. Everyone wanted this encounter to end.

Sean held the take-out bag up. "Well, this is getting cold, so we should get back to my place."

It didn't make any sense to Kat that they would be eating french fries at Sean's house if she was studying their eroded beach, a mile away. Was Sean seeing her? Was he capable of moving on that quickly?

"Yeah, of course," Kat said. "I'll call you this week, Sean." It sounded strange coming out. So formal. They had resolved nothing and, though she didn't want him around as she sorted through the Kyle stuff, she didn't want him with this woman, either.

"Sure, okay."

"Nice meeting you," the woman said.

"Nice meeting you."

They turned and walked away.

Kat watched them disappear around a corner before breaking into a speed walk in the other direction. Minutes before, she'd been so eager to get home and back to her Kyle obsession, but suddenly she wanted a friend to commiserate with. Sean just seemed so content without her. It was devastating. It was also the moment at which she realized what it all meant: she might be losing Sean for good. Because of her secret about Kyle and all the hiding out and the weird discussions with Hunter, this might be the end for her and Sean. It had been such a distant possibility last week when all she wanted to do was get a little space to clear her head. But now, with this woman in the picture… Perhaps she'd overestimated Sean's patience.

Kat walked quickly through the rest of town in the dark drizzle. She trudged up the hill, passed the glass shop and saw Orla talking to a customer inside. Poor Orla. But she couldn't think about that for now.

She kept going until she got to Hunter's house, a giant in a row of giants. These fucking people. They pushed all the real people to the waterless center of the island and could hardly be bothered to occupy their empty cavernous homes for more than a few weekends a year. Kat had grown to resent so many things about Hunter that she never cared about before. She didn't used to care that he was rich or bored or blissfully ignorant of how most people lived. But now. Now he was the source of all her problems and the embodiment of all the privileges she'd been locked out of in this world. Now their differences mattered.

And still, she was at his door, hoping to find him.

"Finally," Hunter said as he opened the door.

Kat stepped inside the foyer and took off her wet coat. "What, finally?"

"I knew you'd emerge from hibernation eventually. You can't avoid me forever."

She nodded. After the Sean interaction, it was satisfying to know that someone had noticed her absence.

"You want a latte?"

Kat nodded again and they went into the kitchen. It was deceptively tidy inside Hunter's house, which she knew was a result of continuous housecleaning services and not Hunter's state of mind. He could go nuts in there and the army of women his father employed would maintain an orderly facade to the very end.

"Do you know anything new?" Hunter asked from the kitchen counter, his back to her.

Kat watched his shoulder muscles move around under his shirt as he tamped the espresso. "No, nothing. Local news has pretty much stopped covering it, but I think the case is still open. Maybe they've moved on to some new terrible thing."

Hunter frothed milk. "Maybe. Let's hope."

Neither of them wanted to talk about it, but it was unclear whether they were capable of small talk.

"I'm sorry I freaked out at you last week," Kat blurted. She had no intention of apologizing about their argument and didn't really believe he deserved one, but she wanted peace.

Hunter poured cognac over two picture-perfect heads of foamed milk. "It's my fault. C'mon."

She followed him and the coffees out of the kitchen and into a small den lined with bookshelves. Hunter had the Cognac bottle tucked under one arm.

They sat down on opposite corners of a leather couch and turned toward each other. Kat had never spent any time in this room.

Hunter crossed his left leg over his right knee. He studied Kat. "Anything else going on?"

Kat sipped the boozy coffee. "I think I really screwed things up with Sean. He seems…I don't know…*done* with me."

"I'm sure that's not true."

"Have you talked to him?"

Hunter shook his head. "No, he's definitely done with me. He doesn't want to blame you for anything, though. He's breaking up with one of us, but it's not you."

"I don't know about that. I saw him today with this woman and…" Kat sighed. Maybe she was making too much of it all. They had been together for years. Was it possible that this was it? She was as heartsick as she was exhausted.

"I probably shouldn't say what I think." Hunter took a long gulp.

"Why? What do you think?"

He shrugged and topped her off. "Kat, Sean's a good guy, but he's very rigid. He's difficult, in his own way."

"He *is* rigid, kind of moralistic. But he's also genuinely good. Maybe that's what being good does to you."

Hunter uncrossed his legs and stretched them out on the couch, so his socked feet touched the edge of Kat's thigh. "But you're good and you're not like that."

"I'm not that good. I don't think you can be truly good if you come from bad people."

"I refuse to believe that. We're fucked if it's true."

Kat picked a red thread from the tip of his socked toe. "We're fucked either way."

Hunter leaned back and closed his eyes. Kat wondered how much of the bottle he'd ingested before she arrived. It was the sort of thing she would have worried about weeks before, but now seemed so minor. Whatever kept them each afloat—that was the new standard.

Kat closed her eyes too and felt the full weight of her exhaustion. Going to Boston had taken a lot out of her. Every day she seemed to have less energy than the day before, her sleep deficiency more pronounced. She kept her eyes shut until her breathing slowed and she could almost feel her body drift toward something like sleep. And just as it seemed she was surrendering to it, Kyle's face flashed before her. It was the same terrified expression he'd worn in his last moments, but this time his eyes were enormous saucers, as wide and white as baseballs. She jerked upright and spilled the latte into her lap. "Oh shit."

"Don't worry about it." Hunter went quickly to the kitchen and brought her a dish towel. No explanation needed. He understood everything.

He sat back down beside her on the couch and they listened to the sound of their breaths for another minute.

Finally, Hunter turned to her. "What's your full name?" He'd never asked before.

"Kathleen."

"Hmm. *Kat* suits you better. Why didn't I know that was your name?"

"Because it's not. Not anymore. I changed it when I left home."

"You hated it that much?"

"I hated the life that came with it. Changing my name seemed important for starting over. New name, new story."

"Did it work?"

Kat thought about that. "Yeah, it did. Seems like it shouldn't, but it did."

Hunter was watching her as she explained it all, and she felt a wave of gratitude for his genuine attention. She still hated him a little bit for the circumstances of their lives. He was still the cause of all this horror. He was a piece of it, anyhow. But their circumstances also made him seem like the only person in the world that she could be fully herself with. She didn't know if that feeling had always been there or whether it was a new thing, a consequence of their mounting problems.

And then Kat did something. She leaned in to Hunter and let her head fall upon his shoulder.

He put a hand on her head and stroked her hair gingerly. The weight of his hand was almost imperceptible, as if he thought she might burst into flames if he pressed too hard.

It was the most overtly *not* platonic thing they had ever done and the danger of it sent a tingle through her body. She could feel the warmth of his shoulder, the drag of his hand in her hair. She was aware of every inch of her arm that was in contact with his and those parts were on fire now.

Hunter leaned in closer and she tried to control her breath. The only sounds in the room were the distant din of appliances and the outside wind.

Kat glanced up at him. She felt embarrassed doing it, as if all accountability for that moment could be avoided by looking away and pretending it wasn't happening. But she looked up and saw that Hunter was gazing down at her. He was really taking her in. Kat had the fleeting notion that Hunter had made the very same face for hundreds of women before her and they were all similarly flattered by it, but she let the feeling pass.

And then his face was closer and his breath mixed with hers. And then Hunter's mouth was on her mouth and they were kissing gently. It wasn't the kiss of people overcome by lust, though there was desperation in it. They wanted it as much as they regretted the wanting. It was soft and shameful, tender and vile. The tension was so arousing that Kat felt her head throb as blood rushed around within her.

She closed her eyes...and saw Kyle. And that wave of panic gave way to the deep pool of guilt and confusion she reserved for Sean. Kat's heart sank and she forgot about the lips that had moved to her neck, up toward her ear. She pushed Hunter and he pulled her in, mistaking the gesture for something else.

"No, let's not," Kat said, pushing him from her.

Hunter drew back and wiped a hand across his mouth. He nodded emphatically as if he were on the brink of making the same declaration. "No, right, sorry."

"No, *I'm* sorry," she said. "I'm just confused and not thinking straight."

"I don't think you're confused. But you're right."

Kat stood up and rubbed her temples. "We both are, I think. Because of everything that's going on. We're, like, hiding out together and that's not really the same thing as…"

Hunter waited for her to finish the thought, but she did not.

"And I don't know," Kat said, shifting directions, "maybe I'm reacting to Sean and that blonde scientist. I don't know…"

Hunter's face changed. "Wait, what?"

"I think I'm just confused."

He stood up. "No, what was the part about the blonde scientist?"

"I don't know." She waved him off. "I saw him earlier with this woman and it seemed like there was something there, but maybe I'm losing my mind. It doesn't matter."

"This was a blonde woman who studies beach erosion?"

"Yeah, it was." Kat knew where he was going with this.

"That's Ashley. Fuck! That's Ashley."

"*Your* Ashley?"

"She's not mine! But yeah. What is she doing with Sean?"

"They were just walking together. They were going to his house."

Hunter folded and unfolded his arms. "To his house?

That's weird. Did she seem, I don't know, interested in anything strange to you?"

A burning panic rose up in Kat's esophagus. She tried to think. "Well, she said she'd been talking to Orla. She's looking at our waterfront. But that's her job, isn't it?" Kat realized then that she *had* met Ashley before. On the morning of the buckling. She'd been hovering around their lives for weeks, apparently.

"I don't really know what her job is. She's a doctoral student. But she was so focused on Kyle when we talked. It seems weird that she just found Sean out of nowhere, doesn't it?"

"Maybe… But not if she's really just looking at our cliffs. That wouldn't be weird." But it *did* seem weird. "Wait, you were supposed to be keeping an eye on her. Did you take her out?"

"No, I didn't." Hunter was not interested in apologizing for this oversight. "I was going to—despite the fact that she seems kinda nuts—but I just haven't yet. But Jesus, I didn't know she was going to get to Sean. What does this girl want?"

Kat chewed her lip. She'd forgotten entirely about the awkwardness just minutes before. "I don't know. Do you think she knows something?"

"I guess she could have gone to the cops with that theory about the currents."

"I don't know, Hunter. That feels like a stretch. There's nothing weird about her studying the cliffs."

"Jesus, I don't know." Hunter scratched his scalp, searching for clarity.

"Maybe we should call them."

"What? Why?"

"To get a read on the situation. What if I just called Sean

and asked him about a bunch of stuff, really normal stuff, and tried to feel around for anything strange."

"I guess you could do that."

"It can't do any harm, right?"

"Not unless they already know something and are just looking for suspicious behavior. It might seem suspicious to someone looking for suspicious behavior."

Kat thought about this. She truly couldn't tell anymore where rational thinking ended and paranoia began. Sean had met an attractive young scientist who was here to study a real phenomenon. Nothing strange about that… Except for the fact that this scientist was preoccupied with the story of Kyle and she claimed to be an expert on local tides. If she wanted to get closer to the truth, she certainly could.

"Let's call them," Hunter said.

Kat went for the phone.

CHAPTER 8

"That was weird." Sean returned the phone to its wall mount in the kitchen.

Ashley looked up from her magazine. She was sprawled out on the couch in the living room of Sean's small carriage house. "What?"

"That was Kat. She just wanted to chat."

"So?"

"So, it was weird. I don't know. We aren't really doing that lately. She asked about the boathouse and my old back injury, and about my mom, even though she sees her more than me. It was very...I don't know...polite."

Ashley stared at Sean, unclear on what made this story noteworthy. She always froze up a little when Kat's name was mentioned. She'd been trying to avoid the topic ever since the two of them started hanging out almost a week earlier.

Sean still couldn't tell if Ashley annoyed the shit out of him or he wanted to kiss her. It was a little of both.

She went back to her magazine.

"She asked about you too, actually."

The magazine came down again. "What did she say?"

"She was wondering if you'd learned anything new about our cliffs. Oh, and she asked if there was anything else you were investigating."

Ashley raised her eyebrows. "Investigating?"

"Yeah, weird word, right?" Sean was still standing in the doorway to his galley kitchen.

Ashley sat up straighter. "That *is* a weird word."

"I don't know. Maybe it's not that weird." Sean turned and opened the fridge.

"Hunter used the same word, *investigate*."

He walked back into the living room, rubbing an apple against his shirt. Sean hadn't explained to Ashley that he suspected Kat and Hunter of cheating. It wasn't a secret, but it felt disloyal to discuss Kat too much with her. Plus, Ashley seemed dangerously prone to drama, which made him nervous.

"Kat and Hunter spend a lot of time together these days," Sean said.

"They do?" She had the same conspiratorial look in her eyes as when Kyle came up. It had something to do with secrets. She wanted to know everything, it seemed. "Is something going on there?"

"Maybe. I confronted them about it last week. That's how all of this weirdness started with Kat. But I have no real evidence."

Ashley got up and fetched herself an apple. "So the two of them are hanging out, talking about how I'm *investigating* something."

"Well, we don't know that…though she was definitely there with somebody. I could hear sounds in the background."

Ashley nodded, like she'd expected this. "Yep. She and Hunter called you to ask what I'm investigating. Hunter called me a 'citizen investigator' when I brought up Kyle. I think this is all about that guy Kyle Billings."

"Whoa," Sean said with a full mouth. "That's a stretch."

Ashley rolled the apple around in her hands. She was getting excited. "So these two are together, they're probing you for more info and they're both being cagey. *Something* is happening here."

It made Sean nervous to see Ashley enjoying this little breakthrough. He'd only been hanging out with her for six days and the full scope of her intensity was starting to come into focus. Still, even accounting for her intensity, something did seem to be going on with Kat and Hunter. There was no denying that now.

"We should talk to them!"

"No," Sean said. "I can talk to Kat, but this isn't your problem."

"But *I'm* the one they're talking about! Of course it's my problem. And I think they might have some connection to Kyle Billings's death. I really do. Why else would they be asking about this? Why would they be concerned about an *investigation*?"

"Ashley, this isn't an investigation, and you're not an investigator. Something might be going on with them, but that's my problem. None of this has anything to do with you."

"Hunter is a selfish prick." Ashley took a large, loud bite of her apple.

"Is that what this is all about? You want to get back at him for hurting your feelings?"

Her face fell. "No. I *am* pissed off at him, but that's not what this is about. It's not *only* what this is about, anyway. I think those two are hiding something more than just an affair."

Sean sat down and studied the apple core in his hand. "There was this one night…"

"What? Tell me."

"A couple days before they found Kyle's body, there was one night when I left them at the bar. I never really got the story about what happened that night. Everything started to fall apart after that."

Ashley's eyebrows went up again. "They were together?"

"I don't know. Maybe."

"That's interesting."

"We were all at The Undertow."

"Kyle's bar."

Sean nodded. He didn't feel good about this. Whatever was going on with Kat and Hunter was—he had assumed—something that could be explained or apologized away. He'd been sick over the state of things and was beginning to approach the stage at which he would take her back no matter what the story was. She'd need to grovel, of course, and beg for his forgiveness. He'd be done with Hunter for good. But after enough apologies, Sean believed he could take Kat back and they could be as they were. But this theory was… this was something else entirely. And while he wanted to dismiss it as the wild ideas of an imaginative woman, it carried an element of plausibility.

"C'mon." Ashley threw a coat at Sean and slid into her own. "We should find them."

He shook his head. "I don't like this."

She pulled her wool hat on—the same one she'd worn the first time Sean saw her. Ashley was a real challenge for Sean. She was simultaneously too young and adorable for his comfort, but also whip-smart and dogged. She was more emotional than he preferred—erratic even—but that emotion also made her knowable. Ashley required no distance from him and made no attempt to hide her vulnerability, which was nice for a change. He did want to kiss her, but he was a little afraid of her too. He wanted to kiss Ashley; and he knew she was trouble; and he missed Kat so fucking much. These feelings were all related, but he couldn't quite figure out how.

"We're just going to pop in," she said. "We're not going to do anything crazy. Just, you know, make a surprise visit to catch them off guard and see how they react. If everything seems normal, then it will just be a normal visit."

"So if it's normal, you'll let all this go?"

Ashley smiled. "Sure."

There would be nothing normal about Sean and his new friend dropping in on Kat and Hunter. It was confrontational by definition. But as they walked toward Island Glass, and Ashley talked about her theories, Sean felt himself growing angrier and more convinced of them. Something real was happening between those two. He was sure of it now, and he deserved an explanation.

Orla greeted them outside the glass shop. "Hi, love. Hi, Ashley. What are you guys up to?"

"Is Kat upstairs?"

She shook her head. "No, she went into Boston for supplies. I thought she'd be back by now, but I haven't seen her."

Ashley looked at Sean.

He avoided her eyes.

"Okay, thanks, Mom."

Orla gave his arm a squeeze and went back inside.

The sun was almost down and the temperature was dropping. Ashley stuffed her hands in her pockets as she led the way toward Hunter's house. Sean followed. They didn't even need to discuss the next stop. They were on a mission now.

"This isn't like her," Sean said as they walked. "She wouldn't normally just leave my mom hanging at the shop."

Ashley made a face that Sean understood to mean she didn't think much of Kat.

"What if she's not at Hunter's?" he asked.

"I think they'll both be there."

Sean did too. And now he *wanted* Kat to be there with Hunter. He wanted to catch them, and have all his suspicions and resentments validated. He wanted to plant it on them, to assign most of the blame to Hunter and a significantly smaller portion on his misguided girlfriend. If they weren't there, this anger would continue to eat him up.

They banged the brass knocker on the front door over and over, but no one came. The door was slightly ajar and lights were on throughout the house, which made it seem like they were hiding inside.

"This is pretty weird," Ashley said, stoking Sean's ire. "I mean, they're obviously here."

He scratched his beard three times. "Well, screw this. If they're not coming out, I'm not going to stand here all day."

Ashley looked around. "Wait, did you hear that?"

They stood with their eyes locked on each other. It was beginning to get dark. Not a soul around, but Sean could definitely hear the distant laugh of a woman's voice over the soft lap of water. It was Kat's.

"C'mon," he said, and he headed back down to the road. Sean knew where they were.

With Ashley behind, he crossed the street and started down the steep stairs to Hunter's private waterfront dock. Their boots clomped loudly on cold wood and Sean felt an anger mounting with each step.

And there they were. Hunter was hunched over the motor of his boat and Kat was in the cockpit staring intently at the controls. They looked up when they heard the descending footsteps.

Kat made a noise, almost like a gasp.

Hunter bolted upright, then waved. "Oh, hey, man."

They both stood stick straight.

"What's going on out here?" Sean said as he approached them. He wanted to sound casual, at least at the start. He didn't really know what he was there for, so he wanted to go slow and be cautious. But there was a catch in his throat that made his voice sound pinched. His fists were clenched inside the arms of his coat.

"Did you guys see the weather alert?" Kat asked. "Sleet tonight."

"I must have missed that," Sean said through his teeth. He looked up at the sky, then at Hunter at the stern. "You gonna put the boat in the boatyard for the winter?"

Hunter folded his arms across his chest. "I don't know. Might sell it before then. I hardly ever use it."

"So that's why we're covering the boat," Kat inserted. "Because of the sleet."

It didn't look to Sean like they were covering the boat.

No one spoke for a moment.

Ashley stood behind Sean, watching him. Why was she there? It suddenly seemed strange to have her in tow. No one had greeted her, though they seemed to acknowledge her presence.

Hunter climbed out of the whaler and walked right up to Sean on the dock. "Yep, thought we should get out here and cover things up."

"The two of you?" Sean asked. Every muscle in his back stiffened.

They were just three feet apart. Kat and Ashley watched

from behind each of the guys. Salt water lapped gently at the hull.

Hunter took one more bold, unnecessary step closer to Sean. "Well, we're all friends, right?" It was a challenge.

"Anyhow," Kat cut in. "He needed two people because the motor seems a little jammed up. It's probably nothing. I was just here to turn the ignition while Hunter checked the motor."

She was rambling; trying to distract or delay what was happening between Sean and Hunter at that moment. Sean hadn't heard a word of what she said and he didn't fucking believe it anyway.

"What are you guys really up to?" Ashley said from behind.

Everyone turned to her.

Sean wished he hadn't brought her.

"Why are you here?" Hunter asked coolly.

Ashley glared. "Fuck you, Hunter."

He nodded in agreement. "Fine, yes, fuck me. But really, what are you doing here, Ashley? On my dock. On this island."

"Don't be an asshole," Sean said. He may not have known for sure what Hunter's crime was, but he did know that Hunter was famously promiscuous and known for disappearing on women. And Sean may have had mixed feelings about Ashley, but she didn't deserve this.

"Ohhh." Hunter stepped back and smiled at Sean. "I see what's going on here. You two… That makes sense. It's cute, actually."

"Hunter, stop," Kat said from behind him.

Sean stepped closer. "No, Hunter. You're wrong. Because, you see, I'm not like you."

Hunter leaned in. "And what does that mean, Sean?"

"I'm a good person."

Hunter clenched his teeth and watched Sean. Their faces were inches apart.

"I would never do what you do." Sean went on, "What you're doing right now, with Kat…"

"Sean, I told you it's not that," Kat said.

Hunter said nothing, but he smiled tauntingly.

The fury rose up in Sean's chest, turning every fiber in his body on high alert. Kat said they weren't sleeping together, but the look in Hunter's eyes said the very opposite. The smug, satisfied grin of victory was all over his expensive face, and Sean couldn't bear to look at it anymore. He couldn't stand there for another minute feeling helpless and unsure about what the fuck was going on, and so he had to do something.

Hunter relaxed slightly and laughed, like he'd won the standoff.

Sean felt his arm pull back before he could think to stop it, and then the skin around his knuckles was tightening, and with one furious swing, his fist exploded into the side of Hunter's left eye.

Hunter's hands rushed to his face just as his knees buckled and the blood around his cheekbone started to pour. "Fuck, man!" He fell to the dock.

Kat ran toward him.

Ashley ran in after her.

This wasn't how it was supposed to go down. Sean looked on in horror as the women tried to pry Hunter's fingers from his face so they could examine the damage. They looked at his busted eye, and then back at Sean, and then back to the eye. This wasn't what he'd intended to do. It wasn't Sean's plan.

"Fuck, man!" Hunter yelled again as he stumbled up to

his feet. He let his hands drop to his sides and everyone took a good long look at what Sean had done.

It was hard to make out the injury in the moonlight, but not impossible. Hunter's eye was red, the socket soon to be bruised and the broken skin beneath it was a bloody mess. But it was a standard punch, probably no permanent damage incurred.

Sean was relieved to see that he didn't seem to have broken anything, but was no less ashamed. He hadn't thrown a punch since ninth grade, and even then—after he caught Bryan Alpo trying to steal his bike—he couldn't believe he had it in him. There may have been times in life when a punch was justified, but that didn't mean all men possessed such an impulse. Sean always thought he wasn't the punching type.

Hunter stared at Sean, and everyone held their breaths. Would he punch back? If he wanted to, Sean wouldn't block it. That wouldn't be right. He would let Hunter take a big, premeditated swing as he stood there. He *wanted* it now because this was almost worse than a punch. Hunter just stared in anger, like he was considering every revenge possibility, and the longer he stared, the more violent his busted eye looked.

Just fucking punch me, Sean thought.

Hunter drew a wet breath. "I'm not sleeping with Kat," he whispered. "I'm not."

Sean looked at Kat, who had been watching him. He believed her. He believed both of them now. He turned back to Hunter and suddenly felt more horrible than he had ever felt in his whole life. They really weren't sleeping together. Something was going on with his girlfriend, but it was clear now that it wasn't an affair. And he'd allowed himself to be seduced by outlandish theories from a near stranger. Ashley. She was still there. Jesus, why was she still there?

Sean nodded at Hunter. "Okay. I'm sorry."

Hunter was still staring, but his anger had softened. "I get it," he said. And he didn't say any more.

Hunter's response perplexed Sean. *I get it*, he'd said. Did that mean that Sean's suspicions had been warranted? That Hunter was guilty of something else? Or was it simply that Hunter was the most forgiving chump he'd ever met. That seemed unlikely. He'd just been punched in the face, so maybe Hunter wasn't thinking so straight. Whatever it was, Sean was grateful for it. He felt deeply remorseful about the punch, and, although he wasn't sure that he deserved forgiveness, he would take it.

"Sean, can I talk to you?" Ashley said quietly. She wasn't satisfied with this outcome.

He turned to her. "No, Ashley. You should go home."

She looked around. Everyone was watching her. She pulled her hat down farther on her head and looked back at Sean. She was pissed. "But what about—"

"Go home."

Hunter and Kat watched as she considered the order.

Finally, Ashley spun on one heel, walked the length of the dock and stomped her way back up to the street.

When it was just the three of them again, Hunter cracked a small grin. "I always did know how to pick 'em."

Kat laughed first, and then Sean. Things were maybe okay.

"I'm so sorry, man," Sean said again.

"I know, you fucking animal."

Kat smiled at Sean, and he smiled back. It felt like a real moment of intimacy and apology and regret for all the weirdness of the past week. It made him hopeful.

"Let's forget about the boat," Kat said.

Sean stepped past her. "No, I got it. You really do need to cover her up tonight. You want me to look at the motor while I'm here?"

Hunter and Kat exchanged the briefest glance. Sean saw it, but he reminded himself to let go of all the suspicion. A look is just a look.

Hunter rubbed the side of his head. "Uh, yeah, that'd be great."

Kat began snapping the stretchy cover into place at the bow while Sean fiddled with the controls. He turned the ignition on, pushed buttons, then turned it off again. Then he walked to the stern and leaned far over the edge. Sean could feel Kat buzzing around him. She was saying something about how it didn't matter…they could all go inside… don't worry about it. He couldn't quite hear with his face right up close to the engine, but it felt like she was trying to shoo him away.

Must be the propeller, Sean thought with his face over the edge. Yes, it was the propeller. Everything seemed to be working, but it looked as if the propeller itself wouldn't spin. He couldn't tell for sure. It was about ten inches under the water, but the grinding sound it made when he accelerated was classic propeller problems. Sean pushed the sleeve of his coat up to his elbows, bent farther over the back of the boat and plunged his arm in. If he could just get his hand closer to the blades, to feel around for whatever might be jamming it up… Goddamn, the water was cold. He walked his fingers along one of the blades, down to the center. He needed to get just a little closer to really know…

"Careful, buddy," Hunter said from the dock. "Bad night for a swim."

And there it was! Sean's fingers landed on something soft

and ropey. Something was tangled up in the propeller. It wasn't seaweed or fishing line. He didn't know what it was.

Sean stood back up. "You got a knife?" he yelled.

Hunter climbed into the boat with his bloodied face and opened a compartment in the cockpit. His nerves must have been running high—on account of the punch—because his hands were shaking so hard he dropped the knife twice. "Here."

Sean went back to the stern with the little jackknife. Hunter and Kat watched from the dock. He leaned far over the back of the boat and put his hand down into the frigid water and started sawing. It didn't take much—the knife seemed like it had never been used. He sliced right through whatever it was on the first few motions, then turned the propeller slightly and started sawing another section. It was really tangled up in there. With one more slice, he freed the last section and everything loosened in his hand. The propeller turned easily and he pulled the long, wet object out with his numb fingers.

"What is it?" Kat asked.

Sean held the skinny, dripping strip of fabric up to his face to try to make out what he was looking at.

"It's probably nothing," Hunter said.

"Garbage," Kat agreed.

Sean squeezed water from the clump of cloth, then unfurled it and held it up to the moonlight. "Some kind of fabric. Clothing. I don't know. It's blue with little, like, flecks of white in it."

The next thing they heard was Hunter's head hitting the dock.

CHAPTER 9

Hunter's eyes opened to the sound of the doctor's heels clicking on hard laminate. He blinked twice into the glaring hospital light and took inventory of the people standing around him. Three bodies came into focus.

"Look who's up," a woman in a starched white coat said. She stood between Sean and Kat at the edge of the bed. "Hunter, my name is Dr. Boardman. Do you know where you are?"

He scanned the room. "Vineyard Hospital," he whispered through parched lips.

"Right." Dr. Boardman looked down at her clipboard. She didn't seem nervous about Hunter's state, which was reassuring. She was all business, with her tidy white coat and every hair in its perfect place.

Kat watched Hunter's eyes as they moved around the room, putting the pieces together. The clock on the wall said 4:07 a.m. Hunter had been in that hospital bed for several hours while Kat and Sean watched him, stewing in all their private anxiety. It was impossible for Kat to know what he understood about their circumstances at that moment. A puffy square of gauze had been taped beneath his left eye, where Sean hit him, and the skin around it was turning purple. Kat could see fear in his swollen face. She hoped the others could not.

"What did I do?" Hunter asked.

Kat put a hand on his blanketed thigh. "You didn't *do* anything, Hunter. You fell and passed out, so we brought you here."

His eyes moved from Kat, to Sean, then Dr. Boardman.

"Hunter," Kat said, trying to keep his focus. "Everything is okay." She said this slowly and with emphasis. She wanted to convey to him that all their secrets were still kept. He didn't need to panic. She knew that he'd be racing through the events of that night in his mind, and that when he got to the part where Sean found a piece of Kyle's scarf tangled in the propeller of the boat's motor, he would panic.

Hospitals aren't the same thing as police stations, but Kat figured that you didn't want to be in either of them if you were evading the authorities. They had ways of talking to each other, doctors and cops. Kat knew that Hunter would be wondering what he'd said in his delirium. He'd want to get the hell out of there.

"You're going to be fine." Dr. Boardman placed her clipboard on a nearby table. A tiny silver necklace with the word *Kamila* in swooping cursive shimmered at her collarbone, revealing just a whisper of humanity. "You passed out. Standard vasovagal syncope, which means that your heart slowed down and your blood vessels opened up too quickly. It was probably brought on by stress."

Sean exhaled. "That's good, right? I thought he had a concussion."

"He might," she went on, "but there's no reason to believe it's serious. Someone should stay with him for a few hours to keep him awake and make sure he doesn't vomit or lose any feeling in his limbs."

"Of course." Kat nodded.

"What you're feeling right now is a mild sedative, Mr. Briggs." As Dr. Boardman spoke, she removed the blood-stained gauze from Hunter's cheek, peeling medical tape from tender skin with great care. "We needed to keep you calm while we stitched your cheek. When that and the topical anesthetic wears off, I want you to take a double dose of Advil."

Hunter's hands went up to his formerly perfect face and moved along the four little Frankenstein stitches.

Dr. Boardman pulled his hand down from his face. "Try not to touch it." She turned to Kat and Sean. "I'll need a moment alone with Mr. Briggs."

They left the room and let the door click behind them.

The hall smelled of disinfectant. There was no one else in sight. Somewhere far away, fingers clicked on a keyboard.

"What do you think this is about?" Kat said, though she knew.

Sean looked worried. "It's about his face, right? She's trying to get the story on how it happened, so we have to stand out here like his abusive parents."

Kat wished that were the case. What a quaint problem to have, she thought, to be guilty of punching someone and nothing else at all. "I'm sure it will be fine."

They looked at the blurred figures talking through the frosted glass window, then at their feet. It was their first moment alone in over a week. There were so many things to discuss between them, but now was not the time.

A janitor walked past them, pushing a large bin, and a gust of human odors wafted by. Kat's stomach rolled over on itself. This episode—and the conversation with Dr. Board-man—would be either no big deal or it would be the end of everything. What was Hunter saying in there? Was he capable of handling himself? What if the painkillers inspired a loopy impulse to unburden himself on this doctor? It would be over for them.

Kat remembered the wet scrap of Kyle's scarf still in the pocket of her jacket, which was hanging over a chair in the hospital room at that moment. No one saw her take it while Hunter lay face-first on the cold dock, and Sean called an ambulance. Kat had grabbed the scarf and then ran back to Hunter's side. When Sean returned to report the ambulance was on its way, he seemed to have forgotten about the scarf.

Maybe it didn't matter to Sean. Maybe he didn't see the connection between the thing he'd pulled from the motor of the boat and Hunter's sudden fainting. There were other explanations for it, Kat supposed. Hunter had a gash in his cheek after the punch and had lost a little blood. People pass out after things like that, right? Maybe that was enough for Sean. He hadn't asked any questions about it, so Kat hoped that meant he had none.

Why had she let Hunter take her down to the boat last night? He'd become obsessed with the boat. He wanted to give it one more scan for anything incriminating they may have left behind. They were just going to give it one last look, check to make sure everything was running normally. But then the motor wouldn't start, and things just got away from them...

The door opened and Dr. Boardman appeared. "You can come back in now."

Kat and Sean followed.

The doctor folded her arms across her chest and made a scolding face. "Well, Mr. Briggs insists that this assault was just a misunderstanding, and he's in no danger with the two of you. I'm not sure I believe him, but I can't make him press charges if he doesn't want to. I'll need you both to sign this form and write your full names beneath, please."

She handed the clipboard to Sean, who got to work.

Kat could see that Sean was taking this hard. He *had* assaulted Hunter, technically speaking, but he wasn't the kind of guy who got reprimanded by doctors for being an assailant. That was a different sort of person, and Kat knew that such distinctions mattered a lot to Sean.

"Thank you," Kat said to the doctor when she was finished. "We promise to take care of him."

"They will," Hunter said groggily.

"Alright." The doctor frowned. "Then you're all free to go. Mr. Briggs, don't sleep until after noon and don't use any drugs or alcohol for a week."

Everyone nodded.

The door clicked behind Dr. Boardman and then they were all alone together.

"Let's go," Hunter said.

The other two helped him up and into his jacket. They walked quietly, but quickly, out of the hospital and into the predawn cold, each shouldering one of Hunter's long arms. He was wobbly on his feet.

"I'll call a cab," Kat said when they were outside, her phone already to her ear.

What a bunch of degenerates we must look like, Kat thought, standing in the enormous empty parking lot of the MV Hospital at five o'clock in the morning. She wanted to be anywhere else.

"How's your head?" Sean asked.

"I think it's fine." Hunter picked a crusty piece of dried blood from his hairline. "I guess I'll know when the meds wear off."

Kat pocketed her phone. "Cab will be here in five."

Sean blew into his hands and rubbed them together. He was thinking about something. Kat could tell. "So what's the story with that rag?"

"What?" Hunter looked at Kat, who said nothing.

"You fainted when I pulled that thing out of the motor. What does it mean?"

Kat tried to keep her eyes on the pavement.

"I don't think it means anything," Hunter said. "I don't know. I had just been punched in the face. Remember?"

Sean nodded slowly. "Yeah, I remember." He looked over at Kat. "Is that your story too?"

She pushed her hands deep into her pockets and tried to breathe. Up to that moment, she had avoided and evaded Sean, but she hadn't really lied in a big, deceitful way. This was a crossroads.

"Kat, what's going on here?" Sean asked again.

Hunter kept picking at the dried blood in his hair.

"What the fuck is going on!"

A white Ford Focus with Island Taxi written across its side pulled gracefully up before them.

Kat looked at Hunter. He nodded almost imperceptibly.

The sun was beginning to come up and the colors of maturing bruises on Hunter's face were clearer now. He was as hideous as she'd ever seen him. Not only the purple bruising and the little black stitches, but also the defeat and shame in his bloodshot eyes. She wore it too, though she didn't realize it until she saw it on him.

The driver glared impatiently.

"We'll tell you," she said to Sean. "Let's go home. When we get to my place, we'll tell you."

They climbed into the cab and it pulled out of the parking lot. But Hunter gave the driver his address from the passenger seat.

Sean sat beside Kat, his mouth set into a firm, unhappy line within his beard.

She put a hand on his knee—a gesture of affection, a plea for trust—but he didn't budge. She didn't deserve his kindness.

It was a short car ride, but it didn't feel so. No one said a word as they snaked along the empty roads, past the closed shops. It was almost November and the sun was in no hurry to rise. The driver side window was down a few inches and the cold air stung in Kat's eyes as they sailed around each curve. The smell of a just-smoked cigarette still lingered in the upholstery of the car.

Finally, they were at Hunter's house.

Kat paid the driver and they walked in a line up to the broad front door of the Briggs beach house. It was open—not just unlocked, but actually open several inches, which explained why the entire first floor was freezing. Their breaths puffed ahead of them as they walked to the kitchen and Hunter turned up the heat.

"I guess we forgot the door," he observed. "We were just going to be down at the water for a minute. I don't know how we forgot."

It sounded nuts in the light of dawn. What was wrong with them? Kat wondered.

Sean sat down at the table with his coat still on. "Tell me what's going on."

Kat adjusted the thermostat and peeked in all the rooms. There was no reason to believe anyone was there, but it still made her nervous, all those cavernous spaces for anyone to lurk in. She came back to the kitchen and looked at Hunter, just to be sure they were doing this.

He nodded. There was no putting it off any longer.

"That night we were drinking at The Undertow," she started. "After you went home…something happened."

"An *accident*," Hunter added. They were standing side by side in front of Sean.

"Right, an accident. Anyhow, we went out in the boat, and everything seemed okay, but then it started raining and—"

Hunter shook his head. She wasn't telling this right. "Kyle was with us."

"Oh God," Sean said. He rubbed his beard with two hands.

"Kyle was with us and he was getting very aggressive with Kat. He was practically assaulting her, and she had no choice but to protect herself."

"He was sitting on the edge of the boat," she added.

"Oh God," Sean said again.

"Right," Hunter agreed, his voice growing stronger. "He was already right on the edge, and drunk as fuck, and all we really did… It was just defense…defense of Kat…because he was about to do something pretty fucking terrible, we both knew it…"

Sean put his head in his hands. "No, don't tell me this."

And then, just as Hunter was about to continue, Kat grabbed his arm to silence him. She could see it all now. She could see the whole thing again, just as it had been playing on a loop in her mind, but this time with a new detail: the scarf. Kyle's bulging, white eyes in the black night; his body jerking back violently and disappearing into the cauldron of cold water. But this time, she could see the thin, blue scarf with the tiny white flecks tighten around his neck. It had been waving behind him as he yanked her close. He didn't notice, but she could see it. It made one loop around his skinny neck—not knotted in any way, just a single loop. The long end that had been waving in the wind, fell to the water. It floated languidly on the surface until, suddenly, it was tight. The moment at which Kat thrust her right hand into Kyle's chest, the scarf became a taut line from his neck to something beneath the surface of the water behind him. The propeller. During their struggle, the scarf must have gotten caught in the propeller of the motor, and then it choked tight around his neck, causing his eyes to bulge and his breath to cease, and then yanking him back with a fierce urgency that remained unexplained in Kat's mind, until now.

"It wasn't us," she whispered.

Hunter looked at her. "What?"

"It wasn't us." Kat felt a tug inside of her as she recalled another detail: the drag of the boat. In those moments just after Kyle went over, she had the distinct feeling that the boat was being held back. It was maybe only thirty seconds, but it was long enough to notice. She thought it was all in her mind, but it wasn't. They'd had something in tow. Kyle. The boat's drag was her sickening confirmation of what really happened to Kyle.

"Kat, it was me," Hunter said.

She shook her head. "No, it was never you. I thought it was me, but it wasn't me, either. It was the scarf. It pulled him in."

Hunter could see it now too. "In the propeller."

Kat nodded. "It must have been fast. At least there's that."

"And then, he must have just…broke free. It tore off."

Neither of them said how grateful they were that the other end of the scarf wasn't still on Kyle's body when he washed ashore. But they were very, very grateful for that.

Sean stood up and his chair tipped over behind him. "Wait, Kyle Billings died on that boat? Is that what you're telling me? Someone pushed him over?"

"Yes, he went over, but we're telling you we didn't kill him!" Kat felt almost relieved.

Sean was dumbstruck. "Am I missing something? What

did you do next? Get to the part where you're not responsible for his death. Did you call for help?"

Hunter stepped closer to Kat, creating a sort of wall of solidarity with their bodies. "Sean, we made a mistake. We didn't kill him, but we did make a mistake."

Sean stared.

"We went home," Kat said quietly. "We were so scared. And, Sean, you have to understand that we thought maybe he was alive! We were so scared…and it was raining so hard… and there was nothing we could have done. We thought he could swim back."

"Did you really think that?"

Hunter looked at his feet.

"We were wrong about it," Kat said quietly. "Clearly, we were wrong. But now we know that he died instantly, which is—in a way—better than the alternatives."

Sean glared; his face was growing red. Everything they said made it worse. "This is not better. This is… I don't even know what to say."

"It's a nightmare." Kat fought back tears. "It's still a nightmare. But you have to understand that we thought we killed him, Sean. And now we know that it wasn't entirely our fault. I mean, it wasn't ever our fault, exactly… Jesus, it's so fucked up." Kat rubbed her forehead. "It was an accident, Sean."

"Actually," Hunter cut in. "I thought *I'd* killed him." He stepped away from Kat and looked at her. "And you let me believe it. I offered you the money."

Kat shook her head. "No, no, no. I was never going to take that money. I didn't know what happened! You said you did it and so I believed you!" She could have cried in that moment, but it would have been a manipulation. This wasn't her tragedy. Even in her panic, Kat knew this wasn't her tragedy and she deserved no one's sympathy. So she didn't cry. "I didn't know who did it, Hunter."

"What money?" Sean looked back and forth at them. "Kat, what money?"

"Hunter wanted to bribe me for my silence."

"Don't use that word. And it was my father, not me."

Sean began pacing. It was hot in the house now and his face was beet red. "Let me get this straight. You two watched Kyle Billings fall into the ocean. You drove the boat back to the dock, called no one and went to bed. And for more than two weeks, you've been watching the news and hearing all the speculation, and you've said nothing. You've been lying to me. To everyone. Do you understand what this means?"

Sean was in flames. He was out of his mind with horror and indignation. And this was almost more frightening than the memory of Kyle or the police investigation, or any of the threats they'd been worrying over. Sean was a righteous man with all their secrets, which made him the most dangerous threat of all.

Hunter stepped forward. "You aren't going to do anything crazy, right, Sean?"

Sean walked to the window and looked out at the covered lawn furniture in the dim backyard. "Ashley kept saying it, but Jesus, I never imagined it could be real."

"Sean, please, you can't say anything to anyone," Kat pleaded. "You really can't say anything to Ashley."

He clenched his hands into tight fists, then released them, over and over. "You need to go to the police."

Hunter shook his head. "No, we can't do that now. It's too late. We need to just stay the course."

"Stay the course? Jesus, can you hear yourselves?" Sean sat back down. "Kat, this isn't you. Is he making you do this? Is he paying you to do this?"

"No, Sean. This is our only option."

Kat watched a line of sweat form above Hunter's purple eye as he stared at Sean. Everything was in Sean's hands now.

"I can't know this. I don't want to. Why did you tell me?" Sean shouted at her. "Why did you have to tell me this? What am I supposed to do with this information, Kat?"

She went to him and took his hand. She could feel it trembling in her own as a fresh wave of that panic washed over her. Sean was in control of everything.

Kat took a breath. "I'm asking you to do nothing, Sean. Just go back to *not* knowing this. That's all I'm asking for."

"I don't think I can do that. It's so wrong."

"I know. We know that it's wrong. But Kyle is already gone and his family has already mourned. Nothing we do today will change that. What it will change is our lives. There will be trials and media attention, probably prison for one or both of us. Your mother will be dragged into this, and the glass shop will suffer. Weeta will know, and all her friends at school. It will ruin all of us."

The full weight of it all was setting in. Kat could see that she was making headway with Sean, but she was also coming to terms with just how comprehensively she'd damaged their lives.

Sean looked like he was in pain. He was resigning himself to do nothing rash at that moment, just as she had resigned herself to Hunter's appeal, but it pained him.

"I don't think it's wrong," Hunter said.

Sean looked up at him. "What?"

"I don't think it's wrong. We're past 'right' and 'wrong.' This is so much more complicated than that. It's illegal, but it's the better path for everyone, which makes it right."

Sean didn't care for this sort of relativism. He stepped away from Kat and looked hard at her, like she was something new and grotesque.

She looked away and forced herself to endure his judgment because she deserved it.

"I have to go." Sean walked out of the room. "I need to think. Don't call me."

"Sean, I think we should talk about what happens next," Kat begged.

"No, I have to go."

They listened to his boots stomp down the foyer. The door slammed.

Kat couldn't hold it in any longer. She sank into a chair and let her head fall to her forearms. Tears were pouring from her eyes to the sleeve of yesterday's dirty shirt. She was crying with fear and also relief. Kat hadn't killed Kyle and neither had Hunter. With the discovery of that scarf, she was exonerated, not for everything, but for the very big thing. And as she let the truth of that night sink in, a primal wave of anxiety rumbled through her body and left her. Everything was still all messed up, but it wasn't as bad as it had been just a few hours before, when she still believed she'd killed Kyle, however accidental.

Hunter sat down beside her and sighed. He might have been crying as well, but she didn't look up to see.

"He's going to tell someone," she said into her arm.

"No, he's not."

"We shouldn't have told him."

"We had to, Kat. And I don't think he's going to tell anyone. Not today, at least."

She wanted so badly to agree with him, but she couldn't imagine a scenario in which Sean went on living his life with a secret as ugly as this one. He considered himself too good for that. But also, he was weak. He wasn't strong like Kat and Hunter, people who were more comfortable living with ambiguity. It didn't make them bad people. It made them resilient and adaptive. They didn't create this world, but they could live with its imperfections. Sean could not.

"So you knew I didn't push Kyle over?"

Kat looked up. She could see the hurt on Hunter's maimed face. "I didn't know anything."

"But you let me believe it."

And with that, the shame was back. She'd only had a few moments without it. "I didn't know," she whispered. "It was so confusing."

They sat in silence with one another.

Hunter's breathing was hoarse. Everything about his physical being was suddenly pathetic. Kat used to think he looked like a beachy Ken doll, the salt-kissed waves of hair and tanned, flawless skin. She thought of a night several months before, when they were all swimming out by the lighthouse in their underwear. They'd had a few beers and she caught herself looking too long at Hunter as they stood dripping on the beach under the moonlight. The battered, hunched person beside her was nothing like that man on the beach.

"You need to go," he said.

She put a hand on his hand. "No, the doctor said you shouldn't be alone."

"Kat, go." He wasn't asking.

She stood up and looked around. There was nothing left to say. Sean had stormed away from her and Hunter had kicked her out. She knew so few people on this earth and she loved even fewer. It wasn't something she normally acknowledged, but at that moment she felt the unavoidable truth of her shrinking universe. She barely existed at all without these men.

Kat walked out alone into the cold island morning.

CHAPTER 10

Hunter had only been waiting for ten minutes at The Lobster Claw, but had already ordered his third ginger ale. His father made everyone wait. It wasn't a conscious habit. It was simply that he was almost always the most powerful person in any room and had become accustomed to the fact that nothing began without him. Time moved with Senator Briggs. Hunter had endured dozens of parent-teacher conferences and adolescent birthdays that began with excruciatingly long periods of waiting for his father to arrive, all of which ended with his father charming the hell out of everyone and earning back their adoration. He'd been a politician even before becoming a US senator, before he was a state representative, a city councilman. He had always been this way and, although Hunter should have been impervious to his bullshit by now, he was not.

A glass of wine would make the waiting better, but that was not an option. Hunter needed to project an air of serene control under these alarming conditions. His father respected control. Plus, he wasn't really supposed to be drinking at all. His father hadn't spent a hundred thousand dollars on a luxury recovery facility just to watch him pound wine at The Lobster Claw months later. Or maybe he had. It was an unspoken understanding that these stints in rehab were merely expensive detentions out of the public eye. So maybe a buttery Chardonnay wouldn't hurt things at all. Two would really soothe the nerves. But no, Hunter reminded himself, no Chardonnay. Serene control.

Erika appeared with his next ginger ale and gave Hunter's shoulder a little squeeze. He hadn't seen her since that night he went home with Ashley, three weeks before. He wasn't going out much anymore. But Erika didn't need an explanation from Hunter about that night, his subsequent absence or the bruise on his cheek. She was good like that. Hunter considered that maybe Erika was the most *good* of all of them, better than self-righteous Sean. People who believe themselves to be good rarely are, he decided.

Hunter picked up a polished spoon and examined his yellowing eye bruises in the warped reflection. It was better than it had been when he left the hospital two weeks before, but not good by any means. Father would ask about it. Thank God the stitches were mostly dissolved. No way to project serene control with those in.

"There he is!" Senator Briggs boomed through the mostly empty dining room as he approached. This was a standard greeting—loud and gregarious—in full sight of his constituents.

Hunter stood and greeted his father with a quick hug and back slap. He smelled like pine trees, because the second wife favored a woodsy cologne. He used to smell soapy, but now he smelled piney, a change that Hunter imagined had been focus-grouped in advance.

"Are we having oysters?"

Sean forced a smile. *Sure, let's have oysters.* He looked

around for Erika, but she was already approaching with a dozen bivalves on ice.

"Thank you, dear."

Hunter cringed at all the *dears* and *honeys*. "Thanks, Erika."

She squeezed his shoulder again, and he remembered that he'd briefly flirted with the idea of trying to sleep with her. That had been a dumb idea.

"So what's on your mind, son?" Senator Briggs went to work dressing an oyster with horseradish, vinegar and one drop of hot sauce. He had the demeanor of a man on vacation, though they both knew this trip was a monumental fucking inconvenience. Hunter appreciated the effort, even if it was motivated by self-preservation.

"Dad, I wanted to talk to you about…the state of things."

Erika appeared with a glass of white wine for the senator. It was pale and cold, with little impressions of her fingers in the condensation. Maybe a Riesling. Father loved Rieslings with oysters, which the waitstaff at The Lobster Claw apparently knew.

Erika walked away and Hunter resumed. "Nothing has really changed, not legally or anything, but the circle is a bit wider now."

"Someone else knows?" The senator whispered, dropping the jovial vacation act.

"Yeah, it's Sean."

"Remind me of this character." This was how Hunter's father always referred to unsavory people in Hunter's life, as *characters*.

"He's my friend. And Kat's boyfriend—or ex-boyfriend—I'm not really sure."

"Is he the one who punched you?"

Hunter put a hand up to his cheek. "Yeah, but not about that."

"Ah, swell. Sounds like a great friend. Why did he punch you?"

Hunter looked around the room. No one was watching them, but he now lived with the constant feeling that someone was.

"Was it about the girl? Kat?"

"Yeah, kind of." Hunter tried to focus. "Anyhow, so Sean knows now. We had no choice but to tell him. We probably couldn't have kept it from him. It's not good that he knows, but it couldn't be avoided."

The senator chewed and thought. Hunter watched his silver hairline rise and fall with his jaws. He seemed to have more hair than ever.

"What does Sean want?" Senator Briggs asked.

"I don't think he wants anything. He hasn't said—"

"No, I mean, what are his motivations? Does he want to be rich? Does he want the girl? Why does he get up in the morning?"

Hunter removed the straw from his soda and looked into the melting ice. "He doesn't care about money. He wants Kat. I mean, he's angry with her, but I think all he wants is to be an upstanding guy and to marry Kat." It felt strange to say it aloud, but it was true. That was all Sean ever wanted.

"And he punched you over her, right?"

"Right."

"Okay, good. Then he wants what she wants. He's not going to turn her in. As long as the girl keeps a clear head, then he will too." The senator began inspecting the menu as if all the problems had been solved.

"Right, but I am a little worried about Kat now too."

His father looked up over the menu.

"She was fine for a while, but she doesn't seem so clear-headed anymore. She never leaves her house. She's avoiding her best friend. She's been working at the glass shop, but basically not doing anything else or seeing anyone. I think she's been obsessing over…the guy." Hunter didn't dare say Kyle's name in public anymore.

The senator placed the menu back down. "Well, what about the money?"

"She won't take it."

"She has to take it. It's the only way to guarantee her discretion. Forever."

Hunter took another sip.

"Now, son, I don't care if you think it's distasteful. This is our goddamn life we're talking about. The alternative is more distasteful. The very least these characters can do now is take the money and move on."

It was some twisted fucking logic, but it seemed to make perfect sense to the senator.

"Should we offer Sean money too? They'd have to split it, of course. We don't have a bottomless pool of cash for this sort of thing. Should we do that?"

"No," Hunter said. "I think that might provoke him to do something really crazy. He really doesn't care about money."

The senator studied the wine list. "Sure, sure, no one cares about the money until they let themselves care about it."

"He doesn't want the money, Dad." Hunter shifted in his chair and scanned the room again. It felt like his father was enjoying this demonstration of power.

"Okay, okay. Just get your friend Kat to take it. She sounds like a smart girl."

"I just don't know how to convince her. I've tried."

Erika approached and the senator waved her away.

"I don't think she'll take it," Hunter said again.

"Well, what does *she* want? Does she want what Sean wants?"

Hunter really and truly didn't know the answer to this. Kat loved Sean, but he had always suspected that they didn't want exactly the same things. Her motivations were more complicated. "She doesn't want to go to prison," he whispered.

"That's not the same thing."

Hunter looked around the room. "She wants to work, I think. She wants to keep blowing glass. I think she really likes her life as it is, actually. Or the way it was."

"Good, okay." The senator picked his menu back up and began reading. "Then the money needs to be about that. Make it about that."

Hunter hated this feeling, having his father swoop in to solve all his problems and give him assignments. If he had any other options, he would stand up and shake his father's hand, and announce that he'd be handling everything on his own from here on out. But he didn't have any options. And there was no room for error this time.

"I'm going with the filet," the senator announced. "Where's that waitress? I need to get the two thirty back to Woods Hole."

And then he remembered the other thing. "Dad, there *is* some good news."

"Glad to hear it. Tell me."

"It wasn't me," Hunter whispered. "It wasn't either of us, actually. The guy's scarf got caught in the propeller and it pulled him in."

His father stared blankly at him.

"So, it wasn't me who…pushed him."

Hunter watched as the senator considered this information. It could have saved all of them, if they'd only called the police immediately. But this was no longer about how Kyle Billings really died or who was to blame. No one would believe them now. Now it was about two obviously guilty people evading the authorities because whatever they actually did must have been truly awful.

"Well that *is* good news. I'm glad to hear it, son."

Hunter picked up his menu. What he was hoping to hear, he didn't know. But it wasn't that.

"Is the boat in working order now?"

That wasn't what he wanted to hear, either.

"Uh, yeah. I think so."

"Double-check the motor, if you would. I'd hate to have it serviced right now, given the situation. We need to sell it eventually."

"Yeah, sure."

Erika came back and they ordered the filet and the lobster roll. The senator inquired about one of her tattoos and complimented her earrings. She smiled the way she smiled for all the flirtatious older patrons, and Hunter was impressed by her unwillingness to be fully charmed. She was a stellar judge of character.

And then Hunter was alone again with his father, who was mildly pleased to learn that his son was not in fact a murderer. But only mildly. Because the senator didn't really care whether or not his son was a murderer—that's what Hunter realized. He only cared whether people *thought* he was a murderer. To this man, being a murderer was precisely the same thing as having people believe that you were one. The social and political costs were the same, and so it was the same. This was the pull of his father's moral compass. The senator had lived for so long in the political spotlight that he'd lost the ability to see truth through anything other than the lens of public scrutiny. There was no good and bad to him; only the perception of good and bad.

For Hunter, there was something freeing in this grim realization. It meant that he could let go of some of the shame he'd been walking around with on behalf of his family. He'd always assumed that the burden his fuckups placed on his father were predominantly emotional burdens—the weight of watching your child fail—when in fact they were only financial and reputational. In other words, they were fixable. It wasn't personal. When Hunter got arrested for public drunkenness, or got that waitress pregnant, or left that joint in his pocket during airport screening, he was creating new logistical problems for his father's people to solve, most of which went away with the proper fee. The inhumanity of it freed Hunter from a bit of all that sorriness he'd been feeling.

When their plates were nearly empty, Erika appeared and whisked them away.

"Son, it was good to see you," the senator said as he scanned the other diners. "I think you've got some work to do, but nothing impossible."

"Yeah, I'll talk to Kat."

"Good, good."

"So, ah, how's the campaign going?"

His father stood up and took his overcoat off a hook. "Oh, it's a pain in the ass. One high-priced fund-raising dinner after the next. But it's a necessary evil."

Senator Briggs loved to complain about campaigning, though he obviously enjoyed the game of it all, the win in particular.

"Polls look good?"

"Yes, as long as we don't have a terrorist attack or a market meltdown, incumbent democrats should all be okay this cycle."

"Well, good luck."

He looked at his watch. "Son, I gotta run. Good to catch up. I trust you'll take care of things."

"I will."

His father nodded once and went for the door, stopping along the way to shake every hand at a table of tourists who seemed to recognize him. And then he was gone.

Hunter went to the bar and had three shots of tequila. Erika raised her eyebrows but said nothing at all. It was one thirty in the afternoon.

"You wanna talk?" she asked.

"Not really. Thanks, though." He left a twenty on the bar and bid farewell to her.

Hunter went out into the bright, cold day and began walking toward the glass shop. The tequila was doing its job of softening all the things that had been hard inside of him, but it wasn't enough.

He walked down Addison's historic main drag, past the big white church, and the medium white library, and the tiny white post office. Every little house around had been painted to match these iconic structures and someone's idea of authenticity. Everything in Addison was an antique, and the things that were not were designed to look as if they were. Addison was a facsimile of the past, real and fake.

There was no one else in sight. Being alone on the streets of downtown Addison, surrounded by relics of history, made it feel like he was walking through a cemetery. It was a preserved archaeological fossil, dense with the ghosts of a previous era. In the quiet of November, Hunter could feel the ghosts moving about, tolerating his presence on their island.

He turned onto Main Street and followed the cobblestone path northward, with the dark, sparkling ocean to his right.

As he approached Island Glass, Hunter could see Kat inside talking to a customer. He went in and lurked by the back wall as she rang someone up for four champagne flutes.

Kat saw him, but kept working. She wrapped each of the glasses in tissue paper with great care. Hunter thought she looked better than the last time he'd seen her, two weeks ago. She wore a sweater he'd never seen before, and her hair was swept up, exposing her long neck. But her face looked thinner, and her eyes more hollow. She wasn't quite right.

"Hi," Kat said finally as the last customer left.

"Hey. How have things been going?" Hunter wasn't sure what to ask. The last time they were together, he was angry because she'd let him believe that he pushed Kyle. He was still angry, but he was also worried about her. He missed her.

"Fine," she said. "You?"

"Shitty, actually. As you know."

She looked around nervously.

"Kat, are you okay? Seems like you're having a hard time."

"I'm okay. I really am. I've been working in the garage a lot lately. I'm working on some very cool new stuff."

He didn't believe her. "Good. And everything else is okay? Have you talked to Sean?"

"He won't take my calls. I don't know what he's going to do."

Hunter leaned in. "We need to talk to him."

"I know."

The front door jingled and a well-appointed woman in her midfifties walked through the door. She smiled and began moving fluidly among the glass displays.

Hunter walked away as Kat went to greet the customer. He pretended to examine a large blue orb hanging from the ceiling. Garden balls, they called them, though he'd never seen anything like it in a garden. He didn't want to leave until he got a better read on Kat's mental state and the situation with Sean. The phrase *loose ends* kept popping into his head, which made him feel like the depraved fixer in a bad Hollywood thriller, but that was also precisely what Kat and Sean were now, loose ends. Maybe Ashley too. Jesus, Ashley. He'd nearly forgotten about her. What was he going to do about Ashley?

Kat was chatting with the woman in the corner. She nodded along as the lady requested something, and then she excused herself to check the stock in the garage. The woman promptly pulled out her phone and began punching away on the keypad.

With Kat gone and the customer preoccupied, Hunter went to the counter, bound for her overstuffed tote bag that always sat behind the register. He knelt quickly beside it and began rifling through its contents. There was nothing interesting there: a balled-up flannel shirt, an old notepad and a bunch of pens floating around the sandy bottom. He didn't know what he was looking for—maybe a prescription drug, something to help him understand her mental state.

And then he saw it. A dog-eared piece of printer paper had been folded into the pages of some book about Florida. He pulled it out to find a grainy picture of Kyle Billings's face. Hunter's stomach dropped. He stared at the picture of Kyle until he heard the door to the studio close and Kat's footsteps along the wood floor. He slid the tote bag back to where it had been, but pushed the picture of Kyle into the back pocket of his jeans.

"Found it," Kat announced to the woman as she returned to the room with a small box.

Hunter pretended to scroll through his phone while Kat rang the customer up.

When the woman finally left, he walked to the door and locked it.

"Why'd you do that?"

Hunter took Kat's shoulders in his hands and looked directly into her eyes. "What's going on with you?"

"What?"

Her shoulders felt bonier than they should.

"What's with your sudden interest in North Florida? What's with this?" Hunter pulled out the photo.

Kat looked at her feet. "I just wanted to know who he was."

Hunter shook his head. "No, you can't do this. I knew you were obsessing. I could see it. Kat, this isn't like you. You're supposed to be the sane one. What is this about?"

She looked around nervously. "I don't know. I can't stop thinking about him. I can't close my eyes without seeing him. Do I look tired? It's because I can't fucking sleep! I really need to sleep, Hunter, but I can't. I just feel like maybe if I can fill in some holes about who he was, maybe understand his life a little better, maybe I'll get some peace or closure or something. I really need to sleep."

"I'll get you some sleeping pills."

She shook her head. "It's not just that. It's like I can *feel* him around me."

A man came to the door and tried to open it. He looked in at them, then gave up and walked away.

Hunter resumed. "You can't *feel* him, Kat. He's not here. And you never knew him, so you can't miss him."

Kat straightened her stance. "I know that. I'm not losing my mind or anything. I'm just tired. You don't have to worry about me."

Hunter ran a hand through his hair. "No more pictures, Kat. This isn't safe for you to be walking around with. You get that, right?"

She nodded.

Hunter tore the picture into several pieces and stuffed the shreds back in his pocket. Kat winced.

"You need to hold it together. And we need to talk about the money again."

She shook her head violently. "No, I'm not taking it."

"Listen to me. This shop and your glassblowing garage won't be here forever. The money is your only chance to have a future. Orla and Sean too. This money doesn't mean anything to my family. It's nothing. It's just a contract, a cementing of an agreement. It's that transactional for my father, so why not just consider it the same way he does? This is an opportunity for you."

She was looking at him now, listening, maybe considering it.

Hunter wasn't done. "You think it's not right or fair to take money for something like this, Kat. But it's not fair that I have all this, and you have nothing. I didn't earn this, and neither did my father. Fairness is bullshit. There is no fairness. Take what you can. And I am telling you, from the bottom of my heart, that this comes with no stipulation other than our shared silence for the rest of our lives. It's just a contract."

She was definitely listening now.

"Just think about it."

He was proud of this speech. Her body language suggested that he was making progress with her. It was working on him too. Hunter didn't feel quite so disgusting about this proposal after the whole fairness-is-bullshit pitch. It was also true. And, although it didn't make his father any less of a sociopath for trying to control the entire world around him, it was truly a victimless crime.

"What's the number again?" Kat asked.

"One point three million."

"That's a weird number. Why that?"

"I don't know." He really didn't know. He imagined it was chosen for purposes of evading the IRS or laundering campaign funds or some other white-collar mischief that he wouldn't put past his father.

"I didn't say I was taking it."

"I know. Just think about it. That's all."

Kat didn't say a word, but she wasn't as closed to him as she had been ten minutes before. She was open now, and standing straighter. Maybe she could pull it together, after all.

As if reading his mind, Kat said, "I know I have to talk to Sean."

Hunter nodded. "You do. And he'll forgive you. He wants to be with you."

"I don't know if he does anymore."

She looked more wistful than sad about this point, and Hunter felt the most contradictory mix of emotions as they stood there. The safety of their secret seemed to hinge on the coupledom of Kat and Sean. If Sean had Kat, he wouldn't tell. But Hunter was not rooting for their coupledom. He rather hated the idea.

"He'll take you back, Kat."

She looked up at him, but she did not smile. "Let's hope."

CHAPTER 11

"Your wizard is dead."

"What!" Sean scanned the medieval village and the color-ful figurines scattered across the board. This was the fourth time they'd played this game, and he still had trouble with the rules.

Weeta laughed and pointed to the tiny people. "Your no-blemen could have saved him, but they're locked up with the vicar."

"I think you're making these rules up."

She smiled and sat back in her chair. "Dad, I'm hungry. Can we order the pizza now?"

"Yeah, we'd better. Your grandmother should be here soon." Sean walked to the window.

First snow of the season. It was only November, but the snow was three inches deep with no sign of abating. Sean couldn't remember the last time he'd seen snow before Thanksgiving.

"Dad, you think they'll cancel school tomorrow?"

"I don't know. Maybe." He hoped. A snow day would mean one more precious day with her.

Sean filled a kettle with tap water and put it on the stove top. He wasn't eager to get back to their board game, but he'd do practically anything Weeta asked of him in exchange for her company. As long as they were engaged and moving their hands, Weeta would talk to him. She talked about school and friends, terrible teachers, and her plans to make the soccer team. He wasn't deluding himself in believing that they had a special kind of connection, a product of his unbridled affection and the freedom that comes with not being the primary caretaker. Sean tried to adhere to Beth's rules on those visits—bedtime at nine and limited video games—but he didn't try terribly hard. He felt that the only consolation for living without her was the privilege of celebrating her presence without judgment when they were together. And so it was lucky for all of them that Weeta was smart and focused enough not to take advantage of him.

"Daddy, where's Kat?"

Sean poured hot water over powdered cocoa. "I think she's working tonight."

"Are you in a fight?"

He never discussed such things with his daughter, but he knew this was inevitable. Weeta hadn't seen Kat in weeks. "I don't really know. Maybe."

She began clearing the game pieces slowly.

"You don't want to play anymore?"

"Not really," she said.

"I'm sure I'll work things out with Kat, though. This isn't like your mom and me." It might be like that, Sean thought. He wasn't sure.

Weeta carefully placed each figurine into the box. Their little swords and pointy shoes all fit neatly just where they should. It was a perfectly orderly life those medieval characters had. "Yeah, I know," she said.

Through the snowy curtain outside his kitchen window, Sean saw his mother approach. Thank goodness. He didn't know how to talk about Kat with his daughter. "Nana's here!"

Weeta jumped up and went to the door.

"My love!" Orla exclaimed, her snowy arms extended in the doorway.

They hugged and Sean took his mother's coat so she could get right to the business of catching up with her only grandchild. Weeta had already launched into a story about her basketball team and which friends were playing which positions. Orla wanted all of it.

Moments later, the pizza guy arrived and Sean greeted him at the door.

Orla and Weeta didn't look up from their conversation on the couch.

It was an almost perfect moment for Sean—his daughter happy, his mother healthy and all of them together on their snowy island. But he ached for Kat. He ached for her and he hated her. She had become a fixture in their family life, not only as his partner, but also as Orla's protégé. It was a strange arrangement, really. Not the sexiest of scenarios, for his girlfriend to be tangled up with several limbs of his family tree. But Sean didn't need sexy. He needed sex—which they had at a perfectly acceptable rate—but he didn't need intrigue. He just wanted this good life and these good people—and for Kat to threaten it all was just such an unfathomable act of deceit.

Sean didn't want to think about Kat, not tonight. Things were almost great, and he'd done such a good job of putting it all out of his mind for the past few weeks. He couldn't lose himself to that anger on this night, not with Weeta there.

"I'm just going to set the table, honey." Orla went to the kitchen and began opening cupboard doors.

"Dishwasher's clean," Sean said.

She turned to her son. "Have you talked to Kat? Something's not right there."

He froze. Orla wasn't supposed to know anything about Kyle. Is that what this meant—that she knew something? "We haven't talked in a few days. We're still working through things."

Orla nodded. "I understand. But I think you might want to check on her. She's not taking this well. She's distracted and listless. She looks like hell. Whatever's going on with you guys must be harder on her than you think."

Sean looked down at the pizza box. It was hot in his hands. He would have loved to believe it was their separation that was making Kat listless. To have that effect on her would be satisfying. But that wasn't what was wrong with her. "Okay, I'll call her tomorrow."

"I know that's not the only thing," Orla went on, her voice low.

"What do you mean?"

"I know she's concerned about the glass shop too, after the cliff fell."

"She's concerned about you, Mom." Sean was relieved to go down this different, depressing path.

"Yes, and me. But it's a poor use of her energy. The fact remains that none of us is in any immediate danger. And the house might be fine for a very long time. We just can't know, so there's no use fretting over it."

Sean couldn't tell if his mother believed this. "Mom, Ashley said that anything could happen. She's not as sanguine as you about the cliff."

"Well, anything can *always* happen." Orla took the pizza

box from his hands and went to the table. "Dinner's ready, honey."

"I don't know, Mom."

"And anyhow," Orla went on, making no attempt to hush her voice, "that girl has a thing for you, so..."

Sean took a seat across from his daughter. "Ashley? Maybe, I don't know. What does it matter?"

"I'm saying that maybe she has other motives in all this."

"Who has a crush on you?" Weeta asked with a mouth full of pizza.

"No one. Your grandmother's just teasing me."

Sean thought about that day in Katama Bay, the day Ashley had convinced him to go with her. She was looking for some kind of clue to Kyle's death there. She had taken pictures of places where the sand pooled and went back out again. At the time, Sean thought it made her nutty and intense. After what Kat and Hunter had confessed, it made her dangerous to all of them. Sean didn't know what to do with the truth of Kyle's death, but he knew he didn't want Ashley to have it. And yet, he still liked the idea that she might want to sleep with him. He hadn't been pursued in a long time, and it helped with the blow of whatever it was Kat was doing to him.

"Who has a crush on you, Daddy?"

"Your dad's right," Orla said. "I was just teasing him. Don't worry about it, honey. Tell me about school. Who's your science partner these days?"

Weeta explained that her lab partner was Ezra, and he was terrible at taking notes. Sean watched her as she gesticulated, licking greasy pizza fingers midsentence.

Weeta didn't need this. She didn't need change or unreliability in her parents. Sean lived with a low, incurable fever of guilt about the scenario in which they'd brought her into the world. He and Beth were not a great couple and they should have known that before allowing for the possibility of Weeta. And yet, they made thoughtful, co-operative coparents. They were doing this pretty well. But they were also both committed to limiting the variability in their daughter's life as a corrective measure for their earlier mistakes. Kat was a variability now.

After dinner, they played one more round of the wizard game, and then Weeta got ready for bed. She kissed them both and curled up with *Harry Potter and the Order of the Phoenix*. Five minutes later, Sean could hear her snoring into the pages of her open book.

Sean snuck into Weeta's bedroom to turn off the pink conch shell reading light. He pulled the book gently from beneath her smooth cheek and brushed a lock of hair away from her parted lips. She was splendid, more so each time he saw her. Sean had feared the onset of these teenage girl years for so long that he was constantly amazed by just how much he was actually enjoying her growth. He wasn't losing her, not yet at least, and maybe that meant he'd misunderstood what these years were all about. Maybe he could be the thing she runs *to* instead of from as she gets older.

It had always been hard for Sean to imagine the next stage with Weeta. When she was a baby, he couldn't picture her as a toddler. And in kindergarten, he never imagined she'd become an adolescent. Did all parents feel this way about their firsts or was this evidence of a more fundamental deficiency in him? He didn't know. Sean wasn't prone to self-doubt in other areas—just parenting, and only occasionally. The prospect of Kat one day being a wife and parent to Weeta had always reassured him. It allayed his self-doubt. But now, with their future in question, Sean suddenly felt his parenting in question too. Kat was supposed to be a steadying third leg in this parenting tripod.

Sean closed the bedroom door quietly and stood alone in the dark hall of his little house. He heard a cork pop from a bottle of wine, and his mother pull glasses from a shelf. He didn't have the energy to go out there and make small talk. He couldn't bear the weight of this secret, which made him feel like a liar even when he was alone. No one was asking Sean about Kyle, but he was still lying. Is this how it would always feel if he kept quiet for Kat? It wouldn't only be with his family, either. Sean might feel like a liar with his friends and coworkers. He'd feel like a liar with new people, friends he hadn't yet met in this life. It would change him—turn him from an open person to a closed one. And who would he be, then?

Weeta murmured something in her sleep, and Sean heard her flipping around in her sheets before settling again.

He couldn't parent like this. Sean couldn't keep this secret from his daughter and keep Kat in their lives. It wasn't right. And the wrongness of it would be a cancer that ate him up. As Sean saw it, there were three paths before him: turn Kat in and be done with her; keep this secret and be done with her; or keep the secret and stay together. The last option seemed indefensible, but it was the one he wanted the most. He didn't want to live without Kat. But there was Weeta. He had to do the right thing for her. He had to model right behavior. Secrets like this weren't right.

Imagining Weeta's life without Kat, though, made him ill. Sean always thought that, when Kat seemed ready, he would propose. He expected that one day they would be a real blended family, officially.

Sean's mind bounced back and forth among all the terrible choices before him. He didn't want to take Kat from Weeta.

But Kat didn't deserve his daughter. And on that night, as he stood alone in the dark hallway, Sean was, for the first time, grateful that they weren't an official family. He could still walk away from Kat.

CHAPTER 12

Three cars whizzed by and Ashley nearly fell into the snowy ditch along the side of the road. Assholes, she thought. Assholes in luxury SUVs are the worst variety of asshole. Ashley was in a pissy mood, the kind that could only be mitigated by running until her legs hurt so bad she could hardly stand. The subfreezing temperatures were just a bonus on the torture scale. It hurt today. She hadn't run in really cold air yet this season and her lungs were now making a sort of whistling sound. She welcomed it.

A rusty gray sedan crept by slowly, proving Ashley's theory about who was and was not an asshole. As it drove off, the car's color blended with the color of the November dusk. She'd never get back to her apartment while it was still light out, which wasn't ideal. She didn't want to die. She just wanted to sweat until she wasn't thinking quite so obsessively about Kyle and Sean and the explosive, secretive little group she'd stumbled upon in her otherwise boring time on Martha's Vineyard. She wanted to clear her head a little and maybe get some perspective. Ashley always knew what she wanted.

An oncoming car flashed its lights and passed slowly, which she understood to be a scolding for being a lady running in the diminishing light. *Fuck off, this is what ambition looks like*, she thought. She didn't get to the top 10 percent in her class, or the most prolific researcher in her unit, or the hardest-working teaching assistant by not being intense. And intensity demanded some risk. No risk, no reward. That was a thing she only said to herself because she knew it probably sounded a little aggressive for a marine geologist, but she was sure it could be applied to nearly every goal in life.

Ashley liked to tick through her ambitions, the still unfulfilled plans for herself, as she ran through the pain on her runs. It made the burning feel more purposeful, like those ESPN montages of athletes in training. But on this day, as the darkness started to close in and she focused on the dicey footing at the edge of the road, she couldn't quite articulate her immediate ambitions. She still hoped to impose a little pain on Hunter—just enough to scratch that revenge itch for ditching her after they slept together. In the longer term, she wanted Sean, who was a better romantic prospect. The truth was that she couldn't be sure whether the second goal was related to the first. If it was, then she would need to recalibrate her ambition. Revenge and lust sometimes blurred for Ashley when emotions were running hot.

There was also the Kyle mystery, which she wouldn't normally care about, except she knew beyond a shadow of a doubt the cops were wrong. And she felt sure there was a connection between her new friends and Kyle. They were keeping something from her. It was all the secrecy that made her crazy.

This was good, Ashley thought. She was working through the questions in her mind, one by one, making great progress.

Ashley huffed and whistled through her condensing

breath. She watched her feet land out in front of her and thought of that old movie, *Rocky*. She'd never actually seen it, but understood its cultural symbolism. She ran, and she problem solved, and she watched the movie of herself in her head—and then she figured it out. Her obsession with Kyle and this group was mostly about the secrets. She had a keen sense for secrets, as someone who'd spent most of her childhood locked out of every social clique. That's the price of being super intense: it's not cool. She could always tell when the secrets were about her, which was horrible; and she could tell when they had nothing at all to do with her, which was less humiliating, but terribly lonely. Ashley didn't know what the secrets in this strange friend circle were all about, but she was sure they were there. And she really hated secrets.

The sweat accumulating under her hat was starting to chill her forehead, and her wheezing lungs were about to give way. Ashley decided to sprint for the final stretch. There was always a little more fuel in the tank. That was what she liked to tell herself. She decided to focus on Sean for the last leg because she was sure that he would be impressed by her dedication. Sean was a guy who valued commitment. Not like Hunter, who'd been primarily attracted to her good looks, the jerk.

No, Ashley didn't want to go down that path. She was just beginning to gain clarity, and she wasn't going to lose it in another bout of anger over Hunter. Her very first priority for now—in addition to the completion of her PhD and becoming the youngest morphodynamics scientist at Woods Hole—was to track down the secrets. If she hurt Hunter along the way, that was just a bonus. If she seduced Sean along the way, even better. It was important to prioritize one's goals.

Ashley didn't stop running until she got to the edge of her

porch. Then she dragged her aching body into the first-floor apartment and closed the door. She lay there on the hardwood floor for two full minutes, listening to her breath and staring at the ceiling. This was always the best part of the run, when her mind was clear and her goals razor sharp. But it didn't last. As soon as her breath slowed and her muscles relaxed again, her racing thoughts would be back.

Ashley showered and dressed, made an omelet and a smoothie. And then she called Sean.

"Hey," she said tentatively.

"Hey!" He sounded surprisingly excited to hear from her.

"I was wondering if you wanted to get a drink?"

"Sure, where?"

Ashley hadn't even considered an answer to this question. She expected that he would hem and haw, pretend to be doing something else, and then finally agree to one drink. He just seemed so conflicted about her presence all the time that she had come to expect a little work from these conversations.

"It's a Monday," Sean thought aloud, "which means we don't have a lot of options. Do you want to come here?"

"Sure, that'd be great. I'll pick up a bottle of wine."

"Sounds good. Maybe in like an hour?"

"Perfect. See you then."

And that was that. So easy. Maybe Sean had just decided that Ashley was a good match for him, and this would be the night they test the waters. Maybe she should wear something slightly more flirtatious than usual. She could floss again and change into a better bra.

Ashley dragged her finger along the inside of her empty smoothie glass and pulled out a sweet, foamy finger. She licked it and considered Sean. Maybe he was just a slow mover. He'd been thinking about her, weighing all her pluses and minuses, as one does, and had finally come to the right conclusion about them.

Or maybe it was something else. Kat could have done something terrible that put the final nail in the coffin of their relationship. Or maybe she'd moved on to someone new. Tonight Sean could be after revenge sex or rebound sex or self-pitying tell-me-I'm-fuckable sex. It didn't really matter to Ashley.

Sean greeted her at the door with a smile. "Hey, c'mon in." He had cozy lamb's wool slippers on his feet.

"Hi." She leaned in for a cheek kiss, and he obliged.

"Do you want some pizza? It's from last night, but I can put it in the oven."

Okay, cold pizza means no intimacy. "No, thanks. I just had something."

"Okay, cool. I hope you're not offended if I have some later."

"Not at all."

Then again, maybe cold pizza doesn't mean anything.

Sean went to the kitchen to open one of the bottles and Ashley tried to find a position on the couch that made her look unintentionally desirable.

"How are things with you?" she yelled.

He returned and handed her a glass of red wine. "I'm good. Weeta was here through the afternoon because all the city schools were canceled today for snow."

"Oh, that's nice for you." Ashley never knew what to say about his kid. It wasn't one of his pluses, that's for sure. "And everything else? How's work?"

"Slow. How's your research?"

She shrugged. "It's a slog right now. I was writing at the

library all day. I need to piece together all these findings into
a cohesive thesis."

"Can I ask you—" Sean leaned forward on his knees
"—what *is* the story? I mean, what's new about the island
that we didn't already know?"

Ashley took a graceful sip of the not-delicious wine. "The
new findings are about the speed of erosion. That's what
I'm focused on. All the same factors are still contributing to
coastal erosion—wind, rain, waves and some human activi-
ties like agricultural runoff—but it's happening much faster
now than it did fifty years ago, and the speed of change is
sort of exacerbating the problem. As your estuaries disappear
with rising sea levels, the rest of your coastline is becoming
more exposed. So, it's momentum that's new."

Sean watched closely as she spoke.

She liked his attention.

"It sounds boring, but I love it." Ashley shrugged, hoping to seem modest.

"It sounds interesting to me. How'd you originally get
into this stuff?"

She slipped her feet out of her shoes and tucked them
under her body on the couch. "I discovered a rare marine
gastropod when I was twelve."

"What?"

"Yeah, it's like a tiny snail. I discovered this breed that
they thought was extinct while I was working on a school
science project. I was on the local news after that and my
dad got really excited about the whole thing, so I guess that's
how I got excited. Momentum, again."

"Wow, geez." Sean drank the last sip and looked into his
empty glass.

Ashley couldn't read him. He was warmer with her than

before, but she felt a strange distance between them, like he was conducting a job interview.

"Can I get you something else?" he asked.

She remembered the glass in her hand and took two long sips. "No, this is great, thanks." What was going on here? Ashley couldn't tell anymore.

The phone rang at that moment and Sean excused himself to the kitchen to answer it.

"Hello...Yeah, okay." Sean looked at Ashley, then stretched the curly wire around the doorway so he was tucked back into the kitchen, as far away from her as the cord would allow. His voice lowered to a whisper. "Yes, I've seen her... What is it?"

Ashley strained to hear his side of the conversation, which sounded curt and impolite.

"How do you know?" he demanded. "That could mean anything...Fine...Fine...I don't want to be involved...Okay, fine, I'll be careful. Goodbye."

The conversation ended, but Sean didn't budge. Ashley had an image of him standing frozen in the kitchen with his finger depressing the hook on the wall-mounted phone.

"Everything okay?"

Sean hung the phone on the cradle and walked back into the living room. "Yeah, no problem. Sorry about that."

She reclined slightly into a pillow, hoping to change the mood in the room.

Sean looked around nervously. "Yeah, so I was just reminded of a thing I have to do. It's a parenting obligation. I promised Beth. I'm really sorry."

Ashley sat up. "Wait, tonight?"

"Yeah, sorry. I'm so embarrassed. I just have to go."

Ashley didn't budge. She brought her wineglass to her lips and slowly drank the rest of its contents while Sean watched.

No way was she going to let him push her out. Something was going on here and she was not getting kicked out of the secret circle now that she had one foot in.

"Can I tag along?" She wiped the perimeter of her lips with her fingers and watched Sean for a response.

"You want to come? No, no that wouldn't work. Beth and I kind of have an agreement about this stuff."

"Understood." Ashley nodded. She was going to make him squirm. "Well, then, maybe I could meet you afterward. I'm free all night."

Sean's eyes widened like she'd said something crazy, and maybe she had, but *he* was the one lying his ass off. If anyone was crazy, it was the guy with all the secrets. What was he hiding?

Sean sighed and sat down on the couch beside her. "Listen, I'm sorry about tonight. I'll make it up to you."

He put a warm hand on her calf and squeezed slightly. With that touch, Ashley felt a bolt of lightning run straight up her leg and her resolve weakened. She assumed he was trying to manipulate her, but she still liked the feeling of his hand on her leg. "I'm going to hold you to that."

"I would expect it." And then Sean stood up and waited. It was time for her to go.

Ashley stood and slid into her shoes. She was in no rush. She took one more look around the room, hoping for clues about what the hell was going on. Sean got her jacket and helped her into it. Then he put a hand on her back and gently led her toward the door. The electricity was undeniable to her, even if he was escorting her out.

"Thanks for coming over," he said, kissing her on the cheek.

"Call me." It was work to smile, but Ashley did it. She could fume in her car. Fume or fret, she wasn't sure which.

Sean closed the door as Ashley stood beneath the porch light. She could hear the lock turn on the other side, quietly, like he was trying to go unnoticed. He had locked her out.

She walked to her car on the street without any notice of her open coat in the frigid temperature. The ignition turned, the vents blasted cold air at her, and then she was driving away.

"Ahhh!" Ashley screamed, pounding on the steering wheel. Something was happening on this island that she needed to know about.

She drove fast down the empty street. And then, just as she approached the first turn, Ashley slammed on the brakes. She'd seen something in her rearview mirror.

Ashley pulled into a nearby driveway and in two quick motions, reversed course and went back in the direction from which she'd come.

Two blocks down, she saw it: Sean. He was huffing along the dark sidewalk alone in his puffy coat. He must have left mere seconds after her. At first he didn't look up, but Ashley decelerated so quickly that the car nearly stopped in the road.

He glanced, and she panicked, and then they were making eye contact through her window. Shit, she'd been spotted. But so had he.

And then Sean did a thing that made all of Ashley's theories and suspicions seem possible. He broke into a sprint and ran. Down the side road, then onto Main Street, toward Hunter's or Kat's or the part of Addison where Ashley suspected all the action—all the secrets—to be.

She considered following him with her car, but that would have been too aggressive. She wasn't stalking him, after all. She just wanted to know where he was going and what he was keeping from her. No need to alarm anyone.

Because Ashley wasn't a stalker, she sat in the idling car

for a cool count to one hundred, and then she drove slowly home by way of downtown, a circuitous route to be sure.

Sean was still running when she passed him the second time.

CHAPTER 13

Kat pulled the goggles down over her eyes and selected an iron rod from the assortment she kept against the wall. It was almost midnight, but there was no use in going to bed. She never really slept anymore, and she certainly wouldn't now, not after the brief phone call with Sean.

Kat looked at the store inventory list. They were low on paperweights and chachkas, the inexpensive souvenir items for tourists. Normally, she hated making that stuff, but lately the mindless items were the only things she managed to finish.

She twirled the rod in the pool of molten glass, around and around until it was the size of a plum. Then she pulled it out, dipped it into a bowl of aqua-colored glass shards and put the spiky little ball into the glory hole. She twirled again and watched the granular colors melt before the blazing heat. Why had Sean been so quick to get off the phone with her? Why had he been so vague in his answers? They hadn't spoken in three weeks—not since she and Hunter told him about Kyle—and she expected something different from the call: anger, or at least follow-up questions, but this was just haste. She couldn't make sense of it.

Kat didn't want to call Sean on that night. He needed time and she wanted to respect that. Kat didn't really think that Sean was just going to run to the cops and turn her in. Maybe he'd do it to Hunter after everything that had happened, but he wouldn't do it to her. Maybe. But with Ashley in the picture, everything had changed. They needed to be more cautious now. Kat had seen Ashley earlier that day and she had new cause for concern.

She'd been sitting in a dark corner of the Addison Library, examining a road map of Florida, when she heard the bathroom doors swing open, followed by a brief and troubling conversation.

"You've been at that desk all day," the librarian said to someone. "Are you a student?"

"Yes, doctoral," the woman said. "I'm a little behind with my thesis, so I've been cramming."

At first, Kat didn't recognize the voice. They were just beyond her line of vision.

"Well, you seem like a hard worker," the librarian went on.

"I was actually ahead of schedule. But I've been distracted by another research project. Something pretty explosive fell into my lap recently."

It was then that Kat recognized the voice as Ashley's. Kat leaned in toward the stacks that separated them and strained to hear the rest.

"That sounds exciting," the librarian said.

"It is. People will know about it soon."

People will know about it. That's what Ashley had told the librarian. *People will know about it.*

Kat had walked around in the cold for much of the afternoon, stewing about those words. Was Ashley talking about Kyle? Had she found some sort of smoking gun with the tidal patterns? It was possible that she was referring to something else, something related to her work. But what if she was not? If there was even a slim chance that Ashley was going to be a problem, then Kat had to do something.

So she went home, ate some toast, stared blindly at the television screen for twenty minutes and finally decided to just call Sean. She knew he was in the best position to determine if there was anything to be worried about. She just wanted him to do a little probing with Ashley. And she knew that no matter how angry Sean was with her, he would be loyal to her first, before Ashley. She hoped.

But Sean had been weird on the call. Receptive to the information, more or less, but very weird. She didn't even get a chance to tell him what she needed him to find out. It was as if he was having a different phone conversation altogether. He just acknowledged what she was telling him and hung up, no commitments made.

So now, as Kat sweated alone in her garage, she couldn't stop thinking about the big fat possibility that she'd misjudged Sean's loyalty to her.

Kat pulled the hot aqua blob from the glory hole, spinning slowly along the way. She held the rod straight up, letting the blob drip down toward her feet like a teardrop in slow motion. When it reached the desired shape, she smooshed it gently onto the cool cement floor. It looked like a chocolate kiss. She twisted the rod with her left hand and used a blowtorch with the right until the steel pulled away from the hardening kiss. One paperweight, done.

Was it possible that Sean was working with Ashley? The idea seemed unlikely, but it wasn't out of the question. Sean was angry with Kat and horrified by the choices she'd made since that terrible night. And he was always so sure of his goddamn rightness in this world. Who knew what he was capable of? This was new territory.

Kat returned the rod to its resting place and began sweeping. She was forever tracking tiny glass rocks onto the hardwood floors of the shop with the soles of her shoes. She swept ferociously, her anxiety mounting.

Sean was more rigid now than he used to be. It was a subtle change, but she remembered him as being more forgiving at the start. Or maybe that was a trick of the imagination. Kat wasn't in love with Sean because of his ability to forgive; she was in love with him because of his sureness, which actually seemed to inhibit his capacity to forgive. There was a day, probably six years ago, when they went out on a sailboat. Sean had borrowed it from someone at the boatyard. He'd been trying to impress her. They'd brought sandwiches and beers, enough provisions to stay out on the water for hours. They'd stayed out until Sean's shoulders were burned bright red and all the bottled water had been drunk. It had been Kat's first time on a sailboat and she had been nervous, but Sean's comfort and confidence were infectious. He was so unabashedly content with his life. He was content with Martha's Vineyard, and he knew exactly what he wanted from it all. She'd never met anyone like that.

Where Kat came from, people didn't sail, or stare up at the clouds, or talk about the ocean with poetic flourishes. Everyone in Kat's childhood had been working to acquire more material possessions or in the process of losing them— that was the measure of everything. And it wasn't because they had no money, though that was also true. They would have been like that as rich people too, if given the chance. Sean and Orla never had much, either, but theirs was a completely different way of being poor. Sean was grateful for everything. And he—perhaps justifiably—believed that this was the right way to live. Sean had little sympathy for those who operated by a different set of values.

So no, perhaps he hadn't ever been a forgiving man, but there were so many other reasons to be in love with someone.

A knock on the garage door startled Kat. She walked to the entrance and put her hand on the doorknob but did not turn it.

"It's me," Sean said from the other side. "I'm freezing. Can I come in?"

Kat opened the door and took him in. Pink cheeked and panting, Sean appeared to have run there. "Are you okay?"

He walked past her into the garage. "Can we go inside?"

She nodded and led him up the back stairs to her apartment.

The lights were all on and a cooking show droned from the TV. Kat liked it that way now, even in the middle of the night. Kyle's image couldn't break through all that noise quite so easily.

"Wow, it's a real command center up here," Sean joked. He was nervous.

Kat found the remote and turned off the TV. "Yeah, sorry. So what's going on? This is about my call, I assume."

He nodded and sat down at the table. "Yeah, it is. Sorry I was weird on the phone. It's just that…she was there with me."

"Oh." Kat sat across from him in the bright kitchen. She didn't know if this meant that he was allied with Ashley now or that he was sleeping with her. And if it was one, did it have to be the other too?

"She just came over for a drink. We barely talked actually. I got rid of her after you called."

Kat felt her body relax slightly. "Oh wow. Sorry. I swear I didn't know she was there with you. I just wanted to know if she'd said anything. When I saw her today at the library, it seemed like maybe she had some new information or something. It seemed like she was still pursuing this."

"I don't know if she's still pursuing it. We haven't talked about it. But I haven't said anything to her."

"Okay. Well, thanks. I'm really grateful for your...discretion."

Discretion. It was the same word Hunter had used when he offered the money to Kat. *Discretion* is the universal euphemism for *bad secrets*.

Sean furrowed his brow. "Kat, don't read too much into this. I got rid of Ashley tonight because I needed to think. I still need to think about it all. I don't know what I'm going to do."

"Okay."

"And, to be honest," he continued, "I don't know what's going on with me and Ashley. I thought she was actually interested in me, but she's also got this preoccupation with Kyle's death, which sort of confuses the whole thing. I may have misread her." Sean scratched his beard and looked out the window to the black ocean.

Kat didn't want to talk about his feelings for Ashley. "Well, thank you for not telling her anything."

Sean scratched harder. He was fidgety. "Kat, I don't know what I'm going to do with...that information. I just don't know yet. That's what I'm trying to tell you. I'm not going to tell Ashley about it, but that doesn't mean I'm necessarily going to just stay quiet forever, either. This is a really fucked-up position you've put me in."

"Oh."

"And, you know, I have to consider Weeta. I have to be able to live with myself. And if I can't defend this to her when she's older, then it's probably not defensible, you know?"

Kat studied his face. It was apologetic, but it was also pitying. He pitied her poor judgment or her moral weakness.

"Sean, you don't have to *defend* anything. You don't have to *do* anything. That's all we're asking for, for you to do nothing."

"Yes, but that's not right. Kyle's family deserves the true story. That's how society works! Bad things happen, and people take responsibility for their actions, Kat. You're not someone who runs away from this sort of thing."

She wasn't going to let him lecture her about right and wrong. Two months ago, maybe she could have endured it, but the world had gotten more complicated since then. Kat felt the temperature in her body rise.

"No, Sean, that's *not* how society works, though it's a very comforting idea. In reality, sometimes bad things happen and people get away with them…or the wrong people are punished…or the real story is never told. Kyle fell! Hunter and I didn't do it and we shouldn't have to pay the price for it."

Sean shook his head. He was all pity now, nothing apologetic about him. "I bet Hunter told you that."

"Fuck you," she whispered.

Kat didn't want to fight with Sean, self-righteous bastard that he was. She just wanted to go back in time and do a few critical things differently. She wanted to drink less that night at The Undertow. Then she wanted to go home with Sean. She wanted to tell Hunter to go to bed and watch him leave the bar alone. Mostly, she wanted to give Kyle the chance to right his actions on that night, to be only a drunk person flirting with very bad behavior, someone who'd gotten close to the edge and walked himself back. No one deserves to die for their intentions alone, do they? Kat didn't know. Kyle was a monster that night, but Kat's guilty conscience

wouldn't let her off the hook that easily. He hadn't, technically, done anything. And now he was dead.

Kat began to cry.

Sean scratched vigorously at his beard. Then he reached
across the table and put his hands on top of hers. Kat leaned
forward and cried into their intertwined fingers, her tears
falling down along his rough knuckles. He wasn't wrong and
neither was she. Everything was just so intractably fucked-up.

"Are you seeing her?" she muffled into his hands.

"What?"

Kat lifted her face. "Are you seeing her?"

"No, I'm not." Sean paused. "It seemed like a possibility,
but I don't think it is. She's very…intense."

Kat didn't know what to do with this information. She
was jealous and heartbroken, but she was also angry that he
could even consider being with someone who was intent on
bringing her down. It seemed so distinctly male to compart-
mentalize the two concerns in discrete and unrelated catego-
ries. Everything was muddied up, but he apparently thought
a relationship—or at least sex—with Ashley wouldn't spill
into the rest of their lives. Kat was more sad than mad. She
just wanted to go back in time.

"I'm really sorry that you're in this position," Sean said.

"I'm sorry for you too."

They sat at the table in the too-bright house and listened
to their breath for ten seconds before Sean spoke again.

"Do you want me to stay here tonight? You seem on edge.
I can sleep on the couch."

"Yes, would you?"

And so they moved from the table to the couch. They
opened two beers and decided to find a movie on TV. It was
a comedy with a bunch of big Hollywood names, not the
sort of thing either of them would have normally chosen,

but it produced a sense of artificial cheer in the room. They weren't watching it anyhow. They were just looking at the screen, lost in their own thoughts.

Twenty minutes in, Sean stretched his legs out across her thighs. It was a gesture not of sex, but of familiarity. Kat liked it.

She saw the faded old tattoo of an ocean wave on his ankle and moved his pant leg up slightly. "Tell me again when you got that. You were eighteen?"

"Eighteen, yeah."

"And why did you do it?"

"What?" Sean looked from the TV to her.

"Get a tattoo. Why'd you do it?"

"I don't know," he said, shrugging. "I was an idiot."

"That's a regret I'm glad not to have. A tattoo."

Sean's forehead wrinkled. "Actually, no. I wasn't an idiot. I did it because I knew I couldn't take it back."

"That's pretty much the argument against tattoos."

"Yeah, but it's also a good reason. It's like you're holding your future self accountable. Because you can't erase it, a tattoo is a way for your younger self to maintain a hold on your adult life. It's like, 'Hey, remember who you used to be.' It's kind of brilliant actually, that an eighteen-year-old would anticipate adulthood changing them like that. I'm not saying I'm brilliant... You know what I mean."

"I do," Kat said. "But I would never want that reminder."

"Yeah, well, I guess that's the big risk of a tattoo. It's not the ink or the dumb picture you choose. It's whether you want the reminder of your younger self at all."

Kat pulled his pant leg back down and Sean returned to watching the movie, which had apparently captured his genuine interest. She knew this was a difference between the two of them and she knew, deep inside, that he thought there was something sad about her quest to live forever in the present, free of any past. But he'd benefited from this arrangement.

Because Kat left her story behind, they got to live completely in Sean's story. They didn't divide holidays among families or travel across the country for her high school reunions. She wasn't trying to fold her traditions into his or push him to stretch the boundaries of his world at all. He liked it this way, though he'd never admit it. It didn't seem fair that he should also judge her for the arrangement.

Sean got off the couch and walked away. At first she thought maybe he was leaving or he was angry about something, but he was just headed to the bathroom.

"Don't pause it for me," he said as the door closed.

Everything was almost exactly as it had been before— their positions on the couch, their beer, the tattoo on his leg under the same work pants—but there were other things present with them now too. Guilt and blame and fear. And that was the sticking point with this exercise in relationship normalcy. Sean had just gotten up to pee, but Kat thought he might be leaving her. She might have that reaction forever. Because every day from here on out, she would be a person who watched a man die and did nothing, and Sean would be the man who knew. There would never again be a day without all that knowledge between them. So they could arrange all the furniture to look as it did before, but the air in the room would still be harder to breathe.

Sean came back with a blanket. He turned off the lights, watching Kat as he did it to be sure the darkness wasn't too much for her fragile psyche, and then he resumed his spot on the couch. He gave her knee a little squeeze and she let go of some of her anxiety. Maybe if they both tried really hard, she thought, they could get through this. Maybe they'd be even better. Relationships could recover. It could be done.

Kat leaned back into the cushions and felt, for the first time in weeks, a heavy wave of true sleepiness wash over her. She closed her eyes and surrendered to the dreamless dark.

When she woke up hours later, Kat was alone on the couch. She heard a swoosh and then a click—the sound of her door opening and then closing again. Her apartment was dark and the TV was off. She had been sleeping so deeply that only the spring of her locking door could startle her back to consciousness, an adaptation of living alone.

Sean's stuff was gone. In the end, he couldn't make it through the night. Maybe he'd changed his mind about wanting to comfort her. Maybe it hurt too much to be close to her. Or maybe he couldn't live another day with this secret and he was on his way to the police.

Kat picked up her phone and looked at the glowing screen. It was just after three in the morning. She would never fall back asleep now. If she woke up at two, she might get a few more hours of sleep, but when she woke up at three, it was all over. Predictable patterns had emerged to her insomnia.

Goddamn Sean. There was clarity in hearing the door lock behind him. It devastated her, which meant that she needed to fight for him. Kat knew that something irreversible had occurred between them, but she didn't want it to be over. Those final moments before she slept—and oh, that sweet peaceful sleep—were worth fighting for. She wanted more than anything else the chance to prove to him that they could start something new and different and better in the wake of all this horribleness. She could make him understand that honesty would only upend all of their lives. Self-preservation was justifiable, even moral. She could do that. And indeed, she had to. Hunter was right about that. They really *had to* change Sean's mind.

"Just don't do anything," Kat whispered as a sort of tele-pathic request to Sean, or any listening gods. She desperately needed Sean to do nothing.

Sure, their relationship would be complicated in the fu-ture. They couldn't pretend that nothing had happened. But maybe they could use this secret to rededicate themselves to each other. It was proof of commitment. Wasn't there some-thing romantic about that?

Kat went to the sink and drank a glass of water. She re-moved her bra from under her shirt and hung it on the back of a kitchen chair. As long as she was up, she may as well get back to her Kyle research.

Kat opened her laptop and clicked on the little folder labeled KB.

CHAPTER 14

The bell on the entrance door of Island Glass jingled and Kat nearly jumped out of her seat. She'd been sitting there, in a chair behind the counter, all afternoon. The clock said it was just after four, which meant that she'd been sleeping for almost an hour. Customers were increasingly rare in those cold weather months.

"Let me know if I can help you with anything," Kat said to the woman who entered.

The lady smiled and walked along the back wall of display items. She was probably Kat's age—late twenties or early thirties—with a baby strapped to her chest in a designer carrier. A weekend vacationer with a family house on the Vineyard, by Kat's estimation. She seemed like the type who came in for a few days of gift shopping and cocktails around a stone hearth. Normally Kat was grateful for these people. But normally, Kat had more than three hours of sleep propping her up. She wasn't normally haunted by the face of a man she'd watched go overboard, or the paranoia that every loud noise was Vineyard police coming to arrest her. Nothing was normal and she wasn't herself.

"You make these?" the woman asked from across the room. She was reading a small placard on the wall that described their techniques.

"Yes, me and the owner, Orla Murphy. I make most of it in our studio." Kat pointed to the door over her right shoulder that led to the garage.

The woman raised her eyebrows. "Cool job." She pulled a tiny knit cap off her baby's head and rubbed the fuzzy dome as she spoke. "And this space! It's amazing. Like floating over the ocean."

Kat glanced at the water. "It's about to fall in, actually."

The woman stopped and looked at her. "What?"

Kat wasn't sure why she'd said that. The customer was obviously uncomfortable now. She only knew that she couldn't watch this lady, with her shiny hair and her sleeping baby and her limitless holiday budget, swoon over the false romance of Kat's precarious life.

"The bluff is going to fall into the ocean eventually, and it's going to take this building with it."

The woman forced a sympathetic expression as she put the hat back on her child's head. "I'm so sorry. What will you do?"

"I don't know." Kat had the feeling she was watching herself from above. "Nothing, probably. I'm considering prayer."

This was a relief to the woman, who didn't recognize the irony in Kat's voice, and certainly didn't want to talk much about Kat's tragic existence. She smiled. "It does more good than we know…prayer, I mean. I read a thing in the *Times* last year about these studies on collective prayer. People with terminal illnesses have been cured. It's amazing, really."

Kat smiled. *Fuck you and your collective prayer*, she thought. She wished she hadn't said anything about the cliffs.

"The erosion is because of climate change," the woman

went on. "Fossil fuels and rising sea levels and everything... we brought this on ourselves, really."

This fucking woman. Kat didn't know her, but she knew her type. And on this day, she was too overwhelmed by the weight of her problems to indulge this woman's cheap sermon. *Lady*, Kat thought, *we did not create these problems together.* The idea that she shared the same level of blame for damages done to the overheated earth as this wealthy woman. The idea that together, with their comparable lifestyles, they were pushing Orla's glass shop into the sea was fucking outrageous.

"Anyway, I'll take this," the woman said, holding out a whale-shaped paperweight. A guilt purchase to absolve herself of the apparent emotions the episode had stirred in her.

Kat rang her up and the woman left without another word.

"What was that?" Orla said from the doorway of the garage. She'd apparently been quietly watching for long enough to get the gist of the awkward interaction.

Kat turned red. "I, ah, I don't know what that was, exactly."

"Why don't you take the afternoon off, Kat. You can't work like this." Orla's face was a mix of concern and exasperation. "Just relax for a few hours. You seem tired."

"Orla, I know that was inappropriate, but I'm really okay. I won't do that again. Don't send me home."

She sighed. "Okay, then how about a trip to Hyannis? We need to pick up the new shelving. You can take my car."

"I can do that."

"The shelves are huge, so you'll need another hand," she said. "See if Sean can come along."

Kat nodded, but she didn't say more. More than a week had passed since Sean had slept over—or nearly slept over—and he'd been avoiding her ever since. Kat wasn't going to call Sean about this.

"I know things are complicated with you guys right now," Orla went on. "But he cares about you. He'll help you."

Kat smiled and hoped she was right. She still wasn't calling Sean.

Outside, Kat pulled the hood of her coat up over her head and breathed in the cold midday air. Everything was gray: the sky, the water, even the leftover snow seemed to blend into the gray of the concrete beneath it. Kat didn't mind this sort of weather. It seemed to freeze everything in place, a crisp pause on reality. It reminded her of walking home from the bus stop on those dark winter afternoons in Buffalo. The silence between the chaos of her school and the chaos of her home was a relief. It had been cold as hell, but she had good memories of those walks.

Kat wanted to see Erika, her oldest friend on the island. Erika was her therapeutic walk from the bus stop to her house, from one job to the next, one obstacle to another. She was the only person Kat could be with on that day. It had been weeks since they'd had a real conversation, something more than a quick call or text. Erika knew something was wrong and it killed Kat not to open up to her. She didn't want to lie anymore.

Kat dialed with chilling fingers and it rang three times.

"Hey."

"Hi! Where've you been?" Erika yelled through a bad connection.

"Sorry, I've been busy. Do you want to take a little day trip to Hyannis with me?"

The kitchen sounds of pots clanking, running water and ambient music thronged behind her. "Yeah, when?"

"Now! I'll come get you."

"I can't come *now*, bitch. I'm at work. Just started a six-hour shift at the bar."

Right, of course. That would make sense. Kat wasn't thinking so straight. "Uh, sorry. I don't know why I forgot that. Maybe later, then?"

"Definitely. Come by for a drink at the end of my shift."

"Great, okay."

"Hey," Erika yelled. "I mean it. I miss you. I don't know if you're mad at me or what, but let's just talk about it, okay?"

"I'm not mad at you. I swear to God. I miss you too."

"Okay, good. Then come by the bar later."

"I will."

And then she was gone. It was probably a good thing Erika couldn't come along. Kat wasn't thinking straight. She'd be tempted to tell Erika everything, and that would be a very bad idea. She couldn't do that, not ever. Thank God Erika couldn't come to Hyannis.

Kat began walking. The problem was that, now that she'd given herself permission to see Erika again, she wanted to see only her. Erika's presence was—aside from Sean—the most calming, natural and lasting thing that Kat knew on the island.

They met in her first job, when Kat came on as a cocktail waitress at the bar Erika tended. It was a dumpy place in Oak Bluffs that started handing out Jell-O shots at ten. By midnight, some party girl was always getting pulled off the bar or a venture capitalist jerk had started shit with a moody local. The other cocktail waitresses were young and flirtatious. They fit in better than Kat. The clientele came for the vacationland vibe more than the service, and the cocktail girls had plenty of vibe to go around. Kat made plans to get a different job almost as soon as she began, but she'd kept Erika close ever since.

Their similarities weren't immediately apparent to an outside observer. Erika was ten years older, from inland California, and thoroughly decorated with black tattoo ink. But they observed the world through a similar lens of past hardships and a belief in the supremacy of self-reliance. They shared flashes of their childhoods in neat little anecdotes that had been sanitized of their uglier truths. Humor was key. Erika and Kat could drink coffee together in silence or spend hours talking over bottles of wine. They expected only loyalty from one another.

Kat kept Erika laughing with her observations on the inanity of elite tourism, but it was Erika's stories that occupied them most of the time. Erika had countless, practiced bits on the adventures of her younger self. There was the time she carried all her boyfriend's clothes into the middle of the street and lit them on fire. The time she'd been hired to entertain a boat of Saudi billionaires. The time she filled her boss's car with garbage. And the time she helped another boyfriend hide from the police in the ladies' room of the Seastreak ferry. They all carried an element of danger, which was also what made them so good. Erika had survived those years and wasn't interested in elaborating on the specific traumas that made her unstable in the first place. And Kat wasn't going to ask about them. That was their arrangement: friendship without explanation or judgment.

If anyone could understand what Kat was going through—and what she'd done to Kyle—it would be Erika. But Kat loved Erika too much to lay that on her. Knowing about Kyle was a liability and too many people already knew. It would eat her up to stay quiet, but she could never tell Erika.

Kat scrolled through her phone for Hunter's number. She didn't really want to see him, but she did need help in Hyannis and she was nervous about driving alone with her sleepy brain.

"Hey," she said when he picked up.

"Hey. Long time no talk. Did you neutralize all the threats?"

"Jesus, Hunter. Don't say things like that."

"Sorry, it was a joke…kind of. Did you get back together with Sean?"

"No, that's not why I'm calling. Do you want to go to Hyannis with me?"

"Oh, so you're leaving the house now?"

This was his new persona: coiled for a fight. All his joviality had hardened into sarcasm and acrimony in the previous few weeks. It was a bit of a relief to Kat, actually, just to be around someone who didn't expect her to behave properly. They bonded over their bitterness.

"Even vampires need supplies. So are you coming?"

"I'll wait outside for you."

It took fifteen minutes for Kat to walk to Orla's car in the town lot, rummage through the glove box for a hairbrush and drive back to Hunter's place. She found an old box of Altoids in the pocket of the door and chewed two while she waited for him. She hadn't been out much or seen many people in a while, and she was suddenly self-conscious about her presentation.

Hunter swung the door of Orla's Outback open quickly and flashed a big smile when she pulled up.

"Hi."

He looked surprisingly good—rested and clean—which wasn't always guaranteed for the two of them lately. No, it was more than that. He looked *good*. The wound under his eye was healing into a visible scar that made his otherwise flawless face more interesting. He looked older, to be sure, but it suited him.

"Thanks for coming with me."

"I literally have nothing else to do."

"Glad to see you're still an asshole." She was glad she had called him.

Hunter adjusted the seat with a smile.

"We have ten minutes before we have to get to the ferry. You want coffee?"

"Oh, yeah."

Kat pulled up in front of Island Beans and put the car in Park. She left Hunter to scroll through his phone from the passenger seat.

The windows of the hot little coffee shop were steamed up, so Kat couldn't see what she was getting into until the door shut loudly behind her, and everyone inside turned her way.

And there, sitting across from one another at a small table in the center of the room, were Sean and Ashley. They were as startled as she was and as obviously reluctant to have this encounter, but the room was too small to avoid it.

Kat approached their table. "Hey, guys."

"Hi."

"Hey."

"What's the occasion?" She wasn't sure how else to ask why the fuck they were sitting there together.

"Nothing really." Ashley was trying to be cute and it didn't look good on her. "Just a lazy Saturday."

Kat kept her eyes on Sean. "Yeah, lazy Saturday."

A barista shouted something from behind the counter and Ashley said, "Oh, that's us!"

Us.

Sean didn't move, so Ashley went to fetch their drinks, leaving Kat standing above Sean at the table.

"You're avoiding me," she said.

"I'm not, I swear. I'm just taking some time." Sean watched Ashley sprinkle something into a cup from across the room.

"And this is just...I don't know, she kept asking to go out for coffee so I finally just agreed. I don't know what it is, but it's not about you."

"Well, have you figured out if she's still pursuing...the thing she was pursuing?" Kat asked with a whisper.

Sean shook his head. "It hasn't come up. I don't know, Kat."

The shop door jingled with the arrival of more customers and a gust of wind held it wide-open for three seconds, just long enough for Sean to see the parked car outside.

"Is that Hunter sitting in my mom's car?"

Kat really didn't want him to see Hunter. She didn't want him to see anything that might set their chances of reconciliation back even an inch. She needed to do something.

"Do you want to go to Hyannis?"

"What?"

"I'm going to pick up some shelves for your mom. I needed some help, and you were avoiding me, so I had to ask Hunter. We'll just be gone for a few hours."

Kat didn't really want to go to Cape Cod with Sean and Hunter. She could hardly imagine anything more awkward, in fact, but she needed to extend the offer to prove that Hunter's presence was nothing more than desperation on her part. He was just muscle.

But now it looked like Sean was seriously considering the offer. He probably wanted to call her bluff. That was the cynical reading of the situation. She'd love to believe that he just wanted to make things normal between the three of them again and forgive Kat for everything, but the likelihood of that seemed slim.

Ashley returned with two drinks in hand. "So, what are we talking about?"

"I think I'm going to have to take this with me," Sean said, standing up. "I have to go to Hyannis."

Ashley's face fell, and then recovered. "You want a third wheel?"

Jesus, this girl was persistent. Didn't she have any pride?

"Actually, it would be a fourth," Sean said. "Hunter's coming."

Why he said this, Kat would never know.

They watched Ashley's eyes widen and her mood change to pure saccharine. She was as fake happy as she could be. "Fun! I'm totally coming."

Kat looked around, but there was no one to save her. What the hell was happening? She scanned quickly through every possible option at that moment. If she walked out and drove away with Hunter, Sean would be suspicious and they'd never get back together. If they took Sean, it would be awkward, but not dangerous. They couldn't take Ashley. They needed to get rid of eager, probing, desperate Ashley. But if the three of them went *without* Ashley, wouldn't that be proof to her crazy little brain that they were hiding something about Kyle? Wouldn't that make her more suspicious? Kat's head was spinning.

Sean looked almost as pained as she felt. He must have been thinking the same thing about Ashley. If they were going to keep their secret safe, it might actually be better to take her, to prove that they were all just normal friends doing normal things, with nothing at all to hide.

"Sure, lemme grab our coffees," Kat said.

Ashley smiled at Sean, who was pretending to focus on the tiny wording on his disposable cup.

Kat bought two coffees, dumped some cream into each and led them out to the car. She could see Hunter's face change as they approached.

"New plan," she announced, sliding into the driver's seat. "We've got two more."

Hunter gave her a what-the-fuck look, and Kat shook her head helplessly.

Miserable Sean and cheerful Ashley took the back seat.

Hunter turned around to acknowledge them and then sank back into his seat.

They drove silently toward the ferry terminal where a man in a Steamship Authority snowsuit directed them to the car queue. There, the four passengers sat for two long minutes in silence until the line started to move, and they were finally driving onto the massive barge as it prepared for sea.

The moment the car stopped on the ferry, Hunter opened the door and walked away from them, through the tight maze of parked vehicles, to the staircase that led to the upper deck. Sean followed him, and then Ashley.

Kat sat in the quiet car, trying to parse the events of the previous ten minutes. She wanted to go back to the part when it was just Hunter and her being mutually grumpy and genuinely comfortable in the car. No, that's not right. She wanted Sean back. This could still be an opportunity to prove her disinterest in Hunter to Sean. But Ashley. Ashley did not need to be there. Her presence would keep them all on their toes. And no one seemed more annoyed by her than Sean, so why was he with her at all? Kat suspected he liked the attention, though he'd never admit such a thing.

She didn't want to look like she was hiding, so Kat got out of the car and walked up the metal staircase to the main floor of the ferry.

At the center of the room was the sad diner-style vendor that sells hot dogs, microwave egg sandwiches and coffee. Hunter, Sean and Ashley were lined up on stools drinking little bottles of cheap wine.

Hunter slid an individual-sized white zinfandel toward Kat, who picked it up and placed it in front of Ashley. She wanted a drink badly enough to know that if she had one, she'd want three, and she couldn't have three. So Ashley could have it.

Ashley looked genuinely grateful for this gesture, despite the fact that it meant nothing at all. She was so glad to be there with the three of them. Too glad. This was going to be a horrible trip.

The ferry took just over an hour, as always, but it felt longer to Kat. The other three had another round of little wines, which seemed to take a slight edge off the awkwardness for the drinkers. Ashley may have been the primary source of the awkwardness, but she was also pretty helpful in mitigating it. No one wanted to talk much, so she filled the space with a thorough description of her PhD thesis, which was inarguably impressive. Kat was reminded of her initial impression of this bright, ambitious young woman. She almost understood the appeal for Hunter and Sean, who had each been, at some point, eager to sleep with her.

About halfway through the second round of wines—which had no discernable effect on the guys—Ashley started leaning into Sean, touching his hand and trying to catch his eye. Sean wasn't reciprocating, but neither was he rebuffing her efforts. Hunter raised his brows at Kat, who responded with the subtlest nod of acknowledgment. Sean was embarrassed. Everyone was. With every flirtatious gesture, Ashley would watch Kat and Hunter. She was trying to evoke jealousy in one of them, maybe both.

Hunter attempted to order another drink just as the ferry inched into port.

"Forget it," Kat snapped at the man behind the counter.

No one argued with her.

They all headed back down to the car.

It was a ten-minute drive from the ferry to the woodworker's home deep in the woods. Hunter kept the music in the car up loud to avoid any conversational pressure. Rolling Stones, James Taylor, Bonnie Raitt…a steady flow of inoffensive nostalgic sounds filled the air until, finally, Orla's wagon pulled up to a charmingly dilapidated home at the end of a long dirt lane.

"This is it?" Ashley asked.

"This is Orla's woodworker friend, yeah." Kat couldn't mask her disdain for this woman any longer. The trip had been okay so far, but Ashley's unmitigated cheer was maddeningly inappropriate. And Sean's eagerness to fake sleep, which ultimately turned into real sleep, only compounded her anger. Kat tried to remind herself that she was, at the very least, throwing Ashley off the scent of their involvement in Kyle's death by taking her along for this painfully mundane chore. So maybe it wasn't wasted time in the end.

Hunter got out of the car. "It doesn't look like anyone's home."

Kat followed. "This guy never leaves. I'm sure he's home."

"Did you call him?"

She glared back at Hunter over the hood of the car. Kat had not called the woodworker. She didn't know when she woke up this morning that she would be sent on this errand and that, along the way, she'd be forced to take her ex-boyfriend (or whatever he was) and her ex-boyfriend's deranged admirer who was also Hunter's scorned lover. So no, she forgot to call the fucking woodworker.

Kat threw her hands up and walked to the front door with Hunter two steps behind her. They knocked over and over, then walked around the house to the back, crunching through old, undisturbed snow along the way. She was alone with Hunter again and she felt like she could breathe.

"I can't believe you brought them," Hunter snarled.

"Me, either, but I had no choice." Kat jumped up on her tiptoes and tried to see in the windows of the dark house. There was definitely no one home.

"It's like you want to get caught," he said. "We shouldn't be this close to her. She's fishing for something." Hunter rubbed his arms. They weren't wearing coats and the temperature had dropped significantly.

"What? I'm doing the opposite of that. I'm bringing her in. Wasn't that why we decided you should keep dating her... to keep an eye on her? How's that plan going, by the way?"

"I think that's Sean's job now."

Kat glared at him.

"I'm sorry. Forget I said that. And don't worry, Sean doesn't want her, either. That's obvious."

It was nice of him to say, but it wasn't precisely what she wanted to hear. She wasn't sure what she wanted.

"What's going on?" a voice yelled.

Kat and Hunter jumped.

It was Ashley, coming around the corner of the house. "Is this guy home or not?" She stood twenty feet from where they'd been talking, in a thin shirt and winter hat. Neither of them had heard her approach.

Sean came up behind Ashley, looking pissed off. "Great trip, guys! Thanks for bringing us. Let's get out of here."

Kat tried to stay calm. "Yeah, sorry. This is my fault. Obviously. I guess we should head back if we're going to catch the last ferry."

What had Ashley heard? She didn't think they'd said anything too specific, but she really wasn't sure.

"I want to know what you guys were doing back here," Ashley teased.

Sean looked at each of them. He had the same suspicious

look on his face as that night he'd caught them arguing in Kat's apartment.

"We were trying the door," Hunter said with an exaggerated tone. He hated this girl. "C'mon. Let's go."

Hunter stomped toward the car and Kat followed. It felt suddenly like teams were forming among them, which was potentially dangerous.

Kat gripped the wheel with both hands as they pulled out of the driveway.

"You should have called first," Sean said from the back.

Hunter spun around. "What?"

"I said she should have called first. I don't understand why we came all the way out here." Sean was mad, but not about the stupid shelves.

Kat could feel the anger rising up in her throat as she drove. It was coming too fast to stop it. "I don't understand it, either, Sean! Why *are* you guys here?" She tried to keep her eyes on the road.

For a minute, no one spoke.

"Why is *she* here?" Hunter said under his breath, and everyone knew who he meant.

This was the only invitation Ashley needed to join the conversation. "Oh, does my presence make you uncomfortable, Hunter? Does it remind you of what a dick you are? Or maybe you're jealous…"

Kat looked at Sean through the rearview mirror. She thought he would jump in and clarify his relationship to Ashley, but he didn't.

"Everyone here knows what's going on with you two," Ashley went on.

Hunter scoffed.

"We already told you," Kat started.

"You are lying!" Ashley yelled. And then she went quiet again. "I think you're lying about a lot of things."

For five whole minutes, no one talked. Local public radio droned in the background while Ashley watched all three of them squirm. She was right. They were lying. And now, Kat, Hunter and Sean were afraid of her.

"I need food," Kat said finally. She didn't want to spend one more second in the car with this group, but she hadn't eaten all day and she was starting to feel weak. Kat had lost six pounds since the night on Hunter's boat and was experiencing dizzy spells with increasing frequency. She'd never been fragile, but in the past few weeks it seemed like her body was breaking down.

"I could use a drink," Sean said.

Hunter nodded in agreement.

It was dark outside, but not late. The next (and last) ferry was at seven, so they'd have to kill time somehow.

Kat drove for six more miles and then stopped at the first restaurant they saw. And because this was Hyannis, the first place they saw was a white-tablecloth, clinking-crystal, farm-to-table affair where the entrées started at thirty dollars.

"Well, this is romantic," Hunter quipped from behind his menu.

Ashley smiled and ignored the sarcasm. She put a hand on Sean's thigh, and he let it stay there. They were looking at each other in a new way. Kat wondered whether it was actual affection or they were just trying to fuck with her.

"We'll have two bottles of the Grüner," Hunter said before the waiter got a word in. "And a couple of bread baskets or something."

No one objected. Kat hoped he was paying, but she didn't ask.

A bread basket appeared and Kat slowly devoured several

pieces, like someone who hadn't seen real food in a very long time. As she ate, and while the other three studied their menus with the focus of people who really didn't want to talk to each other, Kat watched the bartender across the room. He was a fit guy in his fifties with white hair and a handsome face. He chatted with waitresses while polishing the glossy countertop and filling occasional orders. Kat could tell he was the sort of person his coworkers wanted to be around. They kept coming back. She wondered if Kyle might have been a bartender like that if he'd had the opportunity to age into it. Or if he had other plans entirely and bartending was just a necessary stepping-stone to those plans.

It would be nice to believe that we all died doing the thing that defined us, after we'd arrived at the life we wanted, but that was probably almost never the case. If Kat had died ten years earlier, what would her legacy have been? *Here lies a scrappy kid with an unsure future*—that's what her gravestone would have said. It wasn't like she'd become the president of the United States, but she'd found something that felt worth doing. She'd discovered her purpose in that time, which Kyle never got to do.

The wine arrived and Hunter went through the excruciating process of sniffing and tasting because the waiter seemed intent on doing this by the book. And then, finally, there was alcohol in four glasses and they all drank.

They drank and they drank. As the driver, Kat went slow, but the others did not. And then one bottle was empty and they were deep into the next.

After a while, Sean scratched his beard and stretched back in his chair. "So why was Hunter coming on this trip in the first place," he asked with a casual, snide confidence.

"I told you, Sean, for the lifting. I needed help."

"Right, for the lifting," he repeated.

"Well, no harm done," Ashley said, nuzzling into Sean's arm.

The waiter appeared and they ordered food, and something red to follow the white. The kitchen was taking longer than usual—that's what the waiter warned—but they cared less about the food now that the wine was flowing. Hunter asked Sean about the boatyard and Sean provided a terse answer. Ashley interjected with praises for Sean and polite follow-up questions. Kat smiled at the appropriate times and watched the kitchen door like a hawk. Everyone—even Ashley—was faking, navigating around the multitude of secrets and resentments between them. They were just biding time until the food appeared or they were too drunk to care.

And that's how they came to miss the last ferry. In all the seething chitchat and wine refills, forty minutes passed before the waiter finally appeared with their food. Kat looked down at her watch just as the hot plates were placed before them and realized the time.

"We missed the ferry."

Sean looked up. "Nooo."

"We did."

"Fuck." Hunter shook his head. "We'll have to stay over and get the first one in the morning."

Kat, who'd nursed two glasses through it all, reached for a bottle of the white wine and poured it right up to the rim. No point in holding back now.

Ashley looked pleased.

Sean stood up. "Excuse me." He walked to the men's room with an intoxicated sway.

Ashley folded her napkin on the table and looked around for the ladies' room. "Me too."

It was just Hunter and Kat again, looking down at their beautiful plates. The food had been cut into neat geometric shapes and arranged artfully high. It was preposterous.

Hunter stabbed his fork directly down the center of his precious food tower and pushed the enormous forkful into his mouth.

Kat watched in amused horror.

"This is fucking terrible," he said through his food.

"Your dinner?"

"No, dinner is great actually."

Kat laughed. At first it was just a giggle, and then she was laughing harder, until finally she had to use her white napkin to catch the snot coming from her nose.

Hunter was laughing and nearly choking as he worked to swallow the entire meal he'd just pushed into his face.

"This *is* terrible." Kat wiped an inexplicable tear from the corner of her eye and composed herself. She took a bite of supple, buttery scallop. The evening was terrible, but she was glad to have Hunter there.

The other two returned and they seemed displeased by the scene.

"What's so funny?"

"Nothing," Hunter said.

Everyone ate their tiny food and drank their wine in silence for a while. The reality of this endless evening was beginning to sink in. They would need to rent a room—no, a bunch of rooms—in the adjoining inn and carry this project into the morning.

Kat worried about the cost of this adventure. She didn't have the money for any of it, and she figured Sean didn't, either.

Sean looked miserable, even more so than the others maybe. Kat was angry with him for his association with Ashley, but she still missed him, and it still broke her heart to see him sitting beside this attractive, adoring woman. This woman didn't come with an ugly secret that would hover

over the rest of her life like a dark cloud. Kat couldn't compete with that, even if Ashley was a little nuts.

Hunter made eye contact with the waiter and pointed at an empty bottle. They'd have another of the Cabernet, he said.

Ashley reached for her water glass, hitting her wineglass in the process and sending a wave of crimson liquid across the table.

Sean jumped up. "Oh shit!"

Kat collected everyone's napkins and began sopping up the wine. She must have made a disapproving face because Ashley got defensive.

"I'm sorry! It was an accident."

"Don't worry about her," Sean said, putting a hand on Ashley's back. "It's not you."

"Good thing you got out when you did," Ashley said under her breath.

Kat stopped cleaning. "What?"

Hunter leaned back in his chair, content to watch this fight unfold.

"I just mean," Ashley started. "I'm probably a better fit for Sean."

The waiter approached and Hunter waved him away. Other diners were looking now.

"Whoa." Sean stepped in. "Things are complicated with us, but I haven't... Kat and I aren't officially over... I don't know." He looked at Kat for help.

"Right," she said, happy to receive this olive branch, but also unsure of what to do with it. "We're working through things."

And before all of their eyes, Ashley changed. Her expression hardened and her breath seemed to stop. She stood up quickly, banging a knee into the table and ensuring that every sentient human in the room turned to watch them.

"You three," she said, looking from Sean to Hunter to Kat. "I don't know exactly what you're hiding in this fucked-up little love triangle, but I know it's something. I *know* it. And it has to do with Kyle Billings."

She said the last part as a whisper.

"Two of you were there that night, and none of you wants to talk about it. That body didn't float down from the swimming beach, and there's no possible reason for you to disagree with me…unless you're hiding something. And you are. You're all hiding something from me!"

Hunter stood up and took Ashley firmly by the arm, pulling her out of the restaurant through the front door.

Kat sprang to collect everyone's coats from the back of their chairs.

Sean tried to tip the waiter, but Hunter had already taken care of the bill.

They stepped out into the freezing rain to find Hunter yelling directly into Ashley's face.

"What do you want from us?"

Ashley looked enraged. She'd seemed so drunk minutes before, but now she was searing with hot, focused anger. "I want to know what you're keeping from me. I've been doing the work on my own and I know more than you think. I've been talking to the cops and studying the tide patterns. I have proof that there's no way Kyle was swimming where the cops said he was swimming. And I know the three of you were with him earlier that night. And no one seems to have any proof that he was using drugs or high when he died. All of these things…all of these little pieces! You guys are keeping things from me and I'm going to find out what it is."

The frozen rain hit their shoulders and heads with an audible patter.

Kat began to shiver. This was it. Ashley was close enough

now to undo them all. She looked menacing under the yellow light with her wild, wide eyes. The strangest thing about it all was that she didn't really seem interested in Kyle. This was about them. She was mad and hurt, and she wanted to punish them for keeping her on the outside. Kat had the feeling that if only Ashley had won over Sean, or maybe Hunter weeks before, she would have let all this go. Their fate was in the hands of this irrational girl in search of affection.

Kat looked up at the sky and shuddered. "We have to go inside."

Sean nodded, and the four of them walked around the side of the restaurant to the entrance of the inn. It was crazy that they were going to spend the night together after everything Ashley had just said, but they had no choice. All four of them were drunk and there was no way to get back on the Vineyard at this hour. If there had been any way to get rid of her, they would have. There was no way.

"I'll take care of this," Kat said, reaching for the doorknob.

So Sean, Hunter and Ashley stood outside, dripping under the awning while Kat went in to book four separate rooms at the reduced winter rate.

"Family holiday trip?" the old woman at the front desk asked.

"We missed the ferry."

The woman shook her head like it was a damn shame and she'd seen it before.

"Ice machine's in the lobby. You want a call in the morning? Make sure you don't miss the early boat?"

Kat zipped her credit card back into her wet purse and considered what morning would look like. They had a thirty-minute drive together, followed by the ferry. Maybe she shouldn't get on the ferry at all. If Ashley was so close to figuring it all out, maybe Kat should just run. Leave the car, go out the back door of the inn and try to start over somewhere.

"Yeah, a call would be great. Thank you."

Outside, Kat led the other three to the row of rooms, which were stacked next to one another like an incredibly quaint Motel 6. No one spoke. They just went to their respective doors and inserted their keys. Each room had a special name. Kat took the Sandpiper Room, between Sean and Hunter. Ashley's was on the end, beside Sean's. Whether their rooms were also shorebirds or not, she didn't notice.

Ashley got her key in first. She went inside and slammed the door.

Hunter went into his next.

Sean looked pitifully at Kat as they both struggled with their keys. He seemed sorry about it all, worried for her. It made Kat feel worse to know that he was worried. She wanted to tell him she'd be fine, but that probably wasn't true. More than that, she wanted not to care so much about his feelings. It was her life that was about to end, not his. Sean's key finally turned and he disappeared inside, leaving her alone in the freezing rain before a locked door.

Kat jiggled her key fruitlessly. She'd never been prone to fatalism, believing it was a luxury for people who didn't have real problems. But at that particular moment she had the feeling that she'd already seen all the joy her life would ever know. Everything was going to be different tomorrow. Ashley would make sure of that. And it was with this realization of her life's end that Kat also realized what she wanted to do on that last night of freedom.

She left the key dangling in its broken lock and walked five steps to her right. Kat knocked on Hunter's door.

CHAPTER 15

The phone must have rung ten times before Kat realized it was her wake-up call. The ceaseless trilling from the other side of the wall had to be the old lady at the front desk, just as planned. Kat pictured the woman holding her black office phone in her hand and shaking her head in disapproval—not that the old woman could possibly know she was lying naked beside Hunter at that moment, or that anyone had the right to disapprove of how she spent her likely last night as a free person. It was none of that lady's business.

The events of the previous evening came crashing back to Kat in an instant: the ill-fated car trip, the disastrous dinner, Ashley's meltdown. Her head hurt, but it seemed silly to feel pain moments before an apocalypse. Kat had forgotten all of it in the brief window of unbridled pleasure she'd had with Hunter hours before. Even the memory of that sex was enough to nearly push the problems of her life out of her mind. Nearly.

The phone was still ringing and, shit, Kat realized it would wake Sean up on the other side. And then they would all know that Kat wasn't in her own room, which she didn't need on that morning. She didn't need those new problems.

Kat jumped out of bed and searched around for her clothes. She shouldn't have allowed herself to fall asleep in his room. She realized that now.

"Wait," Hunter said into his pillow.

"No, I gotta get that phone before it wakes Sean up. Anyhow, we all need to make the early ferry."

Hunter rolled over and watched her lace her boots. "Does it matter?"

It probably didn't matter which ferry they got. The earlier the ferry, the faster their demise. Probably. But this field trip needed to end.

"Get dressed," she instructed.

Hunter nodded and sat up.

Ten minutes later, Hunter, Sean and Kat were talking to a receptionist at the front desk. It wasn't the old lady. She apparently didn't work the morning shift. This was a young man with a round face, who Kat figured didn't care whether she had spent the night in Hunter's bed emancipating the weeks of mounting anger, frustration and sexual tension between the two of them. He didn't seem as judgy about stuff like that.

"Your friend checked out about forty minutes ago," the man said. "Seemed like she was in a hurry, so I called her a cab."

Sean and Hunter exchanged a look. They were both puzzled by this information. And for that moment, they were allies. Sean didn't know that Hunter had been naked with his ex-girlfriend moments before, and he had no reason to suspect it.

Kat tried to focus. "Where would Ashley go?"

Sean nodded to the door, indicating that they should have this discussion in private. They all took ten steps away from the nice receptionist man.

"I have no idea where she would have gone, but we should just get back," Sean said. "Nothing we can do about her now."

Hunter ran a hand through his unwashed hair. "Do you think she's going to do something crazy?"

"I don't know." Sean looked at Kat. "Listen, I have to be at the boatyard in two hours. Can we just go back? I'll pick up the shelves another time."

"Yeah, of course." Kat had forgotten about the shelves. She would do whatever Sean asked at that moment to ease some of her guilt.

They walked outside and headed for the car.

The temperature was about twenty degrees warmer than it had been the night before and all the leftover snow piles were washing away to nothing. Sean took the driver side and Hunter went to the passenger side, leaving Kat in the back. The seating made her feel cheap, behind the boys. She tried to sleep as they pulled onto the main road.

When Kat woke up, it was to the sound of the ferry docking on Martha's Vineyard. She had the reflexive relief of being home, followed by the panic of reality. Her head hurt even more than before, and she suddenly felt like she might throw up.

The rain was letting up, so Sean turned off the windshield wipers, which screeched miserably with each stroke.

Hunter reached back and handed her a water bottle. He smiled. Kat smiled back. She wanted to run her hands through his greasy hair and relive the things they had done last night again. It was unbelievable to her that she could feel so terrified for her future and simultaneously so aroused by his presence. Her aching, hungover body was somehow tingling with adolescent excitement at the memory of their night together.

"You okay back there?" Sean looked into the rearview mirror and Kat remembered that she deserved whatever terrible fate awaited her on the island. How could she have done this to Sean?

"I'm fine, thanks. Do you mind dropping me at home and hanging on to the car for your mom? I don't feel well."

"It's my first stop."

Kat wondered whether Sean and Hunter had spoken along the way. They weren't fighting anymore, which either meant that Sean's anger toward Hunter had softened or that he just didn't want to pour salt into the wound of their impending problems. Personal beefs were a rather quaint idea in the face of murder charges. Because that's what this would be, eventually, right? Murder? Manslaughter? Who on God's earth would still believe that Kat and Hunter hadn't pushed Kyle over? They were guilty people now.

Ashley could be at the police station at that very moment, with her proof.

Sean pulled the car up along the curb in front of Island Glass. It would be another hour until the shop opened, so Kat thought she might go straight into the garage and get a few bowls into the furnace before she had to shower and work. She needed to keep moving today. Whatever was coming would come, but she had to keep moving if she wanted to avoid dying of panic. Suddenly, she was desperate to get to work and feel the heavy, hot iron in her hands.

"Hope you feel better," Sean said into the mirror.

"Thanks."

"Yeah," Hunter agreed distractedly. Kat could see the same panic setting in for him.

She got out and shut the door, standing for a moment in

the cold, wet air as the car pulled away. Everything looked just as it had one day before. The only sound was the water lapping on the beach below.

Kat put her key in the lock of the garage door to find that it was already open. Orla was inside.

Orla held a long rod into the glory hole, turning slowly with her strong arms. She nodded at Kat, but didn't look up through her goggles. Kat realized she hadn't seen Orla work glass in months. She'd said she didn't feel the same desire to create any longer, which Kat couldn't fathom. But here she was, creating again.

Orla pulled the rod out and held the cool end up to her lips and blew. Her blast of air moved through the tube, and they watched the glass bubble grow slowly at the other end.

Kat pulled on a pair of gloves and went to assist. It worked better with two sets of hands—so one person could blow and another could shape the glass at the other end. She picked up a nearby paddle and began to flatten the bottom of the bubble. It was already clear that this would be a double-walled bowl. Orla liked to blow them up like balloons and then collapse and invert the walls. It was one of the first things she'd taught Kat.

With large pliers, Orla snipped the balloon off the end of the rod. Kat watched as she used a rounded shaper to depress one side in like a deflated soccer ball.

"Did you get the shelving?"

"No one was there. I'm sorry."

Orla nodded. She seemed unhappy with Kat.

"And Sean has your car."

She nodded again, holding the round shaper firm into the center of the glass.

Kat deserved Orla's frustration, this coldness. She'd been absent in mind or body so much lately that it was a miracle

Orla hadn't confronted her about it sooner. She deserved what Orla was doing to her now, but she wasn't sure she could handle it. No one's disapproval stung Kat more than Orla's. In her entire life, there'd been no one she respected more and wanted to do right by than Orla, not even Sean.

"You should go clean up before we open. You smell like alcohol."

Kat nodded and went for the door, embarrassed. She could hear the furnace slide open behind her and the new bowl being placed inside. She imagined that all the tension between them would be baked into that glass bowl for eternity. It was a superstition she shared with Orla, the idea that each piece carried all the energy it was created with, good or bad. The furnace sealed it in. Before that stage, everything was still malleable and capable of change. But once it was baked, it held those emotions for good. Hopefully, the angry bowl would sell quickly and be gone.

Kat turned the knob of the door that connected the garage with the glass shop. And as she did, there came a sound so unrecognizable, she froze.

Orla bolted upright and looked at Kat.

It was a sort of patter, like hail, but less consistent. It was loud and then soft again: a herd of cows running down cobblestone, which of course it wasn't. But what was it, then?

Orla went for the door to the outside first, and Kat was right behind. They burst through and looked down the wet streets. Everything looked the same outside in the post-rain gloom. But the sound...it was still around them. It wasn't coming from the street side.

They ran around the house, unsure of what they'd find, but awakening to the general doom that was upon them. It was the cliffs.

Kat rounded the corner first, stopping suddenly and putting her arms out to catch Orla, as she took in the surreal scene before them.

Just twenty feet away, the edge of the yard that sat between Island Glass and the sharp cliff's edge was collapsing. The sound they'd heard was hundreds of clumps of saturated clay tumbling off the face of the cliff, bouncing and breaking on their way down to the water. That was the patter. Up close, they could hear the low hiss of the falling sand, as well. The loose sediment that had only minutes before been packed in tight with the clay now fell gracefully with it. And the dead winter grass they'd been propping up now slumped and hung like a vertical carpet off the face of the raw bluff…until it broke and fell too.

With every little avalanche, the glass shop got closer to the edge.

Orla gasped and tried to run toward the side entrance of the shop, through the flimsy police tape that had been put there after the first buckling, but Kat wrapped her arms tightly around her. She knew where Orla was going because it was the same place Kat would go if she were losing her mind to the grief of what they were witnessing. Orla wanted to get in to save the glass, a few of the pieces anyway—the stuff that wasn't for sale: the things she'd made with her late husband, the few pieces that still remained from her father's work in Waterford. She wanted to save the pieces that told the story of her life.

Orla squirmed in Kat's arms. There seemed a pause in the action, but this wasn't the end. It was the moment at which the dragon takes a breath before unleashing his fire. It was the windup. And in the deceptive stillness, Kat could sense an irreversible motion that had been set into place. The earth was moving, and the air was moving, and maybe even the house

was moving. She was watching life through a wobbly cam-
era lens, almost imperceptibly unsteady, certainly not right.

And then, there was motion again. The last patch of frontage grass collapsed, pulling the two old Adirondack chairs
down with it. They snapped like dry kindling as they joined
the crumbling bluffs on their way to the beach, falling so
easily. Left behind was the house, hanging three feet over
the edge of the broken bluff for several breathtaking seconds.
And then, it too surrendered.

Orla screamed as the oceanfront wall of the house began
to pull away from the frame, straight down toward the beach
below. Cedar planks snapped off like buttons.

And then came the windows. Orla's thirty-year-old stained
glass windows exploded like fireworks in the debris, along
with the three clear windows from Kat's upstairs apartment,
and all the rest of them. The deafening sound mixed with
Orla's cries. Kat had the feeling of drowning in the cacoph-
ony. A fire truck screamed from the other end of town, followed by police cars.

There were people too. Kat didn't take her eyes off the
house, but she could feel the people collecting in the street
behind them.

She and Orla were alone, though, just a few strides from
the naked oceanfront side of the house. They were dangerously close to the unsteady cliffs, but incapable of running
to safety. They had to be there.

The front face of the house fell off quickly, exposing the
interior of their shop like a dollhouse in a nightmare. Most
of the merchandise inside had fallen to the floor and broken,
but Kat could see some of the small, solid pieces still intact,
utterly unaware of their fate.

The police tape barrier had fallen to the ground, and was
fluttering with the earth's movement.

Kat was taking it all in as she loosened her grip on Orla—that was how she broke away. Orla jerked her body free and started to run. She ran directly toward the edge and a roar of cries ensued from behind. It would only take a few steps to go over—they were so close to the cliff now—but Kat knew Orla wasn't running toward her death; she was running for the starfish. She could see that delicate glass starfish sitting just a foot from the jagged edge of the broken shop floor and knew it was what Orla was running for. Her father had made it for Sean when he was a child, just weeks before he died. It had a ribbon of gold running evenly through each arm in such a way that neither Orla nor Kat could ever fully replicate. She kept the object on a high shelf for display, and now she was running to save it.

It took less than a second for Kat to spring forward, out of her trance and after Orla. One, two, three long strides, and then she got a hold of Orla's arm and yanked. They were suspended in a moment of tug-of-war near the edge as Orla strained to reach the house. Kat got one nauseating look down at the shore, and the pile of fallen debris, before she overpowered Orla and pulled her back toward her. Orla tried to pry Kat's fingers away from her pinched arm. She screamed out in agony, more emotional than physical, but Kat wouldn't let go.

And then there was movement again around them. A man's voice boomed from somewhere and Kat knew time was up. She tried to pull Orla's body toward the street, but in their struggle, they both fell. Others were yelling now too. Something was about to happen. Kat yanked Orla's body through the muddy grass, inching her farther away from the edge and closer to safety. In the seconds that passed between the stranger's scream and their fall, the earth beneath them turned to liquid and it suddenly felt that they were rolling with waves on the ocean.

With a howl, Kat pulled them both to their feet. And then, they ran. Orla wasn't resisting anymore. A cop and a stranger in plainclothes met them on the quivering edge of the lawn and led them to the road where a small group of onlookers had gathered.

Voices were shouting and the earth was rumbling. Cops herded the spectators farther from the house and into the center of the street. Orla and Kat moved with them. A deep roar from the cliffs silenced them all.

From there, they watched the final moments of Island Glass—Orla's shop and Kat's home. It started with the hardwood floors, which snapped and fell without struggle. Then came the remaining contents of the house. Shelves fell from walls, lamps toppled and everything slid down the planks of the broken floors along the fastest route to the shoreline. It would all join a churning stew of debris, unseen from where they stood. The fall came easily for the smaller things, but the frame resisted. Thick beams twisted and splintered before finally breaking off at awkward angles and plunging. Most excruciating of all was the plumbing. The copper pipes running from toilets and sinks to the island's underground were bending and screaming their way apart, the stubborn intestines of a dying body.

Onlookers watched the undignified death in slow, excruciating motion.

There were objects in the falling wreckage, little flashes of ordinary life—an electric teapot and a sweatshirt that had been left on a hook—that made what they were witnessing feel too intimate for public display. Kat blushed to see the stack of books from her bedroom flutter to its demise. Her notes on Kyle would be in there, along with the recovered shreds of his scarf that she'd tucked beneath the stack. Kat didn't see them, but they must have spent a moment exposed and airborne, before being buried in the carnage below and possibly, eventually, swept out to sea.

When the last roof tile finally fell, it left behind the gaping wound of the garage, their glass-working studio. Three of its walls were still intact, and the fourth side—the one that connected it to the house—had pulled away neatly at the seam of the cement floor. The studio opened to the Atlantic Ocean now, so onlookers couldn't quite see in from the street. Knowing that all her glass-working tools were fully exposed felt to Kat like wearing her beating heart on the outside of her body.

No one in the crowd moved or spoke for another beat. They wanted to see if there was more to come.

Then a policewoman quickly made a barrier out of orange tape and instructed everyone to stay back. More cops appeared to shepherd people away from the sidewalk and behind the roadblocks. Kat felt her body being moved. She lost Orla in the chaos. People began chatting in hushed tones around her, sharing what they knew about the shop and its inhabitants. Kat watched their mouths move—some of them may have been speaking to her—but she couldn't make sounds herself. She was sleepwalking through a real-life nightmare.

Police cars and fire trucks flashed, painting the overcast morning in a carnival light.

"C'mon," someone said from behind.

Kat turned to see Sean as he wrapped an arm around her. She leaned into it and let him lead her down the crowded street. He seemed to know where he was going.

They pushed through the people, many of whom placed a sympathetic hand on Sean's arm or made a face to indicate how sorry they were. Sean received these gestures graciously on behalf of them both.

They walked down the steep road to the muddy lawn of a neighboring house, where two officers and an EMT were talking with Orla. When Kat arrived, they all turned to her.

The EMT reached for Kat's wrist and looked up close into her eyes. "Do you think you need ambulatory care?" she asked.

Kat stared at the woman.

"Ma'am, I'm going to have you lay down, if you'll come this way with me."

She shook her head. "No, no, I'm fine. I'm just surprised, I think."

"You're probably in shock," the woman said. "We'll have the ambulance pull around for you."

Kat looked at Orla, who held a brown wool blanket around her shoulders. She was standing, but catatonic. Her clothes and half of her face were covered in mud. Kat understood now what she must have looked like.

"Can I just stay here, please?"

Sean pulled her in. "She's okay. I'll keep an eye on her."

The cops exchanged a glance, and then the older one began. "That was a crazy thing you did out there."

Were they talking to her? Kat looked around.

"Running for your friend," he said, gesturing toward Orla. "That was truly reckless and it should have killed you both... But it didn't. You saved her life."

Orla looked out toward the ocean. She was barely there.

Kat couldn't find words in her head.

The cop wrote something down in his notebook as he spoke. "Really, the two of you must have a goddamn death wish. Out there on those bluffs. You're lucky as hell. Here, this is my phone number."

Orla took the paper.

"Go home, Orla, and rest up. Call me in a few days when you're ready to discuss what happens next with the garage. Until then, don't come back here. It's a disaster site now. You hear me?"

"Yes."

Then he turned to Kat. "I understand you resided at the glass shop?"

She nodded.

"So, do you have somewhere to stay for a while?"

Kat knew the house was gone. She'd watched it fall. But it wasn't until that moment that she began to grasp the full reality of the situation. She had nowhere to sleep, no bed or clothes or books or toothbrush. She had no alarm clock or computer or electric teapot. It was strange how the big things and the small things were all mixed up together in this wave of grief, but they were. Everything familiar and indisputably *hers* was gone.

Kat felt the pressure of Sean's lips and his scratchy face against the side of her forehead. "She has somewhere to stay."

"Good, then." The officer looked around uncomfortably. "If you'll excuse me, we have to get everyone out of here and cordon it off. I'm...I'm very sorry for all of you."

The two police officers and the medic walked away, leaving Kat, Orla and Sean alone on a stranger's lawn.

Kat felt Sean take her hand. He laced his fingers through hers as she turned to watch the ocean waves.

She had no idea where she was supposed to be.

CHAPTER 16

"Can you pass the cream?"

Kat slid the carton across the little folding table that served as Erika's dining area.

"Thank you. More toast?"

"Please."

"This is fun. You know you can stay here for as long as you need to, right?" Erika said, her black hair piled high on top of her head and her mascara from the night before smudged beneath her eyes.

Kat knew she was welcome to stay forever, but she wouldn't. Erika's apartment was not so much an apartment as a room with a minifridge and a bathroom the size of a closet. Kat was sleeping on the pullout couch. She would have to find somewhere else to go eventually. But it was nice for now, and she was glad she decided to stay there instead of Sean's place.

She finished her toast and stood up. "I have to go see Orla. I've put it off long enough."

"You still doing the afternoon shift?"

Kat nodded. She'd taken on a few bartending shifts at The

Lobster Claw in the three weeks since the landslide. Erika was understaffed, and Kat was at risk of succumbing completely to her paranoid trance, so she'd agreed to do the work.

The first shift had been good. She was moving her body and focusing her mind on something other than the trauma of the previous weeks. But then the visions of Kyle intensified. They weren't visions like you saw in movies, when people talked to perfectly articulated ghosts. No, these were just flashes in the corner of her eye, glimpses of the familiar. Kat felt that Kyle was with her sometimes at the bar, like he was working alongside her. She'd forget what was in a Manhattan or whether you were supposed to shake an Aperol spritz and he'd remind her, sort of. She couldn't *hear* him; she wasn't crazy. She could just sort of feel him gently nudging her to the right bottles, telling her when her pours got too long. It was comforting to have him there with her.

Kat couldn't tell Erika about the Kyle visions because she couldn't tell Erika anything about Kyle. It was horrible to keep it all from her, but it had to be done. As far as Erika knew, Kat's dazed state was the byproduct of her trauma. She'd just watched her apartment and her livelihood fall into the ocean, which was enough to devastate anyone. In a strange way, Kat's secrets got easier once the glass shop fell off the cliff. She was suddenly allowed to behave as oddly as she needed to without any reason for suspicion. And that was a good thing because Kat was feeling odder and odder.

It wasn't just her visions of Kyle; those were almost a comfort. The real danger was the paranoia, which had her jumping with every slamming door and honking horn. Her insomnia kept her in a continual state of edgy exhaustion, and the only way through it was movement. She couldn't be still. There was nothing else to do—now that she had no career—but stay busy for as long as she could. Kat's plan was to just keep working the shifts that Erika gave her and wait for someone to come arrest her. That moment felt perpetually imminent. As far as she knew, Ashley was still out there trying to take them all down. Every moment free was borrowed time.

"I'll see you later." Kat kissed the top of Erika's head.

"Good luck."

She felt her pockets for her wallet and phone. Still there. She was wearing Erika's clothes, which fit okay but didn't feel quite right. Kat was in someone else's life, wearing someone else's clothes. She had nothing now, and she was almost too numb to care. She considered going shopping with the money she'd made on *The Selkie*, but hadn't found the will yet. Plus, there was a certain logic to it: losing all your worldly possessions before losing your freedom entirely. She'd read about how people who knew they were going to die would give everything away, shed their material connection to this earth. Maybe it was like that, Kat thought, as if all of this was prewritten. She also considered that she was losing her mind.

"Thanks. I'll see you at the bar."

It took seven minutes to get from the apartment to Orla's house on Erika's rusty bike. The sidewalks were icy and uneven, so Kat stayed mostly in the road. Every third house had electric candles in the windows. God, Christmas. It was two days away and she had no plans. She'd spent the past six Christmases with the Murphys, so this year might only be marked by the absence of all that. The Murphy Christmases had been wonderful. Kat didn't bring any Christmas traditions with her, so she'd gladly adopted all of theirs when she started dating Sean. They were great at Christmas, with all their rules about how to decorate the tree and what foods to eat when. The rules are the rituals, and it's the rituals that remind you of who you are and where you come from. Who would she be now?

"Hi, love." Orla pulled Kat in from the cold with a weak smile. It was the first time they'd seen each other since the landslide.

Kat sat down on the couch, as close as she could get to the crackling woodstove. "I'm sorry I haven't come to see you sooner."

"Me too. It's been quite a time."

"Yeah, it has." Kat noticed that Sean's vest was hanging from the back of a chair. He'd probably been there a lot, taking care of his mother. She looked away, trying not to think of Sean. She hadn't seen him yet, either. He'd tried, but she needed to think about things first.

"Tea?"

"No, thank you." Kat rubbed her cold thighs. "Orla, have you been back...to where the shop was?"

Orla sat back down. "I've driven by. The town says they're going to demolish it. They have some kind of natural disaster fund to pay for the removal, but we have to get the glassblowing equipment out of the garage in the next month. I don't know where we'd take it. We could try to sell it, I suppose..."

Kat looked at her hands. This was worse than seeing Kyle's face. It was almost worse than thinking you were about to be found out as a murderer or a person lying about not being a murderer. Seeing Orla so lost, and imagining the end of her glass-working business, was almost worse than all the other terrible things.

"I don't know what we should do with it all."

"I'll figure something out," Orla nearly whispered, unconvinced. "So how have you been holding up?"

"I'm fine. I wanted to know if *you're* fine. Orla, is there something I can do for you?"

Orla looked out through a fogged window. "Will you come with me?" It seemed like she'd been waiting to ask.

"To the studio?"

"No, to the beach. Most of the stuff washed away, but I hear some of it is still there."

Oh God, Kat didn't want to go back to that shoreline, the site of every recent tragedy in her life. Those waters just kept taking. "Yeah, okay."

Minutes later, they were parking Orla's car on the road and walking down the stairs toward the place where their house had fallen. Normally, Island Glass would be to their right, but today it was just their three-sided garage, still full of their glass-working tools, sitting before a void.

Orla went first. She was surprisingly eager. Why she hadn't done this on her own, Kat couldn't say, but there was a certain honor in being asked to accompany her. It was the last place on earth that Kat wanted to be, but she was also grateful for the closeness it intimated.

They walked quietly along the water's edge, just out of reach of the waves, but close enough for their boots to leave deep impressions in the wet sand. Kat had one of Orla's scarves wrapped twice around her neck. It kept whipping up into her face with the wind. If only Kyle hadn't worn a scarf on that night, she thought.

"It's not what I pictured," Orla said as they arrived at their heap.

The pile of frozen sand, clay, broken floor planks, glass and domestic flotsam had settled into something semipermanent there on the beach, under a thin coating of fresh snow. Waves lapped at the eastern edge of it, but nothing budged. All the broken parts with their rough edges had fused together into a hideous icicle. It made Kat angry that local authorities hadn't bothered to give this fallen existence an adequate burial. It was a corpse left to rot. No, it was worse than that, because the frigid weather would preserve it for months. It was a frozen corpse, incapable of degrading and deprived of burial.

Orla tucked a gray lock back into her hat. "It looks small."

"You think?"

"I thought there'd be more here. There was so much of it when it fell."

Kat considered this. "Cleaned up. Or washed away, I guess… I wish all of it would wash away."

"No," Orla scolded her. "You don't want that. This is a gift. We can take something from this. And whatever we take can be a proxy for all the things we couldn't take. Stories need a place to live, Kat. I don't know how to take the stories with me without something to hold in my hand."

Kat nodded. She didn't feel the same way, but she liked the idea of it. And she had nothing left to hold.

They examined the pile. The broken remnant of a ceramic mug peeked up through the snow, the handle still intact. This wasn't one of the artful pieces from the glass shop. It was a relic of their real life. Kat recognized the pale blue color and the chipped underside. It was a mug that Weeta had given Orla for some holiday many years ago, before Kat was in the picture. Best Grandma—that's what it used to say. The mug had migrated from Orla's kitchen to the counter of the shop, and up to Kat's apartment somehow. It had become invisible, but now Kat could see it again.

Orla reached down and brushed the snow aside, revealing more clay and part of a console table. None of these sad, broken parts seemed worthy of Orla's stories.

How tiny their life looked, buried in a heap for the world to observe and the vultures to pick at. Kat wondered if others had been there to gawk over the previous three weeks, or worse, if no one had been there at all and the world had already moved on.

Kat hated this pile. She'd owned nothing of value and wouldn't miss any item in particular, but this stuff was evidence of her existence. She'd been here. And then, she'd been wiped away...everything but her body. Kat had the unnerving realization that if in fact she was going to prison and her body disappeared from the free world, she would be effectively erased. Her glass art was supposed to be her proof of existence. Now that it was gone, she would disappear completely.

"You know what I wish?" Orla said, turning toward the ocean. "I wish I'd taken on more apprentices. I think teaching you, and watching you grow, was the most enjoyable part of all this. I should have done it more."

Kat's mind stumbled back to reality. "I'm very grateful for it."

"I know you are, love. You don't have to keep thanking me. I'm telling you that it was as much for me as it was for you. I'm grateful too."

Kat had the feeling that Orla was talking about everything now, not just the apprenticeship. She was grateful that Kat had dragged her flailing body away from the house as it fell off a cliff. She didn't have to say that she was grateful for that, but she was.

"You're a good teacher."

Orla looked back at the pile. "Yes, I think I am. I should have taught classes or held workshops." She pulled the hat from her head and let the chilly wind blow her hair about. "You know, these past weeks, I've been doing my best to move on to the next chapter, to accept that this career is behind me. But I don't feel like an old woman yet. I'm not done. That's the worst part of all this. If I were old and tired and spent, this would be easier. But I'm not."

Kat pushed her hands deep into her pockets. "I'm so sorry."

The ocean waves approached and toppled just a few feet away, unmoved by their loss.

Orla reached down and wrapped her fingers around the edges of a small book about glass-working technique from the 1970s. She jostled it free from the wreckage and inspected it closely. Its pages were frozen shut and its hardcover barely hung on, but it was a real thing that meant something once. "Let's go," she said.

They walked back the same way they came, stepping along the same footprints in wet sand.

When they got up to the road, Kat put her arms around Orla and hugged quickly. It was too brief for Orla to reciprocate properly. They didn't do that often, touch. Restraint was a shared value between them. But Kat had the nagging sense that this might be the last time she'd see Orla—and the last time Orla would see her in this innocent light—and so it was a goodbye hug.

"I'm just gonna walk from here," Kat said. "I'll pick up the bike later."

Orla nodded. "Okay, love. I'll be in touch about the glass-working equipment in the garage. We'll figure something out."

"Okay."

"And, Kat?"

She turned around.

"Call Sean."

"Okay."

Orla got in her car and drove away.

Kat began walking. The sidewalk had recently been salted and each footstep made a grinding sound as the pink granules scraped against cobblestone. She wasn't going to call Sean, not yet. Their dynamic made her uncomfortable. He'd wanted her to stay with him because he was grateful that she'd saved his mother, and because he pitied her, but he didn't really *want* her. She needed him to want her for real. Kat wouldn't see Sean until he truly forgave her for what she'd done to Kyle. She would have to just wait for him to get there on his own. And if she were arrested for homicide before that happened, well, then it would be a moot point.

One thing was for sure, Kat wasn't going to beg for anyone's forgiveness. She'd done what she had to do in the moment. She was beginning to forgive herself for it and she didn't want to walk that progress back one step.

Kat wondered whether Sean was still in contact with Ashley. There was no way for her to really know. She seemed to have disappeared from their lives after the night in Hyannis, but Kat knew better than that. Ashley was too dogged and too hurt to just fade away. She may have given up on Hunter and Sean, but there was no way she'd given up on revenge. She was out there somewhere, still trying to bring them down.

Three guys walked past Kat on the otherwise empty sidewalk, laughing and smoking along the way.

She inhaled through their cloud. Strange how many people smoked on the island, particularly in the off-season. Kat imagined it was the influence of all the Eastern Europeans who came on work visas, but she didn't really know. The smoking contributed to the general off-season mood of gritty survivalism and not giving a fuck for the conventions of the mainland. If Kat were a smoker, this would be a good time to have one, she thought.

Kyle was a smoker. She'd seen him with that one cigarette on their walk to the boat. His long, knobby fingers had held it at just the right practiced angle. He'd looked almost cool, but not entirely comfortable. Like all the mannerisms she'd observed on him that night, there'd been a self-consciousness to it.

Kat blinked and, when she opened her eyes, Kyle was right there in front of her.

She stopped and looked up into his face. He was clearer than usual. This wasn't a feeling or a whisper, but a three-dimensional body. He was real.

Kat couldn't move.

Kyle sucked angrily on the stub of his cigarette and blew a puff of smoke into her face.

She began to cough.

He smirked and blew another puff at her.

She coughed again, lightly at first, and then harder and harder until she was choking. Kat doubled over and put her hands on her knees. She couldn't catch her breath. She was choking and gasping for air while, somewhere above her head, she heard Kyle laughing maniacally. He was watching her choke—maybe to death—and he was just laughing. She deserved it. As the smoke burned through her lungs, it felt like justice. She would die of ghost smoke inhalation right there on the street, and he would watch, and she would deserve it.

Kyle laughed.

Kat's throat was closing, tighter and tighter. The more she tried to gasp for air, the harder it became.

Kyle laughed harder still.

You deserve this, Kat thought as she choked.

"Ma'am," another voice said from afar.

You deserve this.

"Ma'am."

There was a hand on her back, a real human hand. It

barely registered through the panic and delirium, though. She needed oxygen. She would die if she didn't get oxygen. Kat's vision had blurred into nothing and a blackness was seeping in.

"Ma'am!"

She coughed and sucked, coughed and sucked, over and over until—finally—air flooded her lungs. Was she dead?

"Ma'am, are you okay?"

The pale pink salt on the cobblestone came back into focus and Kat could suddenly feel the cold ground beneath her knees. Someone was there, calling to her.

She wiped her mouth. For a half second, she thought she was looking up at Hunter's father, Senator Briggs. He was tall and broad, with skin that had been creased by age, but softened by affluence. He looked happy even through his concern. But it wasn't the senator. This was just another handsome rich man in an overcoat. He looked genuinely worried for her.

"Are you okay?" He helped Kat to her feet. "Do you want me to call for help? I think you had a panic attack."

She looked around. There was no one else there. It was just the two of them: Kat and this impossibly well-groomed creature whose life was nothing like hers. She hated him, based on nothing more than what she could see. That was her first impression of this nice person who was trying to help her—that he was a lucky bastard to have been born him and not her.

The nice man stared at Kat.

She stared back as the world came into focus for her. This man had everything and Kat had less than nothing. She had a deep, insurmountable deficit. And that deficit was proof that the world was unfair. But it was also permission to do what survival demanded. Kat deserved to survive.

And then she knew what she would do.

"Ma'am, do you want me to call a doctor?"

"No, thank you. I'm okay now. I'm sorry to freak you out."

"Please, don't apologize. I just want to make sure you're okay. Can I call you a car?" He searched his pockets for a phone.

"Yeah, thanks. A car would be great."

Kat waited while the man summoned his car service with a few finger strokes. Yes, Kat would be perfectly happy accepting a free ride in a black sedan from a stranger, for goddamn once in her life. She might just ride it around the island for a while. She might sleep in it that night and make it her new apartment until this kind gentleman realized he'd been scammed. But of course, she would not do that because she had other things to do now. She had a plan.

The car arrived less than a minute later, as if it had been hovering just out of sight for whenever it was beckoned.

Kat thanked the man and slid into the dark, leather interior, which looked exactly as she hoped it would.

"Morning," the driver said. He wore a suit and tie, which struck Kat as totally ridiculous.

"Fourteen Common Street, please."

The driver looked into his rearview mirror. "That's three blocks away. You sure?"

"I am, thanks."

"Yes, ma'am. Water and pretzels are in the armrest."

Half a bottle of Fijian springwater later, Kat was closing the car door behind her and walking up the front stairs to Hunter's house. As had become the new norm, there were no visible lights on in the house. Hunter seemed to believe that an unlit home rendered him invisible. He apparently likened the police to a group of children in Halloween costumes. As if, upon coming to arrest him, they might find the porch light off and just move along to the next house instead.

She turned the knob and the door cracked open, so Kat helped herself into the shadows of the foyer.

Hunter was there in the dark. "Hey, I was wondering about you."

"Can we turn some lights on in here? This is ghoulish."

"Yeah, I guess so." He led her into the den where he'd apparently been spending all his time. There were no windows in the den. "So? What's going on?" he asked.

Kat sat at the edge of the couch. Hunter took the chair opposite her. This was the first time they'd seen each other since the morning after their night together, the morning of the landslide. They weren't ignoring each other; that was understood. But the landslide changed the nature of what had happened between them. Their night together seemed frivolous in the wake of the fallen house. They were already in a morally gray area as far as Kat was concerned. She wasn't officially *with* Sean when she slept with Hunter, but she was still trying to patch things up. Sean would have deemed it wrong, and he probably would never have done it himself. Kat felt guilty about it—and the part she felt most terrible about was how incredibly fun it had been. She was almost relieved to busy herself with the ghost of Kyle and her mounting paranoia to not have to consider what great sex with Hunter meant. She had no idea what Hunter thought.

Today, though, Kat was not making any decisions about those things. Today she was fixing other things.

"Hunter, I know we have a bunch of stuff to talk about. And we should get to that stuff—obviously—at some point. But right now, I'm wondering if the money is still on the table."

"My dad's money? Yeah, of course." He was confused.

"Okay, good." Kat unzipped her coat and set it beside her. "I think I want it now. May I have it quickly?"

Hunter squinted like he was trying to read illegible handwriting. "Yeah, my father's been bugging me about it. Of course you can have it. What changed?"

"How much is it again?"

"It's 1.3 million. He said it was the remainder of an old account that he has offshore, something that he wanted to close anyway. What are you going to do with it?"

"Can I just…have it, for now? I'll explain everything later. I'm sorry to be rude, but can I just have it?"

Hunter was dumbstruck. "Yeah, sure. I'll call Lars right now and get it started." He walked into the kitchen and made a phone call.

Two minutes later, Hunter came back and asked Kat to write down her bank account number while he held the phone to his shoulder. She found the number on her smartphone and scribbled it onto a notepad. He went back into the kitchen for more hushed conversation, and then returned.

"Congratulations," he said. "You're rich…for a poor person."

He seemed irritated.

"What happens now?" she asked.

"The money will be wired to your account. Legally speaking, it's a gift. If anyone asks, this was a gift from a friend. Do not report it on your tax return and don't do anything conspicuous with it."

Kat was surprised by how fluent Hunter sounded in this language of white-collar debauchery. "Okay, I get it."

"This means that we never speak of that night again. Sean too. If either of you ever feel a stroke of conscience, know that my father will have you convicted of extortion. The money is probably already in your account, so it's done, and we're in this together now."

Kat felt a little sickened by the terms, but excited too. Hunter would understand in the end…if this worked.

She stood up and put her arms around him. "Thank you. I'm going to explain this really soon. I just need to do this on my own first. I promise I'll tell you everything."

He nodded and watched her go.

Kat nearly flew out of the house, down the front steps and southward toward town. She felt suddenly warm and excited as she walked along the cobblestone, nothing at all like the harried weakling who'd collapsed in a panic on that very street an hour before. Now she had purpose. Because what she saw in the blurry haze of her fear was the opportunity before her: Ashley was going to lead the police to her, and so her life (and sadly, Hunter's) was probably over. She could spend every moment leading up to her arrest in terror, or she could live like someone who had nothing to lose and devote her remaining time as a free person to making things right—or *more* right—for the people who deserved better. She was going to exact her own kind of justice on the world.

Her first priority was to give Orla another chapter in this story. That would be easy.

It was the Kyle piece—phase two—that made her nervous.

CHAPTER 17

"You're cracking them wrong, Dad." Weeta looked up from her book with a bored glance. She was sitting at the table in Sean's kitchen, watching him makes eggs on Christmas morning.

"What are you talking about? This is how people crack eggs."

She rolled her eyes. "We did an experiment in science class and I'm telling you, you're using the surface pressure wrong."

Sean kept cracking egg after egg into the bowl, just as he always had. This was his favorite thing in the world: Christmas with Weeta. He only got it every two years and so it felt extra precious when it was his turn. Particularly this year. All of the eggs had already broken this year. Nothing was as it should be, nothing except his daughter. The morning felt thinner and quieter without Kat, who'd been with his family on those mornings for so many years. She usually made the bacon, in the oven, with maple syrup drizzled over it. Sean had forgotten about the bacon. It was still in the fridge.

Orla walked in, still wrapped up in her scarf and hat. "Is breakfast ready?"

Sean appreciated the effort she was making to be cheerful.

"Almost." Weeta looked up at her grandmother. "Dad's making eggshell omelets."

"Perfect. That's my favorite kind. Let's do presents while he cooks!"

Orla and Weeta went into the living room while Sean finished breakfast. There was a coffee cake from the expensive place in Tisbury, plus eggs, clementines and grocery store eggnog. He'd even bought real pine boughs from the winter farmers market to decorate the table with. It felt a little forced, like overcompensation for their small numbers. But it was necessary.

Sean had decided he didn't want Kat there this year. Christmas was sacred and Weeta was sacred, and he couldn't grant her access to those things until he was completely sure that he could live with their new reality. It wouldn't have been fair to flounder on this. Getting together and breaking back up was for people without kids. He didn't have the luxury of anything short of total assurance. So while he felt really bad about not inviting Kat to Christmas, he was also sure it was the right move under the circumstances.

"Oh-my-God-yes!" Weeta squealed from the other room. "The is *exactly* the one I wanted. Thank you, Nana!"

Sean worried about his mother. He had been doing his very best to keep her close, invite her over as much as possible and assure her that he'd figure it all out. But he had no solutions to offer, only fake cheer. Sean worried about his mother's future more than his own. Orla was too private and stoic to ever cry on Sean's shoulder, but she was approaching something like depression.

That was probably the word for it: *depression*. It was an utterly logical response to the violent way in which Orla's whole life had been ripped from her. It was also the literal state of her life—every material thing that meant anything to her had fallen away. Her work, her shop…it was all frozen in an ice-packed depression on the beach now. Every day Sean had to drive past the place, which was now just a three-walled garage that stood naked to the elements. The police tape was still wrapped around the perimeter of the property, but it had begun to sag and fade. One of the wooden posts that held up the tape was on its side, buried by snow. It looked so much more hopeless now than it had on the day of the landslide, before the sand and reality settled in.

"Daddy, we're hungry!"

Bing Crosby's Christmas album was playing in the other room and Sean was reminded of his role as chief officer of cheerfulness. "It's ready. Let's eat!"

They sat down to the full table and poured more coffee. Bing crooned in the background. It was still okay, just the three of them.

Sean piled steaming eggs onto each plate. "You get extra shells."

Weeta laughed and picked at her coffee cake, apparently too old to just shove it into her mouth like she used to.

A muffled knock came from outside.

Orla looked up. "Is someone here?"

Sean put the egg dish down and went to the window. And goddamn it, there was Kat. She was bouncing slightly, looking chilly and impatient. He couldn't resist feeling a little relieved to see her. She shouldn't be there, but he was still relieved to see her.

"I'll get it. You guys sit," Sean instructed.

He went to the door and opened it just enough to peek out at her.

"Hi!" Kat had an eager, uncomplicated excitement about her. "May I come in?"

He stepped aside, without quite inviting her.

"Kat, I thought we decided we weren't doing this, this year," Sean whispered.

"Oh, I..." Her voice trailed off as she looked around. "Oh my God, it's Christmas."

"Did you not know it was Christmas? Are you okay?"

She looked apologetic, but she didn't move.

"Kat, Weeta and my mom are here."

Her eyes got wide. "Oh God, I'm sorry. I didn't mean to just barge in. I kind of forgot. I mean, I'm all alone at Erika's apartment this weekend...she's with her family, and Hunter's with his...and I meant to do something to celebrate. I've been busy, and I sort of lost track of what day it was."

Seeing her wide-eyed and confused like that was validation that he'd done the right thing—and it made him angry to see her there, undermining his choice to keep her away. "You need to go," he whispered. "This is too confusing for my family."

"Oh, but I have some good news! It's actually better that they're all here. I, ah...yeah, I can tell everyone at once. It's even better this way."

"No, Kat."

"Is that Kat I hear?" Orla appeared in the doorway.

"Hey, Orla!"

"C'mon in and have some brunch, love."

Sean scratched aggressively at his beard.

Kat followed Orla to the dining area, but she didn't sit.

"Hi, Weeta. I'm sorry to burst in on Christmas, you guys."

Sean folded his arms and watched her, afraid of what unstable behavior she might unleash before them.

Weeta looked around in confusion. "Are you having Christmas with your family?"

"Ah, yes. I am," she said, stumbling. "So don't worry about

me. Anyhow, I have some great news. It's a Christmas present, actually! That's why I'm here."

Orla raised her eyebrows and sipped coffee.

"I've found us—well, *you*—a new glass shop and studio."

Everyone stared.

Kat smiled. "It's true. You know that ancient little barn on Winding Hill Road? The one we always say that someone should renovate? It's yours now."

She had lost her mind. Sean was sure of it.

"I bought it! It's being repainted this week. They're going to move the equipment in as soon as the heat shields are up in the back room. Everything should be done in a few months. It's small, but it's beautiful."

Orla was frozen, her coffee mug suspended at half sip. "I don't understand what you're saying."

"I'm saying that I'm giving you this. It's yours. You can teach glass working there, open another shop…whatever you want! It's a gift."

Weeta's mouth fell open. "Whoa. Dad, did you know about this?"

Sean shook his head. He was cautiously angry, sure that this was some kind of mirage destined to create more heartbreak for them later. "I *didn't* know about it. What are you saying, Kat? How did you do this?" But he realized the answer even before he was done with the question. It was the money.

Kat looked back and forth at each expectant face. "I, ah…a distant relative died a few months back and apparently left me some money. I didn't even know him. But I guess he was kinda rich. So this really just fell into my lap. It all just happened very quickly."

Sean wished for her to stop, to minimize the number of lies that she would tell—the lies she would tell badly—

to these people who didn't deserve lies. He could see that she didn't enjoy this part, either. She was talking about the money that Hunter's family offered her for her silence. And if her silence was bought, well then his was too. It made him somehow a party to Kyle's death, or murder, or whatever really happened that night. And now, because his family was the beneficiary of this money, they were all unwittingly a party to it. But Sean wasn't going to contradict her. The look on his mother's face made the lies almost worth it.

Orla stood up slowly, her eyes filling with tears. "Is this real, Kat?"

Kat began to cry. She nodded.

Orla pulled her in and hugged her. She hugged and hugged, and Sean couldn't remember a time when either of them behaved so unabashedly emotional.

Weeta began to cry. She looked up at her father for permission to believe it all. He put his hands on her shoulders and did his best to appreciate what was happening.

The money was ugly, but the rest of it was beautiful. Kat didn't have to do this. And regardless of its origins, Kat needed this money as much as any of them and wouldn't have been faulted for keeping it all to herself. It was a selfless act, if a complicated one.

Orla released Kat and wiped her eyes. "You can't do this."

"It's already done, Orla. I knew you wouldn't let me, so it's already done. It's yours."

"And this rich relative? What's the story with this?"

Kat glanced at Sean, missing hardly a beat. "It just happened. I didn't really believe it myself. But the money was never really mine, so I won't miss it." That part was true.

Orla shook her head. She seemed skeptical about the origins of the money too, but Sean could tell that she wasn't going to press it. It was a gift that she desperately needed and so she was just going to accept it unquestioningly. As rational as she was, Orla also held closely to the wisdom of not questioning God's grace when it presented itself. Miracles annulled explanation.

Weeta kept smiling and watching her father. "This is amazing, Kat. I can't believe it. Daddy, isn't this amazing?"

Sean smiled. "It is amazing, honey. It's amazing." He went to Kat and hugged her. It was the closest they'd been in weeks. He wanted to drink in her smell and the feel of her body beneath her coat. Her wet cheek soaked into his shirt. Their lives had gotten so fucked up, but he felt the same about her body in his arms. He didn't want to let go.

They came apart and looked at each other, aware of Orla's and Weeta's gazes.

"Thank you," he said. And he meant it. Seeing her smile before him, and feeling her tears on his chest, he felt the depth of her love for his family, and her capacity for goodness. She'd always been good, but the past few weeks made him question everything. She'd made one very bad choice on that night, but everything she'd done since then had been bigger and braver than he'd ever been. She saved his mother once. And now she was saving them all.

If morality was measured as a tally, a scoreboard on which points are accrued by the opposing teams of good and evil, then she was surely at a positive balance. That should be enough, Sean thought. That should be enough for him.

"I have to go," Kat said.

"No, stay!" Weeta protested.

"No, I have to do my Christmas thing. Just wanted to stop by to tell you this."

Sean knew she didn't have any Christmas plans. She'd forgotten about the holiday altogether. But he didn't ask her to stay. He was almost there, almost sure that she was right for him and his family, that he could live with the weight of the truth…

But goddamn it, why did she have to go on the boat with Hunter on that night? Why did she always seem to listen to him? Everything would be the same if that night hadn't happened and they hadn't made so many poor choices! And as his racing mind picked up steam, Sean became aware of other resentments he held—resentments that predated that night. Like the fact that she insisted on living alone, instead of moving in with him. She was holding him up, and holding up their ability to be a real family. He wanted to marry her eventually, but she wasn't even ready to live with him. How long was she going to make him wait? What was wrong with her?

The depth of Sean's anger surprised him, but he didn't wish it away. Kat deserved his anger. Because it wasn't *his* fault they were in this position. It wasn't his fault she had to go home to Erika's empty apartment with no plans on Christmas. It was all Kat's. Kat had done this to them, and he couldn't invite her to stay until he stopped feeling so hurt by her selfish, reckless choices.

"I'll walk you out," he said with a hand on her back.

Kat looked like she was on the verge of tears again, though it was difficult to tell if they were happy or sad tears.

Orla pulled her in for one more hug. "We love you."

"I know," she sniffed. "I love you guys too."

Kat and Sean walked out together, just the two of them, into the dim December morning. It was so quiet, you could almost hear the waves hitting the dock from several blocks away.

"Really, Kat, thank you," Sean said when they got outside. "We don't have to talk about how you did it, but I'm grateful."

She nodded, happy but eager to be done with the conversation. "I know you don't approve, Sean, but everything is just more complicated than that now."

"I know." He did.

She looked around like there was something else on her mind. "Sean, I'm sorry to ask you this, but…have you seen Ashley lately?"

"I told you I'm not seeing her."

"I know, I know." She wiped her running nose with a sleeve. "But have you run into her? Do you know what she's up to?"

"Yeah, I saw her once at the coffee shop. She still seemed really mad at me. She said something about Island Glass—that she was sorry, I think—but also that it didn't change anything."

"That's what she said?"

Sean thought again. "Um, yeah, I think she said 'it doesn't really change anything.' I got the feeling she was talking about that night…or, her theories about that night."

Kat nodded quickly and looked around. It seemed like she was in a hurry. "Yeah, well, she's right, I guess. It doesn't really change anything about that night." She pulled her coat zipper up as high as it would go. "Okay, anyway, that's kinda what I thought."

"Kat, are you okay?"

"Yes, I am. I will be. I just have some things to do."

She gave a quick nod and turned from him. Then she mounted an old road bike and skidded away on the icy sidewalk.

Sean went back inside to find Orla and Weeta digging into breakfast. The room smelled of fresh coffee and burning wood. In a matter of minutes, their appetites had returned and their senses had been restored. The gloomy fog they'd been trying to see each other through had lifted completely. Kat had done all that. With her toxic money, she'd given them back their lives.

After breakfast, they would pile into Orla's car, drive out to the little renovated barn that would become her new glass-works studio and envision a future.

CHAPTER 18

"You good?" Erika yelled from the end of the bar.

Hunter nodded.

She was consolidating the contents of the cheap liquor bottles, which meant that her afternoon shift was almost over.

Hunter didn't want to leave, not because he cared much about getting drunk on that day, but because he couldn't stand to be alone in his big house.

Erika walked around and took a seat beside him on a bar stool. They were all alone in the restaurant. With the holiday traffic gone and January's long stretch ahead, they'd probably be alone there a lot in the coming weeks.

"You look good," she said.

Hunter smiled. He felt good, in a way. He hadn't smoked pot or blacked out in three weeks. He hadn't even had a real hangover in that time. Hunter imagined this was what normal people felt like, people who didn't have all the time and money in the world to indulge their vices. It wasn't that he'd quit drinking. He'd just been feeling different ever since the day of the landslide, less desperate for sensorial thrills.

No one noticed him at the landslide, but Hunter had

watched the whole thing from the street. He'd seen Orla rush the falling house, and Kat go after her. He watched them struggle and fall, then cry as it all went down. He'd seen Sean scream after them while two big cops held him back. And he'd felt his heart stop at what looked like Kat running to her death.

Everyone watching thought they would die, Hunter too. And every day since, he could see that clarion image of Kat's brush with death, as fresh as when it had happened. It was his most alive moment, his most frightened and helpless too. But it was the aliveness that stayed with him.

Just hours before the landslide, Hunter had been holding all the small, strong parts of Kat's naked body. He could still feel the hard angles of her hips and shoulders pressing into him, and the softness of her hair in his hands, as he watched her run toward the cliff. It made him want to survive. Even Kyle's death hadn't produced such a loud call to life as Kat's near-death. And that was why he could sit there at the bar in a tempest of anxiety while also feeling slightly more grateful to still be alive. People die all the time in the most thoughtless ways, but Hunter was still alive, and that suddenly seemed miraculous.

Hunter missed Kat.

"Have you heard from her yet?"

He shook his head and sipped his Chardonnay. He'd been trying to stay calm about her absence, but it was getting harder by the day.

Erika reached over the bar and pulled up the full bottle and a glass for herself. She poured and drank. "You haven't told me where you think she is."

"I don't know," he sighed. "I think she probably decided that there was nothing left for her here, now that the glass shop is gone." That isn't what Hunter thought, but it was the best lie he could come up with. What he really thought was that Kat had taken his father's money and left town before Ashley led the cops to them. She was gutsy enough to do it, he knew that. But he was surprised that she'd be selfish enough to do it without so much as a goodbye to anyone. It was a deserved selfishness—self-preservation, really. But it was uncharacteristic.

Erika drank. "Doesn't sound like her. I think she's coming back. It's only been a week."

"Week and a day. Did she leave anything at the apartment?"

She shrugged. "She didn't really have anything to leave."

She does now, Hunter thought. She has more than a million dollars…somewhere.

"All she said was that she was going away for a few days. But it's been more than a few days now…" Erika bit her nail. "By the way, I know you guys had a thing."

"What?" Hunter was shocked. They were close, but he assumed Kat didn't tell anyone about that night, because of Sean.

"I mean, I don't really *know*, but I could tell. You're, like, her favorite person…aside from me." Erika tipped the wine bottle toward him. "You want the rest of this?"

"Sure… But what about Sean?"

"Sean's great. Everybody loves Sean."

The wine tasted cheap and floral upon further consideration. "Yep, everybody loves Sean."

Erika stood up and went behind the bar to get her purse and coat. She didn't like hanging out there once her shift was over.

Hunter stood up from his bar stool. "You need a ride home?"

"No, I'm going over to Buzzy's for dinner." She touched his arm. "Don't worry. I think she's gonna show up."

Hunter nodded solemnly and followed her out to the street. There was one hour of daylight left, but the canopy of clouds made it feel like nighttime.

"Sure you don't want a ride?"

"No, I'll see you later." Erika walked in the other direction, and Hunter went to his car.

The interior leather of the BMW was cold as he slid into the driver seat. It had been ages since Hunter had driven home from a bar. Under difference circumstances, it would have seemed like a real victory to leave with nary a buzz. But the circumstances hadn't been normal for a while and there was nothing to celebrate.

As he drove along the empty winding streets, Hunter remembered the chore he'd been working to forget. He needed to clean the boat. Night after night, he'd resolved to go down to the dock after dark and give the boat a proper cleaning so that his father could sell it. He should have done it by now. If Ashley was working with the cops and Kyle's case was still open, someone would be knocking on his door any day now to take a look at that boat. He needed to be sure there were no remnants of Kyle's scarf in the motor, no empty bottles from The Undertow in the garbage. He needed to check every corner of that godforsaken boat until he was sure there was nothing left of Kyle in it.

Hunter had already promised Kat and his father that it was done. Weeks had passed since then. But the last time he attempted to clean the boat, Sean and Ashley had found them. And Ashley got suspicious, and Sean accused Kat of cheating, and Hunter got a black eye.

He'd almost finished the job, and now he was afraid to go back. Anyone could be watching that boat now, just waiting for him to go down there and give them proof of his guilt. Ashley could be down there. The ghost of Kyle could be down there.

Hunter imagined Kyle's body, still tethered to the murderous machine as they drove back to shore. They'd dragged him for a few seconds. Hunter had felt it, though he didn't know what the drag was at the time. It wasn't he who had killed Kyle, and it wasn't Kat. It was the fucking boat. He couldn't bring himself to be near it.

Hunter considered all of these things as he drove along the winding road in the fading daylight, with the heat blasting onto his cold hands. He hated the boat. The boat was holding so many bad feelings from those months that it was a wonder it hadn't sunk to the bottom of the ocean with everything else. With Kyle. Hunter could almost forget about the specific person named Kyle Billings when he wasn't thinking about the boat. He was always thinking of the distant abstraction of his guilt, but he didn't often think about Kyle's face, his mannerisms, the way he died and the fact that he was a real human people had known—until he remembered the boat. Then it all came back. If he could set the boat on fire and push it out into the waves, he would. But that would look suspicious, so he couldn't do that.

Hunter pulled the car into his driveway and walked into the dark house through the back door. He'd get to the boat tomorrow.

CHAPTER 19

Kat watched as a family of six pulled overstuffed suitcases onto the bus and negotiated the dispersal of their children and luggage. The Greyhound was nearly full. She turned her attention back to flattening her map on the empty seat beside her and avoiding eye contact with the new passengers. She couldn't spare the seat.

"No, honey," the mother whispered to her daughter as they walked down the aisle. "I don't think that seat is available."

They had forty-five minutes to go before the Tampa stop and, although it was rude, Kat couldn't spare the space that her maps, notepads and granola bar wrappers now occupied. She clutched the duffel bag in her lap and tried to look busy.

The person in the row ahead opened a window, sending a blast of hot Florida air back into her face. They weren't supposed to open those sliding windows—because of the air-conditioning—which didn't make any sense because the air-conditioning wasn't working. The driver had been scolding people about it since Jacksonville. Kat leaned forward and took a long gulp of the warm air. It was unseasonably hot, even for Florida.

Kat could have hired a driver for this journey. She had a million dollars now. No, she'd *had* one point three million dollars. Then she bought and began renovations on an antique barn on Martha's Vineyard to give to Orla. Now she had five hundred and sixty-two thousand dollars. In a day, half of her new fortune disappeared, and what a relief it was. It wasn't just the pleasure of giving it to Orla and Sean. It was also that she didn't feel right walking around with the money to her name. It compounded her paranoia and guilt. So she felt a little lighter on this day than she had a week before. But she wouldn't feel right until she accomplished her full plan.

"Next stop, Waldo," the driver announced, just loud enough for the first five rows to hear.

Kat looked at her map. She was close—not as close as she'd be if she'd hired a private driver with her secret fortune, and she didn't have to stop at every depressing outpost in northeastern Florida—but close.

She didn't mind the bus. It was unpleasant, but it was a familiar unpleasantness. Kat thought of her many Greyhound rides from Buffalo to Cleveland when she was thirteen. Her mom's boyfriend at the time had moved there for a supposedly lucrative job, and so they went to meet him on weekends for several months. Eventually, one of them did something terrible to the other that Kat never knew the specifics of, and that guy disappeared from their life, along with the Greyhound trips.

The last Greyhound bus Kat had taken was from Buffalo to Martha's Vineyard—one way, seven years ago. That one took a long time. They always took longer than you thought because of all the stops, and the stops were the worst. When the driver allowed, Kat knew enough to stay on the bus during the stops. A bus littered with fast-food wrappers and stinking of a full toilet tank was still better than most of America's bus stops. The stops didn't used to be so bad, she recalled. Not all of them. Now, though…now they were unofficial homeless shelters, drug markets and bustling intersections of unregulated economies. *Don't look at the girls who look too sexy*—that's what Kat's mom had told her years before. She'd forgotten about that rule and how much it had terrified her, until now. There weren't any sexy girls on this bus for this trip, just people who looked hot and worn-out from trying to get by with what they had.

Kat reached into her pocket and unraveled the note she'd been carrying since Jasper: "22 Juno Lane." That's all it said. Kat didn't need to read it anymore. She'd looked at that piece of paper so many times already that she'd probably never forget it again. But she liked to take it out and read it every now and then to make sure her memory of it hadn't changed—22 Juno Lane.

The whole trip was only supposed to take a few days— and it wasn't supposed to involve the bus. Kat was going to rent a car in Boston and drive down to Jasper with just one overnight along the way. She was going to knock on doors on Kyle's old street, maybe ask around at a few local establishments, and then find Kyle's mom.

It didn't happen that way. And eight days into this ordeal, Kat wasn't sure if she was any closer to her goal.

Kat leaned her head back into the soft cushion of the bus seat and ran through the events of the previous days, taking stock of her failures.

It took several days to drive down to Jasper, including the necessary overnights in cheap hotels. She could have stayed in nicer ones, but it didn't feel right to Kat. This wasn't a vacation.

When she finally arrived in Florida, she'd gone straight to her first destination: an address she'd found through free internet search sites for tracking people down. It came up twice with Kyle's name, which seemed promising. But Kat arrived to find the house unoccupied, boarded up and stripped of anything useful. She would have knocked on a neighbor's door, but only two other houses on the foreclosure-ridden street seemed currently occupied, and there was no one home at either. So she found a motel right off the highway and spent the evening planning her next move.

The following morning, Kat went to a diner in the strip mall closest to the original house and asked the waitress if she knew Kyle. The lady told her that she did not, and that Kat should mind her own business.

From there, Kat drove to the offices of a local construction company, the name of which she'd seen on a T-shirt Kyle was wearing in one of his high school yearbook photos. She figured he, or maybe a relative, had worked there at some point. The large man at the desk with hands that looked like burned roast beef told her that the business had been bought and sold twice in the last ten years and that no one there "knew anything about anything."

As she walked to her car on that fruitless morning, fighting back tears of defeat and frustration, Kat stopped at a parked van with the company's logo printed on the side. She knocked on the window at the man in the driver seat. He rolled it down slowly, taking in her whole body as he did. Kat asked him if he knew Kyle. And the man said, "How 'bout you get in and we drive around a while to find him?" He had a gold tooth that shimmered as he flicked his tongue suggestively at her.

Kat turned on her heel and went quickly back to her rental car, taking not a moment to look around before she peeled out of the parking lot. She drove fast down the highway, her breath quickening with the accelerator. Kat was alone and frustrated and at a dead end. She couldn't go home without doing what she needed to do, but she was running out of leads. She breathed faster and faster, her fingernails digging into the steering wheel. Then her breathing became uncontrollable and her vision began to blur, and Kat realized she needed to pull over. She was having a panic attack—her second, after the one on the sidewalk back in Addison.

It took a few minutes to recover and then, although her body was still trembling, Kat pulled back onto the highway and drove to her motel. She didn't have the luxury of attracting the attention of drivers or police.

The next morning, Kat decided that she couldn't drive anymore. It was too risky in her state. So she returned the rental car and bought a Greyhound bus ticket bound for her next, and likely last destination: Tampa, Florida. The Tampa lead came from a photo posted online that Kyle was in. Whoever posted the photo had it geotagged to 22 Juno Lane, Williamsville, Florida—a small Tampa exurb. All it meant was that Kyle had been there once. It wasn't a great lead, but it was all she had, so Kat decided to follow it.

Kat spent several long days watching television in her hotel room, waiting for her scheduled bus trip. The only person she spoke with in that time was the young woman at the front desk. She'd been tempted to call Erika, just to break up the monotony and hear a familiar voice. But if she spoke with Erika—or Sean or Hunter—they would ask her questions about what she was doing, and she didn't have any answers for them yet. So she turned her cell phone off and kept it off. She planned to explain everything later, after she accomplished this mission. If she did.

It would have been faster to just hire a cab for the ride down to Tampa. It would have felt more private too, less annoying. But Kat didn't think a cab was safe. So many hours alone with a chatty driver would leave a trail. Someone would know that she was in Florida and they would know something about what she was doing. That wasn't an option for this trip.

Which is why, eight days into this ordeal, Kat was sitting on a Greyhound bus, listening to babies cry and teenagers text and the bus driver bitch. Kat closed her eyes and leaned back. She was tired, but too nervous about letting go of her duffel bag to nap. That was another thing she remembered about the bus: if you pretended to sleep for long enough, sleep would eventually come, so be sure that was what you wanted. Sleeping on the bus was risky business for anyone traveling alone—even people who weren't carrying half a million dollars in cash.

God, she wanted to get there and get off that bus. She wanted the entire trip to be a distant memory, a successful mission that she could leave in the past. But nothing was unfolding as she had planned it. Nothing ever did, she supposed. The panic attacks were a real curveball, even more so than her bad leads. Because now she was at the mercy of public transportation, brushing up against all those strangers and their multitude of desperations. There was just no fucking way that walking around with a duffel bag of hundred dollar bills was a good idea. But what option did she have at this point?

Kat chugged water and wiped the sweat from her brow with the edge of her shirt. She'd been wearing the same clothes for three days and they were beginning to stink enough for casual passersby to notice. She'd left her other clothes behind in Jacksonville as a matter of strategy. Her pizza sauce–stained jeans and sweaty T-shirt were going to get her through this.

Kat didn't have much practice at criminality, but she

knew how to move invisibly through the world. Looking poor and just a little bit nefarious granted her some distance from strangers. People made up their own stories from there. Maybe she was homeless, mentally ill or generally antisocial. She was certainly too unsavory for men to hit on or children to be allowed to sit beside. And in this costume, her behavior changed too. Kat was riding the bus as a guarded, streetwise loner. She was playing a role she'd watched as a spectator many times before.

"Tampa," the driver announced. "Last stop on this run."

The bus lurched to a halt and everyone stood to collect their things.

Kat quickly stacked her notebooks, stuffed her printouts and maps between the pages, and zipped them into her duffel bag. She could feel the bricks of fresh hundred dollar bills wrapped in a clean T-shirt at the center of the bag.

It hadn't been easy to get the cash. Kat knew enough not to just go to the bank and ask to withdraw it, which the bank wouldn't have accommodated even if no one reported it as suspicious. No, she'd had to ask Hunter's father's fixer—Lars, with the white arm hair—to get it for her. He hadn't wanted to do it, but she'd been prepared with an elaborate story about how she was planning a long African safari trip. She'd told him that US cash was more reliable in the countries on her itinerary. It was recommended by the State Department, she'd said. *Sure, until you get murdered for it.* That's what Lars had said without a hint of irony. It occurred to her that perhaps that was a desirable outcome to Lars, considering the headache and expense she'd caused the senator. She'd laughed nervously at the grim joke, which wasn't really a joke.

Only now, as Kat stepped off the bus into the Florida sun, did she realize what an improbable story her African safari trip had been. Lars didn't really believe or care what she did with her life as long as she stayed quiet.

Kat felt someone shove her from behind. "Keep moving!"

She turned around and snarled like a wild animal. A bald man curled his lip in disgust, and they both kept walking.

Kat followed the crowd of passengers along a sidewalk as cars whipped by and palm trees moved lazily above them. The bus stop was located on a grassy median between two four-lane highways, which left them unnervingly exposed. Could have been worse. Benches were lined up around the center, which some passengers went to. Others got into idling cars. Kat walked toward the line forming at the cabstand.

In line, a large woman wearing a giant straw hat gave Kat a long once-over to indicate her disapproval, and then turned back around. Kat held tight to the faux leather handles of her worn-out duffel and watched as people got into sedans and minivans bearing signs for local taxi companies.

When it was her turn, Kat took the back seat of a teal Chrysler Neon.

"Afternoon. Where we goin'?" A leathery old man flashed bright white teeth into the rearview mirror, and it took Kat a moment to formulate her response.

"Can you take me to Juno Lane?" She handed him the scrap of paper.

He pulled up his sunglasses and squinted at the address. "That up in Williamsville?"

"I think so."

The man nodded and accelerated into the left lane. Moses was his name, or that's what his cabbie ID said. It was clear that she didn't know where she was and would be paying him whatever pumped up amount he decided to charge her for the trip. But she felt safe in the back of his car and relieved to be away from the traveling crowds, and that was worth a few extra bucks. She held tight to her duffel, pulled out a chocolate chip granola bar and ate it as tropical fronds whooshed by.

Florida wasn't what she'd expected. There were fewer broad expanses of Kelly green golf courses and gated communities with oceanic names. She thought, for some reason, that the palm trees would be arranged in precise lines along the highway, though she wasn't sure why. Most of what Kat knew about Florida probably came from Disney World commercials and *Miami Vice*. She hated feeling so provincial, but it was the truth. No, this landscape was wilder than she'd imagined and she rather liked it.

Twenty-five minutes later, Moses the cabdriver pulled off the highway and onto a broken road surrounded by swampy vegetation. For two miles, they passed only a man pushing a grocery cart filled with empty bottles.

Then Moses took a right turn onto a neglected street that was reverting from pavement back to dirt. Run-down bungalows in faded pastels were packed neatly along the road. They were cute little homes—"good bones," Sean would say—but in grave disrepair. Their overgrown lawns grew right up through stacks of old tires and rusted tricycles. Trailers had been parked on yards. You could see decades of changing fates on display at each residence: from middle class, to poor, to barely surviving. The fates seemed to move in only one direction.

Kat pressed her forehead against the car window to take it all in. Dogs behind fences, windows mended with duct tape, and houses that had been converted to nail salons and then boarded up for good. If this was Kyle's old neighborhood, then she had more in common with him than she'd thought.

"This town's seen better days," Moses offered from the

driver seat. He eyed her through the rearview mirror. "You from around here?"

"Something like this." She didn't want to talk about herself. "Was it always so bad here?"

"Nah, this is uglier and wetter than it used to be. These people got nothin' at all now, but they used to have a little somethin'."

Kat understood. She'd nearly forgotten what this life looked like, the life of people squeezing everything they could from the nothing they've been born into. Aside from the blood money she carried on that day, Kat wasn't much richer today than she'd been as a kid. But she didn't live among the poor anymore, and that had changed her. Kat felt ashamed for escaping it all, not for reinvention, but for allowing herself to forget what this looked like, felt like. And in the time that she'd been away from these conditions, it seemed that America's desperate places had somehow gotten worse. She hadn't been aware of the change, until now. Kyle had led her back here, to something like her childhood.

"Here y'are." The cab pulled up in front of a house the size of a room with a deeply bowed roof. "You want me to wait here, or you stayin'?"

She considered the question. Maybe Moses thought she was asking someone for money, taking something back that was hers, buying or selling a drug. He didn't need the details for such comings and goings, but he was familiar with them.

"You can go. Thank you."

The meter said thirty-nine dollars. Kat pulled three twenties out of her pocket and handed them to Moses.

"You need change?"

"No."

"God bless." Moses reached back and handed her a business card. It had his full name, phone number and a biblical passage beneath the image of a gold dove.

Kat put it into her back pocket and collected her things. "Okay, thanks. You too."

She shut the door behind her and watched him drive away.

A row of cheap pinwheels turned in the breeze on a neighboring lawn.

A nearby dog strained toward Kat, nearly choking himself with the fat chain around his neck.

It might have been a bad idea to let Moses go. If this wasn't the place, what would she do? Even if it was…

Kat could see televisions flicker from inside of houses, but no one was out. God, it was hot. Surely someone was peeking around a curtain at that moment, sizing her up as potential predator or prey. She wasn't afraid of these people. It had been a while, but she wasn't going to be the sort of interloper who was afraid of these people.

She wasn't afraid of whatever she'd find in house number twenty-two.

Kat walked up to the little house with the sagging roof, past an overturned Big Wheel, and knocked on the door. Through the window, she could see a detergent ad play on a large TV. The dog barked from several houses down. No cars in the driveway, but that didn't mean much. Someone was home.

Kat knocked again and waited.

Her heel kicked a stack of unopened mail and she looked down. There it was: Tanya Billings. On the first letter at her feet was the name of Kyle's mother. There could be no coincidences now, not after all she'd gone through to get there. Kat stared down at the mail. They were mostly bills, forwarded from another address.

She waited for a moment, looked around and then knelt

down to retrieve one of the letters. She peeled back the little postal sticker to find the original address. It was the very same street she'd started on, back in Jacksonville. So she hadn't been entirely wrong. But now Kyle's mom lived here, in this sagging house, and she wasn't going to leave until she did the thing she came to do.

"She's in back," a voice said.

Kat spun around to find a young man wearing a stiff baseball cap low over his eyes. He didn't look up or formally acknowledge her in any way. He just said it and kept walking down the center of the street because, she assumed, he'd seen something familiar in her. They were both humans who could use a break.

"Thanks."

Kat walked around the side of the house, through a part of the shaggy yard that required long strides over saturated ground. Florida was as hot as she'd imagined, but the sogginess was a surprise. There was apparently nowhere on earth that the ocean wasn't trying to pull her in.

She peeked into the cluttered backyard.

"What is it?" a short, round woman with fuzzy hair demanded from a plastic lawn chair.

"I'm sorry to bother you." Kat suddenly wished she'd prepared more for this moment. "I'm...I'm a friend of your son's."

"No yer not. You gotta leave." The woman hoisted herself out of the low chair and walked quickly to the back screen door.

Kat was right behind her, stepping in the grassy puddles with her sneakers. "Ma'am, I don't want anything from you. I wanted to tell you I'm sorry. I have something for you."

The woman was inside now, grimacing at Kat through the

screen door. "What are you sorry about? Did you put those drugs in my son? You one of his junkie friends?"

"No, ma'am. I'm not. I wasn't. If I could just—"

"I'm not talking to anyone about my son. You people have done enough. Let me be."

Kat didn't know who this woman thought she was, but she was familiar with "you people." She was assumed to be a drug dealer, a needy girlfriend, a bad influence—or worse, someone in a position of relative power like a parole officer or a debt collector. All of this struck Kat as needlessly tragic. Kyle had died, but not from drugs. And as far as she knew, he hadn't led a troubled life before that night on the boat. How wretched for his mother to believe that he had, to have her grief magnified by this false story. This was something that Kat could give this woman. She could redeem the memory of Kyle.

"Ms. Billings, please let me in."

"Go away or I'll call the cops!"

Kat knew she wouldn't call the cops. They didn't get invited to this neighborhood. But she didn't want to torture this woman further. There was another way to do this.

Kat sat down on the back stoop. She pulled out a notebook and pen, and began to write. She could feel the woman watching her from behind, through the screen door.

Kat kept writing. Paragraph after paragraph, Kat put it all down. The woman watched silently from inside, and Kat kept writing.

Four pages later, she had written the story of Kyle's death, the version she wanted to tell.

This version was for Tanya Billings alone. It explained that Kyle had gone out on a boat with friends. They were drinking a little, but no other substances were involved. Kyle was happy, among people who cared about him. And then a storm came and he fell into the water. They tried to find him, but the storm made it impossible. They should have called the police sooner. They should have gone back in before the storm got too bad. It was all a big accident, but they had made some mistakes. That's why Kat was there—because she felt guilty for not speaking up at the time. She wanted to say she was sorry.

She never mentioned Hunter by name. She left out the part about Kyle threatening her, which was surprisingly easy since she'd nearly edited it out of her own memory. Kyle may have been a rapist, but he also may not have been; both versions were untrue, so she went with the nicer one. And she implied that Kyle had been a real friend to all of them, a close friend even. None of this made it a lie. The only truth any of us had was the story of who we thought we were. We were always making it up. And Kat wanted to give this woman a story she could live with. Kat didn't have children but she understood that the story of your children is the one you most hope will be a good one, better than your own. Tanya Billings deserved the peace of a better story for her son.

As she got to the end of her note, Kat paused. How to sign it? The truly noble thing to do would be to use her name. A confession demanded a name. She was probably going down for this anyhow, so why not go down with nobility? But she didn't sign her name. Kat was still free, and she was still programmed for self-preservation. Only a fool would hasten her own demise in such a way. If someone wanted to find her, they could, but she didn't need to make it so easy. And so she concluded the letter with simply "A friend." It was true and not true. She never really knew Kyle, but his ghost would be with her for every remaining day on this earth. She was something like a friend.

Kat folded the paper and slid it into the pocket of the duffel bag. She ran her hands around the neat bundles inside, pulling two of them out for herself, along with the clean T-shirt that had been wrapped around them. She left the bag and five hundred thousand dollars there on the stoop. Then she knocked once more, and walked around the house.

When she got to the street, Kat waited and listened.

A moment later, the screen door creaked open and slammed shut again. Tanya Billings had the money. And she had the story. And she wasn't going to call the police or chase after Kat or tell anyone the details of what had just happened. Kat was sure of it because she knew this life and its inhabitants, and they were way too smart for that. This money was a gift—a real gift, not like the way it had been given to her. It wouldn't buy anyone's silence. It wouldn't even buy anyone's forgiveness. It was just a kind and utterly insufficient thing to do.

Kat remembered an Easter Sunday with Orla and Sean from years before when the priest sermonized about penance as a sacrament. It didn't make much sense at the time. But now she understood the allure of penance, and she hoped for her own absolution.

Kat walked down the broken road, light as a feather. When she came to a tree-lined curve, she pulled off the stinking shirt she'd been wearing for days and threw it into the woods, replacing it with the crisp white shirt that had been wrapped around the money. She took out her cell phone and turned it on for the first time in days.

He picked up on the second ring.

"Moses? This is Kat. I need a ride to the airport."

"I'll be there in ten. God bless."

CHAPTER 20

Kat felt a tap on her shoulder and she opened her eyes. The man standing above her in a Steamship Authority hat was smiling, but impatient. It was time to get off the ferry. Instinctively, she looked around frantically. It took about three seconds to realize that she wasn't traveling with the money anymore. She wasn't hiding anything that put her in danger or made her every movement potentially suspicious. It was just her now, wearing the Red Sox fleece she'd purchased at Logan Airport, with her full wallet zipped into the pocket, and an open *Boston Globe* in front of her.

"Time to go home, doll."

She blinked and stood up. "Okay, thanks."

Kat got in line behind a handful of people and they walked off the ferry, along the clanking metal plank, into the cold night. She pulled her hands into the soft fleece, which wasn't enough cover for January. She was freezing, but refreshed. It had taken the entire cab ride to Tampa, the flight back to Boston and the cab to Cape Cod for her body to calm down enough to sleep. She understood intellectually that the deed had been done, the mission accomplished, but her body was incapable of believing it. Until she got to Cape Cod, Kat's body was still on high alert, weighed down by half a million dollars in phantom bills and the memory of recent panic attacks.

And then she boarded the ferry. Once they were out on the water, the familiar tinny sounds and salty air, the Brahman voices of vacationers and Southie-accented arguments of ferry workers, all signaled safety to her. She was as good as home once she got to the ferry, and she slept at last.

So now, as she walked away from the port, Kat's rested mind was thinking clearly again. She was beginning to process all that she'd just accomplished in Florida, and she was proud of it.

But having that journey behind her also meant that Kat couldn't ignore the present any longer. She had come back to the Vineyard, her home. Crazy Ashley was surely still trying to tie her to Kyle's death, and local police hadn't closed the case yet. All of these things meant that she was probably breathing borrowed air. Everything could come crashing down soon. Maybe next week. Maybe tomorrow. Soon.

She walked alone from the parking lot of the ferry to the bus stop and considered her next move. There was no rush to return to Erika's apartment, to reality. Why wait for twenty minutes in the cold for the bus now? She had nowhere she needed to be. So instead of waiting, Kat went one block north to a pub with a warm glowing light out front. A drink sounded right.

A bell jingled as Kat opened the door. Two middle-aged guys at the bar gave her a nod. She took a seat at the far end, where the lighting was dimmest and the music most muted.

"Harpoon, please."

The bartender grunted. He had a small, black apron wrapped around his rotund center like the twine on a Christmas ham, a detail Kat remembered from the last time she was in that bar. It was one of Sean's haunts, which made it less than ideal for the moment, but there weren't many options on a Sunday night in January.

The full pint arrived moments later. "You want to start a tab?"

"Yeah, sure." She hadn't planned on it, but why the fuck not? Kat had kept sixty thousand dollars for herself. It wasn't for anything specific—just survival, she supposed. She just wanted to survive the months or weeks or days of freedom still available to her. She was stalling.

She was stalling because Kat knew that the moment she went back to Erika's apartment, she would have to make up a story about where she'd been. And then she'd have to see Sean and Hunter—separately, of course—and probably tell them the real story, which they would both disapprove of for different reasons. She wasn't ready to do any of those things.

Kat finished her beer with gusto and ordered another.

A group of twentysomethings came in, all thoroughly inebriated already. It was still winter vacation for college students—a concept that seemed to Kat, particularly in that moment, the most foreign and gilded of all concepts.

They packed into a nearby booth and filled the room up with rowdy energy. Kat watched them as she finished her second beer. (It was too much beer for her; she could feel it. But too much for what? What did she have to stay sober for?) One of the young women nuzzled into the beefy arm of a broad guy. He dipped a lock of her hair into a pint glass and she shrieked. Everyone laughed. The other girl tried to inject herself into this mating ritual, but the guys didn't seem as interested in her.

They were all beautiful, likely from families rich enough to endow this adventure, and with futures that Kat imagined would take them around the world and then back to the wealthy enclaves of New England. At least two of these people would go home together tonight, Kat thought, maybe more than that. Beautiful, young, unburdened bodies fucking like the gods that they are.

The skinnier of the guys looked over and caught Kat watching them. She turned her head quickly to find the old man at the other end of the bar watching them too. She was just like that old lecher, staring at the beautiful young gods of a different world. They hardly even saw her world, hers and the old man's. They were invisible to these kids.

Kat was drunk, too drunk. This was the sort of thinking she didn't care to indulge. All this us-and-them business wasn't the lens through which she wanted to see the world. Envy was for angry and self-pitying people. Kat didn't want to be angry.

Kat took another sip of her third pint and stood up and headed for the door.

"Twenty-four bucks," the bartender called.

Shit, she'd forgotten to pay. She thought she could feel everyone in the bar watching her drunkenly fumble through the bills in her wallet. She left two of them and walked out.

It was cold outside, but it felt warmer than it had when Kat walked into that bar thirty minutes earlier. She looked up and down the cobblestone. Nothing. She should probably call a cab, but then she'd have to take it somewhere. She wasn't ready to go somewhere yet.

Kat sat down on an iron bench with ornate armrests. She'd walked past that bench a million times, but she'd probably never sat on it before. It was cold as hell.

Kat pulled out her phone and took a deep breath, knowing what she needed to do. She hadn't answered a call or checked a message in over a week and the idea of looking back at the record of ignored names was growing less appealing with each hour. But she needed to look before she went back to her life.

Erika had texted three times and called twice. Based on the texts, it was all just "Where are you and let me know you're okay" stuff. Jesus, it hadn't really occurred to Kat that people would be worried about her safety. She felt bad about that.

Hunter had reached out twice as many times, more frantically than Erika. He was worried about her. He wanted to help her with whatever she was working on. And he was sorry for anything he may have done. He was sorry for everything.

Sean had called twice. Just twice. No texts. Kat's heart leaped at the number, which made whatever he had to say seem more meaningful, somehow. It was withholding—just two calls—which made her want more of him. Kat held the phone up to her ear and listened.

The first message was just an inquiry: "Where are you and can we meet for coffee?"

The second message, from three days later, she could see from the screen of her phone was going to be very long.

Here was Sean: "Kat, I don't know where you are, but I'm trying to respect your privacy. I know this has been a hard time for you—for all of us. I was going to say this in person, but I feel like it needs to just be said, so here goes. First, thank you. On behalf of my mom and Weeta and all of us, we're really grateful for the glass studio. The renovations look amazing already. Better than the old place. Even Mom says that. We don't have to talk about where the money came from…we probably shouldn't…but I want you to know that *I know* that this wasn't easy for you, and I'm grateful. That's really why I wanted to talk to you. Because you know I've had reservations about all this. Everything's gotten so fucked up and I wasn't sure if I could get on board… But I want you to know that I've decided that I *am* on board. I forgive you. We can put everything behind us now because I forgive you. And I don't mean to sound like a dick about it—I know you didn't mean to do anything bad—but I couldn't move forward until I really felt okay with it all. And now I do. So I hope you'll come home. I love you. That's all. I love you."

Kat slid her phone back into her pocket and looked around. A woman in heels clicked along the cobblestone a block away.

Sean forgave her. He forgave her and wanted her to come home. It was what she wanted to hear—or something like it. What she wanted was to go back in time to the relationship that didn't feel so weighed down with guilt and shame. But if he really did forgive her, then maybe it was possible to rebuild their relationship. That was the best anyone could hope for at this point. It was great news if you adjusted for the circumstances.

Kat stood up and began walking. She should have gotten a cab five minutes before. Now she felt nauseous. She just needed to walk it off a little, maybe throw up along the way. Then she would get a cab.

Focusing on her feet, Kat stepped slowly and deliberately. Right foot. Left foot. Her sneakers made almost no sound at all. They were worn-out, but she felt appreciative of the faded running sneakers that had taken her all over Florida. She hadn't been running in them in quite a while. That would be a good thing to do tomorrow… No, no it wouldn't. In her spinning mind, she'd nearly forgotten that she needn't bother with quaint resolutions like jogging anymore. Those things were for people without real problems. Jogging was a dumb idea.

She realized that this was why troubled people drank. Not

the kind of drinking that she usually did—wine with dinner and occasional overindulgence—but, like, *real* drinking. Fast and alone drinking. Because of those three pints, she'd forgotten for a few moments that she'd watched a man die and done nothing to save his life. She'd forgotten how that night had changed all the relationships that mattered most to her. And she'd forgotten that someone was working at that moment to prove that she was responsible for Kyle's death. It was a fucking brilliant reason to drink. It actually worked, if temporarily.

A middle-aged couple walking a tiny dog gave Kat a disapproving glance and kept going. Fuck those two for judging her for being sloshed on their precious cobblestone road. She was drunk for a *reason*.

God, she was nauseous. What a dummy she'd been for having that third pint.

A cab pulled up beside her and rolled down the window.

Kat shook her head.

He drove off.

She needed that cab, but she really needed to puke first. If she puked in the cab, he'd drop her on the side of the road and probably demand another twenty dollars. It struck Kat as a little funny that she did actually have the twenty dollars now. She had plenty of money for puking in cabs, which was probably how people like Hunter went on doing dumb shit year after year—because they had infinite funds for fixing all the consequences of that dumb shit.

Right sneaker, left sneaker. Right sneaker, left sneaker. Kat kept walking. She got to the end of the cobblestone street and turned left onto the main road that would take her back to Erika's place. It wasn't the kind of road pedestrians were supposed to use—there was no shoulder, just dark woods, and the cars drove fast. But there was hardly anyone out, so she figured the risk was minimal.

Two minutes later, a car zipped by with blinding lights, apparently unaware of the hunched walker moving along the road's edge.

Five minutes later, the nausea lifted a little and Kat's toes started to go numb. She started walking faster, which helped with her body temperature, but not her toes.

Eventually, she began to jog. It was a hobbled sort of jog, but it had the benefit of warming her body and getting her closer to her destination. She regretted walking.

As Kat considered calling a cab on her phone, she hurdled over a downed branch. She cleared it, but landed weird on her left ankle and fell to the ground.

At that moment, another car rolled up from behind and slowed beside her. Kat looked over to see a police officer in his cruiser.

"Ma'am, you need some help?"

She straightened up and tried to sound breezy. "No, thanks, just tying my shoe."

The young officer watched her for a moment, then got out of the car. "You don't look like a late-night runner to me. I'm going to help you up now and give you a ride home."

Kat let the man help her up. She suppressed a howl as her left foot came down onto the pavement and she nearly collapsed again.

"I must have twisted it," she said as he eased her into the back seat.

"That'll happen after a few pops."

The officer closed her door, then slid into the driver seat.

It was warm inside the cruiser, thank goodness for that. But the trees were going by too fast. Kat closed her eyes and tried to breathe deeply. She didn't even care anymore if the cop knew she was drunk. She just didn't want to throw up in his car.

"You can take me to Addison… Church Street. I think it's number six." She had no idea what Erika's address was.

"Ma'am, I'm gonna take you into the station first, just to sober up."

Kat opened her eyes. "What? I haven't done anything! Being drunk isn't a crime."

"No, but I can take you into custody for public intoxication if you pose a risk to yourself or someone else. And you clearly pose a risk to yourself. You could have frozen out there with a sprained ankle."

"I'm going to the drunk tank?"

He laughed. "We don't really call it that around here, but yeah."

Kat slumped in her seat and closed her eyes again. She was having a hard time wrapping her mind around what was happening. She was in a police car, but not for a crime. This guy didn't know who she was, not yet, anyway. Was it possible that this was a ploy to get her into the police station? Maybe. But it was too late to resist now.

Kat looked around at the car doors. They just had normal handles like the inside of a normal car, but they were probably locked. Criminals would try to escape too much, so you'd have to lock them. And anyway, jumping from a police car was something that only a guilty person would do. She needed to behave like a not-guilty person. She *was* a not-guilty person.

It felt like a thousand years ago that Kat had been standing in water, under the hot Florida sun, pleading with Tanya Billings. The days were all sort of melting together in a wavy timeline. She was guilty and not guilty, liberated by what she'd just accomplished and still chained to the story of that night. She wondered where the ghost of Kyle was. She hadn't felt his presence since she'd left his mom's house. He hadn't traveled back with her on the ferry and he wasn't sitting beside her in the police cruiser. Was he gone for good?

"Here we are."

Kat's door opened and the young cop used a surprisingly gentle hand to lead her toward the picture-perfect little police station. She still didn't believe there wasn't someone waiting for her with handcuffs and Miranda rights on the inside.

There was not.

As police stations went, it was adorable. In the seven years she'd lived on Martha's Vineyard, Kat had never been inside the Addison station. It looked just as she'd imagined it would, from the tasteful muted walls to the natural wood beams. Lovely, but still a police station.

"Make yourself at home on that bench right there."

Kat frowned.

The cop shrugged. "Just for a few hours. Warm up for Chrissake."

"Can I pee first?"

He pointed to the door behind her.

For a moment, Kat thought the officer would insist on coming in, like they did in movies when suspects were trying to escape through bathroom windows, but he didn't.

There weren't any windows in this bathroom, anyhow. Just a toilet, sink and a pine tree air freshener that made her feel nauseous all over again. It was as bright as hell in there. Kat tried not to look in the mirror as she washed her hands. It had been a few days since her last shower—an intentional choice as part of her streetwise Florida persona—but now it seemed so disgusting. Her hair was greasy and her pants stained. She wondered if she would have been taken to the police station if she looked like a pretty young woman after a rowdy bachelorette party. They probably took those girls straight home and fluffed their pillows for them.

When Kat returned from the bathroom, the cop was still there, and he pointed to the bench. She sat down and let her head rest against the wall behind her. It was about fifteen feet away from the counter where an ancient-looking woman was stamping things. Behind the old lady, an older cop riffled through files. The young cop left Kat and joined him at the files. They weren't doing the things that Kat imagined cops did, but what did she know. They were just puttering around, indifferent to her. She was really and actually only there for public intoxication, it seemed.

It was almost funny, that she was going to spend a few hours at a police station for being drunk. It would make a good story one day, if she were to have the kind of future where you told lighthearted stories like that at dinner parties with your friends. She probably wasn't.

Kat closed her eyes. The bench was pleasingly long and broad, not the worst place to rest for a few hours. She wasn't going to sleep, of course. She was too nervous for that. But she was warm and safe, which was something.

The cops talked softly to one another about their lives. It sounded nice from a distance, like dozing off to an old movie. Henry was looking forward to his granddaughter's christening next weekend. Josh was looking for another player on the softball team. The lady at the front desk stamped things and threw in her two cents now and then. It was hard for Kat to imagine these men busting up drug rings and wrestling people to the ground. Or finding dead bodies on the beach. Those things probably didn't happen often on the Vineyard. Maybe there were tougher, more hardened cops to handle them when they did.

A new set of shoes walked in, followed by the sound of

files smacking on a desk. "The tox report finally came back from Boston," New Shoes said.

"Took long enough."

"Yeah, the backlog's a mile long."

"Hey, Manny," the younger cop said.

There was a pause and Kat imagined them looking over at her, reminded of their mixed company. She kept her eyes closed and tried to make her face go slack. It was interesting to be a fly on their wall, so she wanted them to believe she was asleep.

"Yeah, we'll give her a few hours," the other one said. He didn't seem so concerned about the sleeping girl. "So, the tox report?"

"Fentanyl."

"All three?"

"Aliya Bergeron and Brad O'Connor were fentanyl and oxy. Kyle Billings was just oxy."

Kat's muscles went rigid. She wanted desperately to open her eyes and somehow confirm that she'd heard what she thought she just heard. *Kyle Billings…toxicology report…oxycodone.* Kyle Billings's body had oxy in it. Kyle was on oxy when he died. She tried to be still, to keep her eyelids relaxed and her shape in a drunken slump, but every nerve in her body was alive now. She focused on her breath, long and slow and like a sleeping person.

"Alright, close 'em out," the old cop said. "Notify the families quietly. We don't need any more press on this garbage."

"Yes, sir."

Shoes scuffled around and then there was the sound of coffee brewing.

"Jesus H. Christ, if this shit is still going around when my grandkids are in school…" the older cop said.

"I know it."

Kat murmured and turned her head, so her cheek was pressed up against the cool wall. They weren't interested in her anymore.

Close 'em out. That's what he'd said. This was over. The file was closed. And it wouldn't matter anymore what crazy Ashley had to say because Kyle was using drugs on that night and everything the cops thought they knew about his death had just been validated. The story made sense and it didn't matter what was true.

There was a sick relief in knowing that Kyle was the user he was rumored to be. It almost made his late night drowning true, like it *could* have happened that way, so it may as well have happened that way. It was a tempting line of reasoning for Kat. If he hadn't died on the boat with them, he would have killed himself in some other undignified way... or so the thinking went.

She couldn't commit to that logic, though. For one thing, Kat knew that Kyle wasn't high on the night he died. They would have noticed. He may have had drugs in his system, but he wasn't high when he was out with them on that boat. More important, Kat had grown to like the ghost of Kyle, so news of his drug use made her sad. Kyle hadn't died because of his drug use and his future wasn't foreordained by it. No, she couldn't allow this revelation to ease her guilt.

But! This revelation of Kyle's drug use and the decisive closing of his case meant that she was free. This was over. Was it possible? Kat seemed to recall that there was something about reopening cases if new evidence was uncovered, but that may have come from the movies too. And what new evidence could there be? The scarf was gone, buried under the wreckage of the glass studio. The boat was clean. Now it was just Ashley's theories about tidal patterns against everything else. And who the hell was Ashley? She was nobody.

She was certainly not as authoritative as a *tox report*—that was the final word. Kat went around and around in her head about what had just happened and the only logical conclusion was that, yes, this was over. She was free.

"What's the story with the sleeping girl?" the new cop asked.

"Few too many. My guess is boyfriend troubles."

"It always is."

Kat smiled to the wall and opened her eyes.

At first, no one noticed her. And then, the lady at the desk raised her eyebrows. "Well, look who's up."

"Ma'am, do you think I could call someone to come get me?"

She frowned and looked over her shoulder. "Josh?"

The younger cop walked over. "You have a safe place to go tonight?"

"Yes, a friend. He can pick me up."

"Yeah, alright. You can use the phone on the wall."

Kat walked over to the big telephone hanging on the wall. This part was just like the crime shows. She smiled at the realization that this could now be a story that she could tell one day—a story about how happy, normal, not-incarcerated Kat had been detained for public intoxication and used her one phone call on a big old-fashioned police station phone.

She put two quarters into the coin slot and waited.

Hunter picked up immediately.

CHAPTER 21

When they finally opened their eyes, the sun was already high and the room flooded with light. Kat rolled over in her cocoon of down bedding and blinked. What an exquisite room it was. Bright ivory walls with pale yellow toile accents. She'd seen the room from the end of the hall, but she'd never been in it.

"How'd you sleep?" Hunter rolled over and wrapped a bare arm around her waist.

"Really well. I think I slept really, really well."

The white of his grin was magnified by the bleached light. Something smelled of lemons. Maybe it was her.

Kat's deep, dreamless slumber had been so immersive and disorienting, it took a moment to find her memories of the night before. Hunter had picked her up from the police station. She remembered that. And she told him everything. From the station to the house, and through half of the turkey sandwich he'd put in front of her at his kitchen table, she kept talking until the story of how she'd spent the previous eight days was fully told. Not a detail edited, softened or massaged. If there was such a thing, she wanted Hunter to have the truth.

He'd been angry at first, relieved that she was safe, but angry about her silence while she was away. But as the story unfolded, his anger dissipated. He wasn't even mad about the money. Kat had been worried that, in giving it away, she was violating some aspect of her agreement with Hunter's father. She wasn't worried about it a week before—when she'd thought they were to be found out for Kyle's death and it was all going to end terribly. But with the case closed, she no longer felt the same kamikaze urge that had hurled her into the risky and righteous plan she'd just completed. She wanted to live again and protect her relationships.

Hunter wasn't mad about any of it. He was astonished by the stupidity, luck and craftiness of it all. But he wasn't mad. Just as Kat was no longer offended to sell her silence, Hunter wasn't offended when she laundered the payment for her own purposes. The world was too complicated for such prudishness.

She'd told him everything the night before and he understood it all.

And now, they were finally alone, weightless without their secrets.

"Do you still feel bad about it?" Hunter asked.

Kat knew what he meant. "No. Not anymore. I was defending myself. We both were. Do you still feel bad?"

"No."

She couldn't be sure, but Kat had the distinct feeling that it was the last they would ever say about Kyle Billings.

Hunter pulled her in closer.

"We don't have to do anything today," he said into her hair, taking a long breath in. "We can get started tomorrow."

It was her hair that smelled of lemons. After she'd explained the story to Hunter and answered all his dumbfounded questions, she'd finished her sandwich and taken a shower. The shower at Hunter's house was quite possibly the best shower Kat had ever experienced. It wasn't only her desperation after so many unwashed days in Florida. It was the deep claw-foot tub and dueling showerheads, the imported French toiletries and the blanket-sized towels to dry off in. In the old days, Kat wouldn't have allowed herself to enjoy such temporary luxuries from someone else's unattainable lifestyle. Nothing good came from such pleasure. But last night, she'd felt no hesitation. While she was there, standing under the gentle pressure of that water, it was hers.

"I have to do a few things today," she said. "Just a few."

Hunter kissed her ear, her neck. He moved down her naked body to her breasts and stomach. She'd never gotten dressed after that shower. She didn't have anything to wear.

Hunter's lips moved along her thighs. His hands wrapped around her waist.

When she'd finally finished her story the night before, she'd asked Hunter if he thought they were safe now. And he'd laughed. *Don't you know*, he'd said. *Ashley is gone.*

Apparently, in the time Kat had been away, Hunter had been busy. He'd sold the boat. (Thank God he'd sold the boat.) And he'd tried to make things right with Ashley. His plan was to beg for her compassion, or convince her that she was certifiably nuts. He was armed with both strategies when he'd gone to see her. But before he had a chance to administer either of them, she told him that she was leaving Martha's Vineyard. She'd been offered a job on a new commission for coastal erosion. It was her *dream job*, she'd said, and she would be working with the *best people*, on a *world-class team*. Those were the words she kept using. She wasn't even mad at Hunter. He said she hadn't seemed mad at any of them.

Hunter came back up and rested his head on Kat's bare chest. She liked the weight of him there, pressing her firmly in place. She was so close to being comfortably still. Ashley was gone, and the case was closed, and she was almost still. Hunter wanted nothing more from her than her presence, which was all she had left. They were there together—just as they were, not as they should be. That's probably all Ashley ever wanted too.

The crazy thing about Ashley—the part Kat still couldn't quite believe—was that Ashley would have ruined their lives if she had the chance. And it was all because she'd been rejected. Her feelings had been hurt. Ashley didn't want to be a vigilante; she wanted to be a part of something. She wanted it so badly that she would have ruined them for it. This was never about Kyle for her. She wanted to do something big and be seen. So if she couldn't have Hunter, or Sean, she wanted to be known for having ruined them completely. It was fucking nuts, but it made sense too. If what she wanted was to prove her existence, to beat invisibility, well then being in love was about the same as taking revenge. She got seen either way. She left a mark and something to be remembered for. It was only dumb luck—hers and theirs—that she was offered this job. The job allowed her to be and do something big in the world. There was no logic to that luck, but Kat was grateful for it.

Kat ran her fingers through Hunter's hair and felt his breath on her breasts. "I have to do a few things," she said.

"I know." Hunter kissed her and rolled over into the cloud of covers. "Take the car."

Kat went to the bathroom to splash water on her face and brush her teeth. That house had every amenity one could hope for, replenished regularly by an invisible army of house cleaners. She opened and closed cabinets until she found a hairbrush, then a roll of floss, and it occurred to her that all the secrets of the island were being kept by that invisible army

moving among all the enormous summer homes. The help.
It was impossible to know what they knew about her secrets,
but it didn't worry her. She was the help too. Most of her
life, she'd been the help. The help didn't need new trouble.

Kat opened dresser drawers in various bedrooms before
finding some forgotten yoga clothes of Hunter's stepmother.
She put on the strange clothes, followed by Hunter's big coat.
She laced her old sneakers. Her ankle still hurt a little from
the night before, but the swelling was going down.

"I'll be back in a little while."

Outside, it was bright and cold. Kat was alone on the
sidewalk.

She didn't take the car. Instead, she started walking, knowing full well that it would take forty minutes to get to Erika's apartment. Kat savored the fresh tonic of subfreezing
air in her lungs, even with a slight limp. She was hungover,
which was strange because it felt like weeks had passed since
she'd been sitting alone at the pub in her dirty jeans. A lot of
things had happened since then. She'd gotten her life back.

Kat walked through downtown Addison and out onto a
lonely main road. She passed a row of grand beach houses,
closed up for the winter, followed by a row of gnarly, worn-
out little shacks that served as year-round homes for others.

At the last driveway on the block, Kat watched a woman
in a beige uniform tug a winter coat onto a toddler. The
little girl played a video game while her arms were directed
into the sleeves. They fussed over seat belts and the mother
issued a series of directives while scraping ice from the windshield of their sedan.

It was easy to forget that there were kids on Martha's
Vineyard, real people growing up in vacationland just the
way real people did everywhere. Rushed mornings and harried mothers, packed lunch boxes and braided hair. That was

how Kat imagined such mornings, anyhow. It wasn't the way hers had been. Kat didn't remember her mother ever packing her lunch or fussing over her hair. She just got up each day and figured it out for herself, which never seemed especially tragic until these rare moments when Kat was looking in from the outside at other people's lives. Flashes of other childhoods from a distance tended to have a dangerously melancholy effect on her. To imagine a stranger's life in romantic sepia tones only served to make the memory of her own seem more deprived. And it was a lie. She didn't know those strangers or their story. She wasn't looking at the truth.

The driver door closed and the pale blue Ford backed out of the driveway.

Kat stopped and smiled at the little girl through the window, just a few feet away from her now. There was something purple staining the rim of the girl's lips, jam perhaps.

The child waved and then frowned. Something on the ground had caught her eye. Kat followed her line of sight to a pink mitten lying in the driveway. She didn't miss a beat, running to grab it as the girl cried audibly from her seat.

The car stopped abruptly and the mother jumped out, jogging around to retrieve the mitten from Kat's hand.

Her face was a surprise. She seemed about Kat's age, which didn't make sense because the age of motherhood felt perpetually three years ahead of Kat on some imaginary timeline.

"Thanks," the woman said. "It's always a mitten, isn't it?"

Kat smiled, but she couldn't think of a single word to say in response.

The woman bounded back to her seat and they drove away quickly, the little girl fully recovered and smiling again.

Isn't it? The woman meant it as a gesture of camaraderie, of shared experiences. She'd assumed that they were alike in some way. But what way? Kat wasn't a mother. But she could be. And she wasn't living in a nine-hundred-square-foot salt-ravaged ocean bungalow. But she certainly could be. They were as alike as Kat allowed herself to believe. She was as close to the rest of humanity as she chose to be. She would have to stop looking in at it from the outside, though. That was a prerequisite for closeness. And something about having her life back made her want to try it.

Kat walked for another twenty minutes until she was once again walking along narrow village streets in a neighborhood less tony than her own.

The windows of Erika's second-floor apartment glowed invitingly as Kat slid her key into the storm door. She walked up the stairs and heard the artificial sounds of TV chatter.

"Hey," she said weakly into the room.

"Jesus Christ!" Erika jumped up from the couch where she had one set of painted toenails elevated and another set still in the process. She ran to Kat and threw her arms around her. "Where the hell have you been? You scared the shit out of me!"

"Sorry, I had to clear my head." Kat collapsed into a chair.

"What? Clear your head? Where have you been?"

"I'm so sorry, Erika."

"Okay, fine. Tell me or don't tell me where you were. Whatever. I'm just glad you're safe." Erika sat back down, the little nail polish wand still in her hand. "Do you know that I've been trying to talk everyone down these past few days? Sean called me about it. I've been trying to keep Hunter from going crazy with worry."

Kat smiled. "I've seen Hunter. It's okay."

"You know that he loves you, right?"

"Yeah." Kat looked out the window at the swaying trees. You wouldn't even know they were on an island from this part of town. "I know it."

"Well?" Erika wanted something, some explanation for where her friend had been and some validation for all her heartache. She deserved that.

"I went to Florida."

"Ooh la la."

"Yeah, I just kind of roamed around in the sun. I had to clear my head after everything that had happened with Sean and the house and everything."

"Okay... It's kinda nuts, but okay."

"I know. I'm sorry." It wasn't a great story, but Kat figured that if she couldn't tell Erika the truth, then she needed to adhere as closely to it as possible. This felt the least deceitful.

"I'm just glad you're back. Do you have any more spontaneous trips planned that I should know about? Is this, like, a thing you do now?"

"No more surprises. But there is another trip I'm planning."

"Where?"

"I don't know yet. I'll tell you all about it when I figure it out myself. But I won't disappear this time. I promise."

Erika shook her head and finished the pinkie toe. She couldn't stay mad.

Kat looked up at the kitchen counter. "Is that coffee fresh?"

"Yep." Erika blew dramatically at her splayed toes.

Kat poured two cups and added cream to each. She set one beside her friend's feet on the coffee table, taking a long sip from her own. "Hunter and I are going away."

Erika considered the news for a moment. "Good."

"Good?"

"Yes, good. That seems right to me."

"You never told me that before."

"Well, yeah, because there was Sean. And everybody loves Sean..."

Kat's stomach turned. She felt the warm coffee moving

down her throat and into her empty insides. "Yeah, everybody loves Sean."

They drank in silence for another minute. Then Erika put the cap on the nail polish and exhaled loudly. "You really scared me."

"I know, I'm sorry."

Erika rolled her eyes and smiled. She leaned forward to fan her drying toes. Things would be okay between them.

Finally, Kat stood up. "I actually have to go. I'm not running away again like last time. I just have another stop I have to make."

"Can I drive you?"

Kat really didn't want to walk another forty minutes in the freezing cold. Even in Hunter's giant coat, she felt like she'd never get warm again. And the thing she'd been avoiding doing suddenly felt like it needed to be done. "Can you bring me to Sean's house?"

"Of course."

The thermometer on the wall said it was twenty-four degrees outside, but Erika slid her feet into flip-flops to protect the fresh pedicure.

They warmed up her truck and five minutes later, were driving along the same road Kat had just been walking, the hot air blasting at their bodies. Kat had a canvas grocery bag at her feet containing the few items that were still hers: the clothes she'd been wearing on the day of the landslide, an old pair of boots from Orla and the cheap drugstore cosmetics she'd purchased downtown.

"I'm glad you're doing this," Erika said from the wheel. They hadn't discussed exactly what Kat was doing, but she knew enough.

"I'm glad you're glad. But why?"

"I don't know. With Sean—and all the Murphys—it always felt like *they* picked *you*." Erika pulled into Sean's driveway and they sat in silence for a moment.

It had started to snow and a light film of powder was settling onto the steps of Sean's house.

"I think I wanted to be picked by the Murphys."

"Well, you got it. Now you can want more than that."

Kat leaned in and kissed her friend on the cheek. "I love you."

"I know. I love you too."

She got out of the truck and waved goodbye. Erika turned her music up loud, waved and peeled out of the driveway.

Kat walked up to the front door. She rang the doorbell once. The snow was falling harder now, dampening her hair and driving the cold deeper into her bones. No one seemed to be inside. There was one light on by the front window, but that didn't mean anything. Sean always kept that light on. The Murphys thought it was bad luck to let a house go completely dark.

Kat rang again and knocked. It was around ten o'clock in the morning. Sean did paperwork from home on Monday mornings. He was supposed to be there. There was a very thin possibility that he was still sleeping, of course. Maybe he'd had too much to drink the night before. Maybe he'd gotten up early to go ice fishing on the pond and crawled back into bed afterward. Those were the only scenarios Kat could imagine in which he'd still be sleeping.

It was strange to know so many things about another person. All these little rules and habits to hang on to; they could disguise themselves as intimacy. People fell in and out of love all the time, but they didn't forget the rules. The love is fickle; the details indestructible.

She rang again and waited. Sean wasn't there. He would have heard her by now.

Kat was alone on the steps of Sean's home, the snow piling onto the broad shoulders of Hunter's winter coat. She didn't want to come back here. She didn't want to do this again. Most of all, she wanted to turn this page.

Kat reached into her tote of meager belongings and pulled out the notebook and pencil that had accompanied her up and down the East Coast. And just as she had done two days before in Tanya Billings's swampy backyard, she sat down and began to write.

In all of her life, Kat had probably written less than a dozen letters. There had been a pen pal assignment in middle school, a few thank-yous sent after job interviews and one postcard exchange with her mother after she left Buffalo for good. Kat couldn't remember any other times in which she'd written an actual letter. She wasn't confident with the written word. But here she was, again, writing letters. And like last time, this wasn't so much a letter as it was a story to hold on to, with all the power of inclusion and omission.

She thanked Sean first. She thanked him for his kindness and generosity, for the joy and beauty he'd introduced her to, for his unbreakable commitment to family and friends. She said that all of these things had made her a better person, though she secretly believed he'd only awakened dormant qualities inside of her. But this wasn't a letter for complete honesty. It was a story to leave him with, and in this story, he'd made her better. It was true and it wasn't true.

She wrote about how much she loved his family. Weeta— and his devotion to her—had opened something in her heart that she'd never known. She wished all the best for Weeta. And she wrote a lot about Orla. She wrote it knowing that Sean would share this part with his mother, and so she considered them both in the writing. What Kat really wanted to do was write a letter to Orla alone, because it may have been Orla's influence and not Sean's that had really changed her. But she couldn't ever let Sean know that, so she wrote of her gratitude to them both.

There was more Kat wanted to say about them all. She couldn't ever fully thank them for giving her a chance and a craft. She would benefit from their love for the rest of her life. As Kat wrote, she had to keep reminding herself that she'd done a lot for these people, as well. She didn't need to beg for their forgiveness, though she felt guilty for so many things. She still felt as if Kyle's death was a bad omen that clung to her, cursing everything she touched, including the Murphys. But the landslide wasn't her fault. She didn't need to feel guilty about it. It wasn't punishment from a god or a curse that she carried with her. It was just the weight of water.

Kat didn't write anything about Kyle. She knew beyond a shadow of a doubt that no matter what happened between them, Sean wouldn't endanger her. Her involvement in Kyle's death had been a challenge to his moral compass, but only because it confused his understanding of who she was. Sean was never going to tell. They would never discuss it again and he would never use it to punish her. He was a good guy. Everyone loved Sean.

In the end, all Kat could say about why she had to leave was this:

I love you, Sean. And I'm glad to have your forgiveness. Thank you for it. But forgiveness isn't enough for either of us. We can still want more.

Kat folded the note twice and slid it under Sean's door.

And then she walked away. With the note beyond her reach, she needed to go. There was no reversing things now. She couldn't reach back and change her mind, edit the story or change the ending. It was done. And it was frightening to consider all that she was walking away from: loyalty, safety, a sense of belonging. But she didn't regret it.

Kat couldn't be in a relationship premised on the granting of her forgiveness. She didn't believe that there was any length of time that would equalize the power between the two of them, that would erase the feeling that she should be grateful for his forgiveness, that would mitigate his sense of magnanimity for granting it. Forgiveness wasn't enough for either of them.

There was also the matter of love. Maybe it was the events of the previous months or maybe it was just the natural progression of things, but Kat wasn't in love with Sean anymore. She didn't really care that he forgave her, not in the way a lover should. She told him that she loved him because, in a way, she still did. And it seemed a kinder story to leave him with. Placing the blame for their demise on outside forces was tragically romantic, whereas falling slowly out of love was mundane and insulting. She would never completely stop loving him, but she didn't love him enough anymore. It was true and it wasn't true.

As Kat turned the corner for the main road, she pulled the hood up over her head and took one last look at the house.

And then, a light in the kitchen came on and a body moved past the window. Sean had been there all along. He'd been there and he hadn't opened the door.

It stung, but only for a moment. Maybe Kat wasn't the only one with reservations about their forgiveness arrangement. Maybe she was just the braver one for saying it and releasing them both.

CHAPTER 22

Hunter slammed the back door and blew onto his cold hands. "The trunk is full. What else do we need to fit in there?"

Kat looked around his expansive kitchen. The notion that they needed anything was a bit ridiculous at this point. After everything she owned fell into the sea, and she'd been living out of a canvas grocery bag for three weeks, she wanted everything, but she was sure she needed very little. "Let's take the espresso machine."

"Really?"

"Yeah, why not."

Hunter kissed her cheek and began the delicate process of unplugging and partially disassembling the hulking device.

Kat watched him work. There was very little for her to do in this project of packing up. It wasn't her house and she had nothing to pack. She wandered into the living room, then the study and the grand dining room. She wasn't looking for anything in particular, maybe a stray sweatshirt or a book that Hunter would want to take along. Mostly, she was trying to make a mental photograph for the future.

The beach house would still be here if they wanted to

visit. Hunter's father, the senator whose reelection bid was looking like more and more of a sure thing, would hold on to it forever. But Hunter would never live there again. He'd promised himself that. Neither of them would.

"You want the little cups too?" Hunter yelled from the other room.

"No, don't worry about those," she yelled back.

"I'll grab them anyway."

When Kat proposed this adventure to Hunter—after she'd explained her absence, and they'd made love, and any shred of doubt about their rightness melted away for good—Hunter didn't need to think about it. He said yes immediately. It wasn't even a real plan, just a vague idea to move away together, and he leaped at it. Because it wasn't only Kat who needed to start a new chapter. Hunter did too. He wasn't the bored screwup he'd been six months before. Like her, he'd seen death, and near-death, and he'd been sobered by the unvarnished cruelty of fate and nature. It was all so fucking precarious. He needed to *do* something.

"Let's go to a new place," Kat had said as they'd lain in bed. "Somewhere with a glass studio, maybe near water… but different water. We can get jobs."

"I want to find a kitchen to work in." He knew this immediately. Hunter already knew what he wanted to do there, wherever *there* was.

"It's not running away," she'd added. "We can stay in touch with everyone, visit someday. But we can't live here anymore."

Hunter felt it too. The people and the memories and the ghosts of the Vineyard…it was suffocating them.

They never did discuss what it meant for the two of them, their new status. It felt so natural they forgot to acknowledge it. The rules and routines and labels could come later.

Kat turned off the light in the study and walked out for the last time.

They locked all the doors and got into Hunter's car. It was a nicer car than she'd ever owned and he'd done exactly nothing to earn it. This fact didn't seem to bother Hunter. It wasn't his right and it wasn't his fault. It just was. And Kat believed that he'd paid for this privilege in other ways—not because she thought the world is a fair place or there is some sort of cosmic leveling in the end. There is not. She simply believed that the payments and rewards of this life are more complicated than they seem.

They drove past the collapsed bluff where the glass studio used to be, through downtown Addison and past the boatyard. Kat had the feeling that she was already looking at it all from a distance, like a tiny scale replica of the town where she'd once lived, familiar to her but powerless now.

Hunter put a hand on her knee and squeezed. He looked like his old self again, healthy and happy. But he would never be his old self. Neither of them would. A small, puckered scar beneath his left eye was testament to that.

Hunter pulled down the sun visor and offered Kat a pair of sunglasses, which she accepted. They gave the world a pleasing pinkish glow.

A man jogged past from the other direction and raised a friendly hand at their car. Hunter did the same. There was an unspoken message among the men, it seemed. *This world is ours, and isn't it grand?*

But Kat felt now that it was also her world—because she was going to make it so. She was choosing to be unbound from the story of her past. The place from which she came did not define her, and the choices she'd been forced to make after Kyle's death didn't, either. She was who she said she was. And she was a survivor. And she knew that the only way to survive the next chapter was to forgive herself and to believe this world was really hers. There would be no asterisk by her name. She'd done what she had to and she'd learned from it. And, like Hunter, she was going to fully avail herself of any blessings that came her way. She'd paid for it all.

Hunter followed the ferry workers' signals and pulled into the line of cars. A man in a Patriots hat came to the window to accept their tickets. Hunter made a comment about the game the night before and they both laughed. And one minute later, the lot of vehicles was weaving slowly onto the enormous ferry.

Unfazed locals and winter vacationers with carloads of kids drove on, along with a postal truck, a fruit truck and a pickup filled with rusting machine parts.

A dozen ferry workers went about their practiced dance of directing traffic and unfastening the enormous barge from its port. Every day they did this, for large crowds and small; like castle guards at the drawbridge, they controlled all passage in and out of the kingdom.

From the passenger seat, Kat felt the final nudging of the boat away from the shore. This time, it felt something like a push. They had officially left Martha's Vineyard.

Hunter turned off the car and they both got out.

They walked along the narrow lanes between parked vehicles, to the rear of the ferry. A bitter wind pushed against their chests as Hunter took Kat's hand. With her other hand, she held the cold metal rail before them—the only barrier between their bodies and the vast water.

Their island grew smaller as the boat picked up speed. It would be gone to them in minutes.

Kat wanted to see every last second of it, to understand the finality.

But she looked away. She thought for an instant that she

could feel Kyle beside her—the way she used to—and she turned to see if he was there.

He was not.

And when she looked back at her island, it was already gone.

Kyle, and the invulnerable tide that had pulled everything in, was behind her now.

★ ★ ★ ★ ★

ACKNOWLEDGMENTS

I'm grateful to all the people who helped bring this story into the world including my agent, John Silbersack; my editor, Kathy Sagan; my publicist Shara Alexander, and everyone at MIRA Books.

I couldn't have had more fun researching this book and I met some fantastic people along the way. Thank you to the Luke Adams Glass Blowing Studio for your patient instruction. Thank you to the good people at the Martha's Vineyard Transit Authority, who ferried me around their lovely island and answered my incessant questions. Thank you to The Writers' Loft of Sherborn, where I spent most of my days drafting this story. I love you, Massachusetts.

None of this would be possible without the support of my family. To Josephine, Annabelle, and Dan (especially Dan): thank you for your sacrifices on this journey. I'm grateful for your love, humor, and insights.

I'm grateful for everything.

EVERYTHING THAT FOLLOWS

MEG LITTLE REILLY

Reader's Guide

1. What motivates Kat to defer to Hunter and not immediately go to the police? Do you think their decision to delay is defensible? Is it ever defensible to choose self-preservation over what's morally right?

2. Much of Kat's perception of justice is shaped by her class and lack of power, particularly relative to Hunter. Does that make her behavior more or less justifiable?

3. A major theme of this story is who gets to control the truth and whether it matters at all. Did Kyle's mother deserve the truth about her son? Can withholding some truths be an act of kindness?

4. Sean's deep sense of morality is admirable, but it also makes him rigid and judgmental. Do you think he made the right choice about what to do with the truth? How would you have handled it differently?

5. The setting of Martha's Vineyard is a strong presence in this story; it's both naturally striking and culturally unique for its mix of vacationers and year-rounders. Have you

ever lived in a place where others go only to play? How do you think that dynamic might affect your feelings about home?

6. Kat's guilt and her quest for cosmic justice drives much of her subsequent behavior. Is guilt ever a constructive force? Do you think she is absolved in the end?

7. Memory is a slippery thing in this story as Kat's memory of the night in question—and of Kyle—warp and change over time. How reliable do you think her memory would have bee

8. The
   agg
   pe
   giv
   in

9. In
   it
   th
   it.
   d
   re

10. W
    p
    H
    p
    a